POISON AT THE WILD HAGGIS BOOKSHOP

JACKIE BALDWIN

Storm
PUBLISHING

To request permissions, contact the publisher at rights@stormpublishing.co

Ebook ISBN: 978-1-80508-845-5
Paperback ISBN: 978-1-80508-847-9

Cover design: Dawn Adams
Cover images: Dawn Adams

Published by Storm Publishing.
For further information, visit:
www.stormpublishing.co

A Grace McKenna Mystery

Murder by the Seaside

Murder at Castle Traprain

Murder at Whiteadder House

The Highland Bookshop Murders

Murder at the Wild Haggis Bookshop

Poison at the Wild Haggis Bookshop

Dead Man's Prayer

Perfect Dead

Avenge the Dead

PROLOGUE

Nora jumped as she heard the front door open. She turned her head slowly and painfully as the person she had loved paused in front of the hall mirror, rearranging their cold, hard features into a mask suggestive of caring. A flare of pain tore at her soul. She had placed her trust in one who was unworthy. It was not the first time she had loved unwisely. But it would no doubt be the last. Admittedly, she had made grave mistakes, but she hoped that the fire with which she had taught at school and her many years of voluntary work might weigh against them. It was out of her hands now. Nothing more to be done except to graciously accept her fate.

She heard the kettle boiling and a tray being assembled in the adjacent kitchen. Her paper-thin lips parted in a faint smile as she heard measured footsteps approaching.

It was time...

ONE

'I'm starting to feel like I'm on a factory production line.' Morna scowled. 'There's a reason I never watched Blue Peter as a child.'

'You're doing great,' soothed Beth. 'Just another four boxes and that will be us done for the month.' The large table looked like a nursery class had visited – tissue paper, books, beads and micro samples from local suppliers were all bundled into one gigantic mess.

'Stop moaning, Morna,' said Chloe, deftly scrunching up tissue paper. 'You'd know all about it if you worked in a real factory.' She placed the lid on the red candy-striped box and tied the ribbon with a flourish before adding some beads and tucking in a sprig of heather to finish it off.

'It's all very well for you,' continued Morna, glaring at her friend and colleague. 'You probably do origami with the bog roll every time you go to the loo. I'm just not *good* at all that stuff.'

'I don't know whether to feel complimented or offended by that,' said Chloe, one perfectly manicured eyebrow shooting up.

'It's so sexist that Lachlan's been allowed to escape the glitter fest,' Morna continued. 'Just because he's a bloke.'

'That's simply not true,' said Beth, stung. 'Someone had to hold the fort by dealing with customers while we're all in here getting the subscription boxes ready. Lachlan does more than his fair share.'

'Anyway,' said Chloe, leaning in for the knockout blow, a gleam in her eye. 'Whose idea was this?'

'Mine,' growled Morna, rolling her eyes.

'And a great one, too.' Beth smiled, unfazed by the bickering. 'The subscription box scheme has really taken off. I think what makes it really special is that we get to showcase local products by including soaps, chocolates, a bath bomb or a miniature whisky, whatever our partners decide to offer. And all attractively packaged with their business card inside.'

'The bit I like is choosing the books for each individual customer,' said Morna. The others nodded in agreement.

Every month the staff chose three books for their assigned customers based on a detailed questionnaire completed when subscribing and also on the feedback forms from the previous month's selection. This was where Lachlan's encyclopaedic knowledge of the book trade and extensive local knowledge came into play. He had stopped them making many faux pas over the last three months. For example, sending a psychological thriller called *The Mistress* to someone whose marriage had just broken down due to an affair.

Finally, they were done; the mess had been cleared away and the book boxes set to one side for delivery after work. Beth had opted to deliver them personally as it gave her an opportunity to check up on their elderly or housebound customers.

The door burst open bringing with it a blast of cold spring air. The crepe paper lifted off the table as though trying to fly away before settling back down. A vivacious girl with long jet-black hair and bright red lipstick rushed towards them. It was Kathleen from 'Time for Tea,' the pop-up shop situated a few doors up from them.

'Sorry, Beth, I'm not too late, am I?' she asked. 'I've been run off my feet this morning. There was an article in one of the nationals today about the health benefits of particular kinds of tea and it's caused a mini stampede.' She flopped down at the table beside them, rummaging around in her embroidered carpet bag and fishing out samples of tea. The packaging was exquisite with ten muslin teabags gathered up in patterned silk in an assortment of colours with a tea-stained card detailing the forest the mushrooms had been foraged from, written in beautiful calligraphy.

'These are so gorgeous,' breathed Beth, picking one up to examine it. 'They'd make lovely presents.'

'I've been selling a lot of them,' Kathleen admitted, her face dimpling in a way that briefly reminded Beth of someone. 'Unfortunately, not so many takers for my kombucha bar.' She sighed.

'Ugh, I'm sorry but you couldn't pay me enough to try that,' said Chloe, pulling a face.

'Sorry, Kathleen,' said Morna, nudging Chloe in the ribs. 'This one's not known for her tact and diplomacy.'

'But it looks like a monster in a jar,' protested Chloe, 'as if it might not even be from this planet. Maybe, if you hide it behind a curtain or something then people might be more willing to try it.'

'I could take a large jar for the café in here on a trial basis,' said Beth, taking pity on Kathleen. 'If anyone likes it, I'll send them up to you.'

'That would be great,' said Kathleen. 'Are you sure you don't mind?'

'Not at all. It's always good to diversify. Just send it down to us along with an invoice and I'll feature it.'

'As long as I don't have to touch the slimy monster,' muttered Chloe.

Beth and Morna both glared at her.

'I like your necklace,' said Chloe, pointing to the beautiful gold J resting in the hollow of her throat.

'Oh!' said Kathleen, her hands flying to her neck. 'Thanks.'

'Why do you have a J instead of a K?' asked Chloe, curiously.

Kathleen blushed. 'It sounds a bit tragic, I know. But my boyfriend wears mine and I wear his. His name is Jack.'

'That's SO sweet!' enthused Chloe, putting her hand over her heart.

'Coffee and cake?' asked Beth. 'On the house, of course, as a thank you for the samples.'

Kathleen reluctantly shook her head. 'Thanks, but I need to get back up to the shop. It's only me. Another time?'

'Sure,' said Beth, and waved her off as she rushed away, leaving a vapour trail of perfume and an assortment of dried tea leaves behind her.

The rest of the afternoon flew by as now they were heading into March, the large number of tourists were making the town feel busy again. The winter could be a lean time for small business owners in Oban and Beth felt grateful that her bookshop hadn't fared too badly. She tried to support others who weren't quite so lucky any way that she could with joint initiatives.

Pulling the door closed behind her, she glanced up at the sign above her head: 'The Wild Haggis Bookshop'. It never failed to raise a smile. She only wished her mum could still have been alive to enjoy it with her. After years of having Beth as her carer, her lovely mum, knowing that her time was limited, had set about making her only child's dreams come true. Her mum had fond memories of growing up in Oban, feeling that it was a warm and welcoming community that would take her daughter into its heart and so she had arranged matters such that, on her death, their house in Glasgow would be sold and the bookshop and a small cottage purchased with the proceeds. Now, after a rather rocky start when someone had been murdered in her shop, she was finally living the life her mother had wanted so badly for her.

Suddenly, she was dragged from her thoughts by the sight of Detective Sergeant Logan Hunter walking along the High Street towards her. Her stomach performed an impromptu somersault as she cast her eyes wildly around seeking an avenue of escape. No such luck. All the shops were closed. Nope, it was happening. The gods were not on her side today. Ever since he'd regarded her as his chief suspect in a murder case last year, she'd been both wary and simultaneously drawn to him which felt excruciating. Whenever she saw him, it threw her into complete disarray, and made her feel like the teenager she had never got to become. His footsteps slowed until he stopped in front of her.

'DS Hunter,' she managed, her voice sounding squeakier and more high-pitched than normal.

His dark eyes sought hers and she was mortified to see amusement there.

'You can call me Logan, you know, unless we're meeting in a professional capacity.'

Couldn't resist that little dig, could you? she thought, glaring at him.

'What have I done now?' he protested, holding his hands up in mock surrender.

'Nothing.' She sighed. 'Anyway, I don't have time to chat, I'm off to deliver this to one of my customers,' she said, indicating the large box she was carrying.

'Is it her birthday?' he asked.

'No, it's our book subscription service,' she explained. 'If you want to know more about it, I have a leaflet.' She rummaged about in her handbag. 'Here you are.'

She thrust it at him so that he had no alternative but to take it. Then grinning at him, as this time she felt she had got the better of the encounter, she bid him a cheerful goodbye and marched off, her head held high. Once she had gone a few steps, she was unable to resist the urge to turn round and saw him stood watching her. She quickly spun round again and carried on, her cheeks burning.

Veering left, she was soon ascending the same steep hill where her newfound family lived. It had been a shock for all of them when she had discovered that her solicitor, Harris Kincaid, was in fact her half-brother but she had been welcomed into his family with an ease and grace that astonished her. Her only regret was that she'd never had the opportunity to get to know her real father, who had died before she came to Oban.

Reaching Nora's house a bit out of breath, she leaned against the gatepost for a few moments, taking in the handsome sandstone façade ahead of her. The last time she had been up here, the garden had been manicured perfection. Now, it was looking distinctly shabby. What's more, the curtains were drawn and it wasn't even dark yet. There were no lights on that she could detect. Had Nora been ill? She couldn't remember the last time she'd made it down to the shop, but she'd been on the phone to her a month ago to voice her pleasure at the latest offerings in the subscription box.

Worried now, she ran up the steps to the front door and rang the bell, hearing it echoing down the high-ceilinged hall. No reply. She was just about to give it up as a bad job when she noticed an upstairs curtain flicker. There was definitely someone in there. Feeling quite cross now, she rang the bell again and followed that by pounding on the door. It had been a long day and her feet hurt. She just wanted to get this done and head home.

Suddenly, the door flew back on its hinges and an angry young man stood glaring at her.

'I've come—' she began, before being rudely interrupted.

'Whatever you're selling, we don't want any,' he snapped, starting to close the door.

Somewhat perplexed, Beth inserted her foot in the doorway. 'I'm simply trying to deliver a package. Where's Nora?'

'She's sleeping, alright?' he hissed at her. 'I'll take that parcel for her and make sure she gets it.' He reached out to grab it.

'I'd prefer to deliver it into her hands,' said Beth, pointedly moving it out of his reach. 'Now are you going to let me in, or should I call the police?' She hoped that her bluff would work. She doubted that he was a burglar or he wouldn't have come to the door. Nevertheless, she had no idea who he was, and his demeanour made her feel suspicious in a way she had yet to identify. She needed to check her customer was safe and well before leaving.

'There's no need for that,' he snapped, face flushed with anger. 'I'm her son.'

'Oh, I see,' said Beth, surprised. Nora had never mentioned having a son.

'She's sleeping in her chair in the living room. Just give it to me!' He stuck out his hand for the box.

Beth hung on to it. There was a fine sheen of sweat on his face although it wasn't a warm day. She could see a nervous tic twitching at the corner of his eye. He moistened his lips and shifted from one foot to another. Something definitely wasn't right.

'I must insist on delivering it to her in person. It's... protocol,' Beth said, taking a step forward so that she was invading his body space. They stared at each other for a few seconds. Beth hoped he couldn't hear her heart pounding with fear as she stared up at him, unblinking.

'Fine,' he huffed. 'But don't wake her.'

'I won't,' she said, with a placatory smile, as he reluctantly pulled the door wider and she stepped aside.

It was gloomy inside the house with lamps dimmed and the curtains drawn. She was probably making a fuss about nothing and, had the man not been so needlessly hostile, she might have accepted his explanation at face value. All she wanted was to get this over with and get home. Peeking in the lounge door, she saw Nora asleep in the chair just like he'd said. There were a number of lit candles dotted throughout the room, all omitting conflicting and rather cloying odours. She advanced further into the room, ignoring the exasperated sigh behind her.

'Right, you've seen her. She's fine. Just give me the bloody box and go!' he snapped.

Beth spun round and stared at him. He had made no attempt to lower his voice yet Nora still hadn't stirred. He moved to grab her arm and pull her out of the room, but she twisted out of his grasp and approached the silent woman in the chair, dread pooling in her stomach, certain now of what she would find.

She placed two fingers on Nora's neck. There was no pulse and her body was cool to the touch, despite the warmth from the radiators. Her face had a yellowy tinge.

Turning in horror to look at the man now blocking her way out of the room, she pulled out her phone and dialled 999.

TWO

The police car drew up outside the house less than ten minutes later. Beth would rather have waited outside, despite the cold, but the man who maintained he was Nora's son was acting so irrationally she felt she needed to stay with the body to protect it. Nora had never once mentioned having any children. Nor had she ever noticed any photos around to indicate their existence. After a standoff lasting a couple of minutes, the man had stormed off and started banging about upstairs, opening and closing drawers violently.

Hurriedly, she ran to the front door and pulled it open to reveal the surprised face of DS Logan Hunter.

'Beth! They didn't tell me it was you who called this one in. Where is the body?'

Beth nodded, biting back tears. To think that Nora was now a body instead of the wise woman she'd been the last time she spoke to her.

'There's a man inside,' she said quietly, fearful of being overheard. 'He says he's her son but he's not behaving rationally. He insisted Nora was only sleeping and he's a bit aggressive. You'd best be careful.'

'Noted,' the detective said. 'The duty police surgeon will be over shortly.' He turned his back on her and disappeared inside the house with DC Quinn, who wasn't her greatest fan.

Beth continued to stand outside the front door, her teeth now chattering with the cold or maybe the shock was catching up with her. He hadn't said she could leave but neither did she want to set foot inside that house ever again.

Another car drew up and out popped her younger half-sister, Dr Fiona Kincaid, looking her usual calm and capable self.

'Beth! What are you doing here?' she asked, her forehead creasing in concern.

'I found the body,' Beth said miserably. 'I was delivering her book subscription box.'

'Oh, that's horribly upsetting for you,' Fiona said, pulling her into a quick hug. 'I'm so sorry but I need to go,' she added, disengaging and picking up her doctor's bag.

'Just be careful in there,' warned Beth. 'There's a man inside and he seems a bit unhinged.'

More time passed. It was pitch dark now and Beth was shaking with the cold. She was surprised that Fiona hadn't re-emerged by now. All she had to do was declare life extinct and there was little doubt about that. Probably a heart attack, she thought, swallowing down the sudden lump in her throat.

'Let go of me! You have no right,' shouted the young man she had heard earlier.

There were sounds of a scuffle and he emerged in handcuffs being frogmarched to the waiting police car between DS Logan and DC Quinn. Both were tight-lipped with anger. What on earth had happened? she wondered in alarm.

'I'm sorry, Beth, but we need to escort this gentleman down to the station. Do you think you could pop down there to give your statement?' called Sergeant Hunter over his shoulder as he went past her.

'Yes, of course,' she murmured, though it was the last thing she felt inclined to do. The last time she had been there had been when she'd been falsely accused of murder.

A tight-lipped Fiona Kincaid followed close on their heels.

'I'm sorry, Beth, I can't stop, I'm needed at the station,' she said, rushing past her and jumping into her small car, reversing in a splatter of gravel.

A burly police officer who had subsequently arrived in another car closed the door to Nora's house and stood in front of it, arms folded.

Beth stared at the door, somewhat at a loss, then turned on her heel to head down to the police station in town. What on earth was going on? Nora had surely died from natural causes, hadn't she?

She walked into the police station feeling her heart rate accelerate. Even though she'd done nothing wrong, memories caused her palms to moisten, and a headache began to thrum at her temple. Steeling herself she approached the front desk.

'Hi, I'm here to give a statement about the death of Nora Kelly,' she said to the world-weary police officer currently on duty. 'It's Beth Cunningham.'

'I know who you are,' he said, subjecting her to a piercing stare. 'Take a seat over there. I'll tell him you're here.'

'Thank you,' she almost whispered, turning round to take one of the shiny black plastic seats. In what felt like an eternity but was more like twenty minutes, the internal door opened and DS Hunter appeared looking creased and tired.

'Miss Cunningham,' he said formally, 'would you like to come through, please?'

She followed him and was relieved when she was shown not into the interview room but a larger room with nicer furniture and a more relaxed feel. She sat in a chair on one side of a small coffee table and he sat down opposite. She explained the circumstances in which she had found the body.

'You surely don't suspect foul play, do you?' she blurted out.

'I'm sorry but I can't comment on an ongoing investigation,' he said, holding up a hand.

'Okay, I'm sorry,' she said, taking a deep shuddering breath.

'It's just been a bit of a shock, finding her like that with that strange man in the house. I mean, I didn't know what to think.'

'How well did you know Nora Kelly?'

'Not terribly well. She used to come down on a Monday and have a good old browse, buying something more often than not. She'd have a cup of tea and a blether after she'd made her selection. Mondays are quiet and I felt she was a little lonely. She never mentioned that she had a family, so I assumed she was all alone in the world.'

'Did she visit the shop last Monday?'

'No, she hadn't been in since just before Christmas. Earlier in the year, we launched our monthly book subscription service with an ad in the local paper. She signed up and the second time I delivered a box, a month ago, it was a carer who came to the door and mentioned that she'd been ill. We had a catch up then, but she seemed rather low and, I have to say, not her usual bright and inquisitive self.'

'This carer, do you know her name?'

Beth shook her head. 'Sorry, I'm afraid I don't. She showed me through to the sitting room then disappeared. She was wearing a turquoise uniform, if that's any help?'

'Her doctor has no record of her having been ill. The last time he saw her was four months ago for a routine blood pressure check. He described her as being fit as a flea. It's something of a mystery how she could have deteriorated so markedly in such a short period of time. Anyway, thank you for coming in to help with our inquiries,' DS Hunter said, getting to his feet. 'I'll see you out.'

Beth walked the rest of the way home, deep in thought. The more she thought about it, the more she worried that Nora had fallen through the cracks and become a victim to foul play. The way that Nora's supposed son had been acting had felt really creepy. There was something off about him, but she couldn't quite put her finger on it.

THREE

The following morning, Beth was in her office doing her monthly ordering when Chloe tapped lightly on the door. Beth waved her in and stretched her arms above her head, stiff from sitting for so long. Chloe slid onto the seat in front of the battered table that served as her desk.

'There's a woman out there who's acting a bit weird,' Chloe said in a hushed voice. 'She keeps picking up books to read but it's as if she's just hiding behind them because she's clearly not reading anything at all.'

'Well, it's a free country.' Beth shrugged.

'Except she keeps angling herself so she's staring in here at you,' said Chloe, widening her eyes.

'What?' Beth laughed. 'Why would she be doing that?'

Her youngest employee was prone to flights of fancy which she usually found amusing but she really had so much work to do. She glanced over Chloe's shoulder through the open door and was startled to see a woman staring at her over the top of a book. Immediately, the woman dropped her eyes and turned her back to them.

Beth didn't have time for this. Rising to her feet she left her office and walked up to the woman. She stood behind her and cleared her throat. 'Can I help you?' she asked.

The woman jumped and spun round. She was tall and elegant in a mid-calf black wool dress with an olive-green leather jacket. Beth guessed she was around her own age. She softened as she realised that the woman seemed distressed and took her through into the office to compose herself, sending Chloe away to make some tea.

'My name is Jane Guthrie,' the woman said. 'I've been trying to pluck up the courage to come and talk to you.'

'What about?' asked Beth. The name didn't ring any bells.

'I gather that you're the person who found my mother?'

The penny dropped. Nora must have had a daughter, too. Strange that she'd never once mentioned having a family.

'Yes, that's right,' Beth said. 'I'm very sorry for your loss. Your mother was a regular customer in the shop, but I gather that latterly she wasn't too well, so she took out our book subscription service. That's what I was delivering when I realised that she... she had passed away.'

'She always did love to read,' Jane said, tearing up. She pulled out a hanky from her pocket and blew her nose. 'Sorry for being so emotional. I knew it would happen one day but not out of the blue like this, and not in such strange circumstances.'

'What do you mean?' asked Beth. 'Have you been in touch with the police?'

'Not yet. I'm due to see them later. I've just arrived up from Glasgow and booked myself into a B&B. Why did you ask that? What do you know? Please, tell me, I'm begging you,' Jane implored, her face twisted in agony.

Beth was cross with herself for blurting that out. She couldn't backtrack now though. 'All that I know is that the last time I saw your mother she was a bit listless and seemed rather low,' she said.

'When was that?' Jane asked, fumbling in her bag for a paper and pen.

'The subscription boxes come out on the first Monday of every month, so it must have been the second of February, just over a month ago. Her carer answered the door to me and explained that she'd been unwell.'

'Wait, she had a carer?' Jane asked, horrified.

'What? You didn't know?' replied Beth, puzzled. 'Anyway, we had a cup of tea and a bit of a chat, but she seemed rather low and subdued and wasn't her usual self. She didn't even open the book box, just put it to one side. Normally, I would have expected her to tear right into it. It wasn't like her at all. Haven't you spoken to your brother yet?'

'My *what*?' Jane had stiffened.

'Your brother?'

'What do you mean? I don't have a brother. I'm an only child.'

Beth realised her jaw had dropped and hastily gathered herself together. 'When I called on your mother, there was a man in the house. He seemed quite hostile and said your mother was sleeping. I had to practically push my way into the house. Looking back, I assumed he was having a hard time accepting your mother's death and that was why he seemed so... odd.'

'Maybe she didn't die of natural causes,' blurted out Jane, invigorated now. 'Maybe that man murdered her?'

Beth felt an electric shock run through her body. The conversation had taken an unexpected turn. The 'M' word triggered all sorts of difficult memories to start cascading through her brain. No, this couldn't be happening again. Jane was simply becoming overwrought. That was it. There was bound to be a perfectly innocent explanation for all of this.

'The police did take him away after a bit of a struggle at the house,' Beth finally admitted. 'But I'm fairly sure that was simply because he was worked up and getting in their way. It's the police you really need to be speaking to about this. They'll probably be able to tell you a lot more as next of kin.'

Jane got to her feet. 'You're right. I'm sorry to have bothered you,' she said stiffly, turning to go.

Beth knew she should simply stand there and let her go. It was madness to get involved but, unable to help herself, she grabbed Jane by the arm.

'It was no bother,' she said. 'Look, I hate the thought of you up here all on your own and in these circumstances. Why don't you come round to mine for dinner later and we can talk properly?'

Jane's face lit up. 'Really? That's so kind of you.'

Beth scribbled down her address on a piece of paper. 'It's a white cottage with a yellow door, on the left, out Gallanach Road. If you come at seven, dinner will be ready.'

She walked Jane to the door, aware of covert glances from the rest of the staff. Once the door closed behind her, she turned to face them.

'I couldn't help but overhear,' said Lachlan, looking worried. 'It's terrible that Nora has died but is it wise to become involved with her daughter given that the dust has only just settled after the murder in the shop last year?'

'How could I not?' sighed Beth. 'She's clearly all on her own and now that her mother's gone, she doesn't have a soul to help her navigate things up here. When my own mother died, I was knocked for six, I could barely function for months. I thought the least I could do was extend a hand of friendship.'

'But you know nothing about her!' he protested.

'Well, I'm sure that will be remedied tonight,' she added firmly. She noticed the two girls exchanging loaded looks. 'Come on, you two. If you've something to say, spit it out.'

Morna nudged Chloe, who put her hand on her hip.

'We're just worried that you might land in bother with the police again,' she said hesitantly. 'I mean, you were the one who discovered the body in the first place. What if the police believe the son that she was only sleeping when he checked on her, and then you pitch up and suddenly she's dead?'

'That's ridiculous,' scoffed Beth. 'He knew fine well she was dead on one level but maybe he was blocking that knowledge from himself because he couldn't face it.'

'I... er... also couldn't help overhearing,' said Morna, reddening under her thick makeup. 'But didn't the daughter say that she doesn't even have a brother? One of them is surely lying then.'

'Or else she simply didn't know,' said Beth. 'After all, look at me. Until a few months ago, Harris Kincaid and I had no idea we were half-siblings.'

'True,' said Chloe. 'But Nora was so old and straitlaced. I just can't see her having a secret love child somehow.'

'All old people were young once, you know,' admonished Lachlan with a stern glance.

As Lachlan was in his late forties, Chloe and Morna sometimes acted as though he was Methuselah himself. Age-wise, Beth fell in the middle of her staff at thirty-four, and hadn't quite worked out where she fitted in. Sometimes she had a giggle with the young ones and felt quite skittish. Other times she felt more aligned with Lachlan and older than her years.

'We know that,' conceded Morna. 'It just takes a bit more imagination to picture it, that's all. Anyway, I think it's cool that you're being kind to her but please watch your back.'

'Yeah,' said Chloe. 'She did look a bit like a crazy stalker person the way she was acting in the shop. Maybe she was just upset but... even so...'

'I promise I'll be careful,' said Beth. 'It's only dinner. Now, can we please get on and do some actual work? Chloe, we've got Easter coming up soon. Can I leave the window display with you?'

'Of course!' exclaimed Chloe, who was incredibly arty and always full of ideas. 'I thought we could have an Easter egg hunt here in the shop for our young readers followed by juice and Easter egg nests while I read them a story? Maybe Lachlan could dress up as the Easter Bunny?'

'Good heavens! Really?' said Lachlan, looking horrified.

'That sounds wonderful!' said Beth. 'Let me know if you need my help with anything.'

Morna cleared her throat. 'I was wondering if we could have a sci-fi and fantasy weekend?' she said, avoiding eye contact.

Beth's heart sank. Morna was good at her job, but she wasn't outgoing. She could be quite morose and carried a bit of a chip on her shoulder.

'How would you envisage that working?' she asked. 'My main concern is that if it involved cosplay, for example, it might be a bit scary for our younger customers who tend to come in for story time on Saturday mornings.'

'They're all away by noon, though,' interjected Chloe. Beth was pleased to see her supporting Morna. The two girls were as different as oil and water, and had clashed horribly at first, but now, despite their differences, had formed a tentative friendship.

'Lachlan, what do you think?' asked Beth, keen to include the former manager of the shop, now her consultant, in the decision-making process. She was conscious, however, that the shop had been rather staid and stuck in the past under its previous ownership.

'I think it's a grand idea,' he said, pushing his glasses up his nose and smiling at Morna. 'The lass has been really building up that side of the business. We're carrying double the stock in that genre now from when she started here.'

'I thought we could start it at six on the Friday and put together some food, maybe get a couple of kegs of beer and a few bottles of wine. Greg Owan, the author of The Iona Chronicles, lives locally and he said he would be willing to give a talk on the understanding that we make him Book of the Month, giving him a featured book table with signed books for a further two months.'

'There's a romantasy author, Penelope Lively, who lives up in Fort William, too,' said Chloe. 'If you offered her the same deal, I'm sure she'd be happy to appear. An influx of girls would make the whole thing a little less sad,' she added, smirking at Morna who glowered at her.

'We could order in some merchandise on sale or return as well,' said Morna. 'I thought on the Saturday night we could hire a couple of films and have a discussion afterwards.'

'I don't know. It's a lot of outlays, Morna,' said Beth. 'In relation to the filming, maybe you could enlist the community cinema though you'd have to open the screening up to everyone if they agreed to it.'

'Why doesn't she ask for an expression of interest first then we could get an idea of projected ticket sales before committing?' said Lachlan.

'That seems a reasonable next step,' said Beth. 'Perhaps you could also cost out the expenditure. I can absorb a small loss if it brings increased sales but anything more than that...'

'It's fine,' said Morna, striving to hide her disappointment. 'I'll do the groundwork then come back to you. Thanks for at least considering it.'

After dealing with the afternoon's last few stragglers, Beth locked the door and headed home to put the dinner on. At least Morna had distracted them all from their concern that Beth was going to get dragged into the chaos that seemed to be brewing around their customer's death. She knew they were right and that she should be washing her hands of the whole affair, but she'd known Nora and liked her. She couldn't just turn her back on her daughter in her hour of need. What kind of person would that make her?

FOUR

Beth was pulling a tray of steaming moussaka out of the oven, supervised by her black cat, Toby, when she heard a light tap on the door. It suddenly occurred to her that she'd forgotten to check whether her dinner guest was vegetarian. She rushed to the door and felt the spring air cool her flushed cheeks.

'Something smells good,' offered her guest. 'I'm ravenous.'

'You're not vegetarian, are you?' Beth asked with some trepidation.

'No, I'm not,' Jane said. 'Is that moussaka? It smells divine.'

Soon they were seated at the scrubbed pine kitchen table tucking in. Her guest had produced a bottle of red, so Beth opened it and poured a generous measure for each of them. She kept the conversation general while they were eating, to help Jane relax. Due to the fact that food was on the go, Toby made polite overtures to their guest, rubbing against her legs under the table.

'Oh! What a lovely cat!' she exclaimed. 'I didn't even see him. He's like a dark shadow.' Suddenly Jane's body convulsed with a loud sneeze. 'Sorry, I've always been allergic to cats. I love them, just can't be around them.'

'That's a shame,' said Beth sympathetically. She carried an unimpressed cat through to her bedroom. He hissed at her and swiped at her ankle as she made to close the door. She'd have some serious grovelling to do later. As she was returning to the table, she suddenly clapped a hand over her face.

'Oh, no! I'd completely forgotten! Your mum has a cat. It's a big ginger tom called Marmalade. I didn't see him when I... err...'

'It's alright, I get the picture,' her guest said drily. 'I didn't know she'd got herself a cat. It figures. Well, I'll just have to try and rehome him, I suppose. That's if he deigns to show up.'

Beth sat back down and thought for a moment. She was surprised by how callous Jane seemed to be towards her late mother's pet. Nora had had him for years. How come her daughter didn't know that? She'd met Marmalade a couple of times and he was a beautiful big boy and very friendly. He would be so upset and confused by recent events. Casting a wary eye towards the bedroom, she made a decision.

'I'll take him. He knows me a little. I'll see if he'll settle with me, or more importantly, Toby. If they adapt to each other, I'll take him off your hands permanently. If not, I'll keep him until the ideal home presents itself.'

'Thank you, that would be great,' said Jane, looking relieved. She fished out a key from her bag. 'Here's a spare key. I found it at the house under a plant pot. My mother was far too trusting.' She shook her head at such folly. 'Maybe I've been living in Glasgow too long. You'd get robbed blind if you carried on like that there.'

'Yes, too right,' agreed Beth. 'I lived in Glasgow for a long time before coming up here. Whereabouts are you from?'

'Oh, here and there,' Jane said vaguely. 'I moved around a lot. It was hard to find a suitable tenancy.'

The conversation petered out as they applied themselves to the homecooked meal. It always gave Beth a great deal of pleasure to see people enjoying food she had prepared herself.

As she carried a tray of coffee through to the sitting room, she sensed the sudden tension emanating from Jane. Once they were seated in a couple of comfortable easy chairs, Beth took a sip of her coffee and asked the question she'd been dying to ask all evening.

'How did your meeting with the police go?'

'The person they've got in custody is still maintaining he's my mother's son. According to his driving licence, his name is Callum Henderson. His date of birth is apparently 13/02/2002, which would make him considerably younger than me. I'm thirty-six so I just don't see how it's possible.' She shrugged helplessly. 'I mean, I could understand it if my father had had an affair and hadn't realised it had resulted in pregnancy, but how could my mother have hidden that she was pregnant? It makes no sense. I was living with her at the time.'

'I assume that they're doing a DNA test if he has no actual proof beyond his name?' asked Beth, leaning forward.

'Yes, but that'll all take time and he's refusing to cooperate.'

'Can't they get a warrant?' asked Beth.

'Apparently not. The police say his biological parentage is a civil matter unless his identity becomes pertinent to a criminal case.'

'I see,' said Beth, though she didn't really. It seemed quite extraordinary. The only person who could have thrown light on the man's true identity was dead.

'What if he's not her son at all? What if he's deluded or some con man who inveigled his way into her home?' said Jane, her voice rising in pitch. 'If they let him out tomorrow after his court appearance, he's just going to return and squat in my mother's house. I won't be able to get him out, will I?'

'Nora certainly didn't mention that she'd a son,' said Beth. Something else occurred to her. She hadn't mentioned that she had a daughter either, and there'd been no family photos apart from a few of her late husband dotted around. Beth froze. So far, she only had this woman's word for it that she was who she said she was. Her staff were right. She should have been more careful about becoming involved. Had Jane, if that was her real name, even been in to see the police?

'What is it?' asked Jane, her eyes narrowing.

'Nothing!' replied Beth with a strained smile. 'To be honest, I was just thinking back and Nora never mentioned having a daughter either.'

'Well, she was only a customer. Why would she get into the nitty gritty of her family life with *you*? Does the butcher know your family tree?'

Beth gave a faint smile but said nothing further. This was beyond awkward.

'What? You think I'm lying and have come here under false pretences?' Jane stood up and gathered up her bag. 'I didn't always have the easiest relationship with her but that makes me even more devastated that she's dead. We'll never be able to fix things now.'

'Wait! I'm sorry, don't go like this,' pleaded Beth, jumping to her feet. 'I'm just struggling to make sense of it all, please don't be angry.'

Jane turned back towards her, her expression softening a fraction. 'Look, it's fine. I overreacted. You've had a shock, too. I can't blame you for not taking me at face value given the circumstances. Thanks for dinner. I appreciate it. Really, I do. Much better than anything on offer at my hotel.'

'You'll stay in touch?' offered Beth impulsively, scribbling her number down on a Post-it.

Jane took it from her but didn't comment, simply walking to the door without further ado and closing it firmly behind her.

Beth flopped on the couch, feeling wretched. She'd made a real mess of things. Feeling the key still curled in her palm she resolved to go up to the house first thing with a cat carrier and rescue poor Marmalade. It would also give her the opportunity to have a little look around to satisfy herself about one or two things that were eating away at her. She owed it to Nora to make sure that no stone was left unturned in determining her cause of death.

FIVE

The next morning, Beth approached Nora's house warily, but the police presence had now been withdrawn. It was after ten and the haar that had rolled in from the sea greatly reduced visibility. The house seemed to stare at her with shuttered eyes as the blinds had been drawn. A mark of respect to the deceased or to avoid people peering through the windows? A crude V shape had been sprayed in red paint on the brick wall surrounding the property. Beth tutted but supposed it couldn't hurt Nora now. She'd come early to avoid meeting up with the man who had claimed to be Nora's son. As far as she knew the police were keeping him in custody until he appeared before the sheriff this morning. He'd most likely be granted bail and she wanted to be long gone before he returned. Glancing furtively around, Beth let herself into the house and put the cat carrier by the door. The air felt heavy and the cloying scents of yesterday had now dissipated, leaving only a faint trace behind. Beth swallowed hard as she walked quietly into the lounge casting a nervous glance towards Nora's chair which was now empty. Only an imprint of her body remained on the cushions. Just like that, she was gone from this world, alive only in the memories of those who had known her. Beth swallowed hard. There was nothing she could do for Nora now, except take care of her cat.

'Marmalade,' she coaxed in a soft voice. 'I've got some Dreamies...' She pulled the packet out of her pocket and rattled it furiously. She had yet to meet a cat that could resist their siren call. A plaintive miaow pierced the silence and was accompanied by the sound of heavy paws thudding down the stairs. In stalked a huge orange cat with a big head and a big tummy to match. Beth sank down onto her haunches and held out a hand for him to sniff, then shook out some Dreamies onto the carpet. The poor cat was hesitant at first but crept closer, tail flicking, ready to turn and flee should anything alarm him. He gobbled up the Dreamies, purring as he ate, and Beth shook out some more.

'Poor cat, you must be starving,' she soothed, not that he was exactly waif-like. He must be confused and upset though. She ushered him into the cat carrier she had brought with her and clipped it shut. Standing up, she glanced around the room now that she had the opportunity to do so. Nora had been houseproud and kept it well. It saddened her to see the dust already starting to settle on the normally gleaming surfaces. The whole house had a feeling of the pause button having been pressed, which Beth remembered well from the passing of her late mother. She mustn't become melancholy. This was not her loss to bear. As much as she had liked Nora, she couldn't pretend to have known her all that well. It was much worse for her poor family, if indeed that's what they were. She looked around the comfortable sitting room. No photos of Callum or Jane. Why didn't she have a single photo of her children? It was decidedly odd.

Beth moved into the adjacent kitchen, which was large and airy with patio doors opening into a beautiful garden. She picked up Marmalade's bowls from the floor and located his basket and a few toys scattered around. He'd be happier with his own things. It would help him settle.

She was busy packing his things into a large plastic bag that she'd brought with her when a loud bang at the door made her jump out of her skin in fright. Instinctively, she pressed against the wall, feeling the urge to hide away. To her horror, instead of the mystery person giving up and leaving, she heard the sound of the front door opening. Heavy footsteps came into the hall then paused.

'Hello? Is anyone there?' asked a male voice.

Beth groaned to herself. Detective Sergeant Hunter had once more caught her at a disadvantage. Red-faced, she peeled herself off the wall and revealed herself.

'Only me,' she muttered, lifting her eyes to meet his which always seemed to penetrate to her very core. Did they learn to do that at police training college?

'Beth!' he exclaimed, clearly taken aback. 'What on earth are you doing here?'

'I've come to take Marmalade,' she said, pointing to the cat carrier.

He bent down to peer inside and received a spine-tingling hiss for his trouble.

'Rather you than me,' he said with a grimace. 'It's good of you to take him. Can I ask how you got in?'

'Nora's daughter, Jane, gave me a spare key. She's allergic to cats. She said she'd been in to see you?'

'Yes.'

'Don't you think it's weird how there's no photos up of her at all?' asked Beth. 'Not even one from her childhood? My mum had an embarrassing amount of mine up.'

'Everyone's different,' he said. 'It's certainly odd that Nora Kelly doesn't appear to have admitted to having a family to anyone up here.'

'Jane seems adamant that her mother didn't have a son and as he appears to be a fair bit younger than her, it's hard to understand how she wouldn't have known of his existence.' Beth glanced at the clock in the hallway. 'Did he get out on bail this morning?' she asked, wondering if he would be arriving any time soon.

'Yes. I've just come from there. He apologised and said he'd lashed out because he couldn't come to terms with his mother's death. If there's no further incidents the procurator fiscal will probably drop the charges. In the meantime, the case has been continued.'

'He's not dangerous, is he?' asked Beth nervously.

'I hope not,' was the somewhat unsatisfactory reply. 'We're still looking into his claims. But, in the meantime, we've taken his key off him. He won't be able to stay here until such time as he's able to prove his entitlement.'

'You don't think it's possible that he killed her?' asked Beth. 'I mean, he was in the house when she died and was clearly trying to conceal the fact. Although whether that was to cover up his crime or because he couldn't face up to her death, I don't know.'

'All yet to be determined. The postmortem will take place tomorrow morning. Hopefully, we'll know more then. I suggest you try to put it out of your mind and leave it to us.'

'But how can I?' burst out Beth. 'I haven't been able to think of anything else since it happened.'

His gaze softened as he looked at her. 'I know it was a shock, but I don't want you getting involved, Beth. I don't want a repeat of last year.'

'When you thought I was a murderer,' muttered Beth, staring up at him defiantly. A part of her despaired. Why was she antagonising the one person she wanted to get closer to? Every time she met him, she felt so conflicted.

Instead of becoming angry, he looked so sad momentarily that she felt the impulse to throw her arms around him. An instinct she hurriedly quashed. With a deep sigh, he walked to the front door and held it open for her. She picked up the cat carrier and associated feline accessories and walked out. The door closed behind her with a note of finality. Fighting back tears, she strode off. She'd barely reached the gate when she realised that she hadn't thought this through. Marmalade was no lightweight. She wouldn't be able to walk all the way back to her cottage with him. She decided to drop in on Susan Kincaid who lived further along the same road. Hopefully, she'd be able to cadge a lift off her. Puffing further up the hill, she soon found she was in luck as the door opened to reveal an elegant woman whose face lit up on seeing her.

'Just the person!' Susan smiled. 'You've saved me from the ironing I was about to start.' She peered into the carrier. 'And who's this handsome chap?' she cooed, receiving a plaintive miaow in return.

'I can't stay long as I need to get to the shop,' Beth explained, sitting down in one of the comfortable chairs dotted about the large sunny sitting room with views over the bay below. The haar was now starting to clear. It was going to be a glorious day despite the nip in the air.

'I'll be back in a tick,' said Susan and, true to her word, she brought a tray of tea through in under five minutes. 'Are you going to let him out?'

'No, I don't dare in case he runs off again,' Beth said. 'He belonged to one of your neighbours, Nora Kelly. I take it you've heard...?' She hesitated.

'Yes, word has spread along the street. Such a shame, poor woman.'

'Did you know her well?'

'I knew her to pass the time of day with, but we weren't close.'

'What about family?' asked Beth.

'None as far as I was aware,' Susan said.

'A son and daughter have arrived on the scene but the daughter claims that he can't be her mother's son as she would have known, since he appears to be younger than her.'

'Goodness, that does sound a bit odd,' said Susan. 'Best you leave it all to the police, though.' Susan gave a worried glance in her direction.

'Of course,' replied Beth, though she wasn't sure she was going to be able to stand idly by, given that she already seemed to be involved whether she liked it or not. The door to the sitting room opened and Beth looked up to see her newly minted half-brother, Harris Kincaid, waltz in through the door. He was dressed for work as a solicitor and was carrying a briefcase and a banana which he waved at her cheerfully.

'Sorry, Beth, can't stop. I was at court this morning and I've only popped back to pick up a file for the office.' He glanced at the carrier. 'A new edition to the family?'

'Looks that way.' She grinned, and he rushed off.

Susan rose to her feet and grabbed her car keys from her bag. 'Right then, let's get you and Marmalade back home. I think you might need to put him on a diet.' She winced, as she lifted the carrier. There was an indignant yowl. 'How's Toby going to react?'

'I'm about to find out,' Beth said, as they walked together out to the car.

SIX

Beth pushed open the door to the bookshop feeling exhausted already and it was only just after ten. She'd left the two cats in separate rooms as it had been hate at first sight. Toby had spiked himself up like a pufferfish and spat venom at the newcomer who wasn't shy about responding in kind. She was glad that she didn't understand cat language as she suspected things were getting sweary. Hopefully, they'd get over it soon but, if not, she'd need to find Marmalade a good forever home.

The shop was busy, she noted with quiet satisfaction, with all of her staff engaged in chatting animatedly to customers. She slipped behind the cash desk as she noticed an older woman, whom she recognised, approaching.

'Morning, Valerie,' she said brightly, as she took the book from her. It was *Anxious People* by Fredrik Backman. 'We've sold quite a few of these in the last week,' she said as she slipped it into a paper bag. 'I haven't read it yet, you must let me know what you think of it.'

'It's for my book group,' Valerie said with a smile. 'They have me reading all sorts.' Her smile faded. 'It won't be the same next time. We lost one of our ladies recently.'

'It wasn't Nora Kelly by any chance, was it?' Beth asked.

'Yes, how did you know?' Valerie asked, surprised.

'I'm afraid that I was the one who found the body,' she said, lowering her voice.

'Oh, how awful!' Valerie said, her hand flying up to her mouth.

'I gather that she'd been ill recently,' Beth said, handing across the book and ringing it up on the till.

'Yes, she missed the last two monthly meetings. but the meeting before that she was happy as a clam and dropping hints about having a gentleman caller. They'd met online and had decided to meet up in person for dinner. She was as giddy as a girl. Of course, we told her to be careful and to meet in public places until she was sure of him, but I suspect she was hellbent on jumping in with both feet. Such a shame she became poorly in the end.'

'Terrible,' Beth agreed. 'Enjoy the book!' was her parting shot, not wanting to arouse suspicion by asking too many questions.

The rest of the morning passed in a blur and it was soon lunchtime. Today was Morna's turn to cover lunchtime in the shop and eat later. The rest of them sat around the table in the staffroom and brought out their packed lunches.

'Oh, I asked my mum about the carer in the turquoise uniform,' said Chloe.

Her mum, Jean, was a nurse attached to a local GP practice in the town. 'What did she say?' asked Beth, her sandwich paused halfway to her mouth.

'None of the regular care agencies use a turquoise tunic. She reckons it was probably someone obtained privately.'

'Oh well, that's that, then,' sighed Beth, taking a bite. 'A dead end.'

'You sound like you've already made up your mind that it's foul play?' said Lachlan, pushing his glasses up his nose. 'Why, may I ask?'

'I'm not sure exactly. It's more of a feeling really. I mean if I'd gone in and she was dead in her chair I would simply have assumed she'd had a heart attack or died in her sleep. What worries me is the way that her supposed son was acting. It was beyond weird. He'd lit all these candles to disguise the... er... smell.'

Chloe screwed up her face. 'Maybe he has mental health problems?'

'Or maybe he's the one who killed her,' said Beth grimly. 'For all we know he's been closeted in the house with her for longer than he let on. The carer that I came across before seems to have vanished. Why is that? Shouldn't she have been in touch with the police already?'

She was conscious of her voice rising and the concerned glances of her staff. They were right. She needed to cool it and leave it to the police to investigate. It would be sheer folly to get involved.

'I wonder who his solicitor was at court this morning?' Beth said.

'Most likely the duty solicitor,' said Lachlan. 'From what you've said he sounds too erratic to have instructed one of the big boys to come up from Glasgow.'

A horrible suspicion took hold. Beth groaned. 'Harris was at the court this morning. I bet he represented him.'

'But that's good, isn't it?' asked Chloe.

'No, it's not,' retorted Beth. 'It means he'll clam up and I won't be able to get anything out of him at all.'

'Look, Beth, I know that she was one of our regular customers, and seemed like a nice woman too, but it's not your responsibility to figure out what happened to her,' said Lachlan, peering at her over his glasses.

'Then why is my gut telling me something different?' she said, shrugging helplessly. 'Maybe if I'd got there earlier, instead of fussing around doing paperwork first, I could have arrived when she was still alive? If I'd only taken the box over before work instead of after, everything might have been different. Maybe I could have saved her...'

SEVEN

Beth was exhausted. It had been a long day. She whipped up a quick cheese omelette with some tomatoes on the side and took it into the lounge where both cats were sitting on opposite sides of the room letting out low growls at each other. She'd fed them in their separate rooms but thought it was time they were properly introduced. Clearly, it wasn't love at first sight. Toby was also cross that she'd temporarily locked the cat flap as she didn't want to let Marmalade out just yet, in case he ran off to try and get back home. The poor cat must be missing his owner and had no idea why his world had turned upside down. Beth felt for him.

'Come on, Toby. Can't you be the bigger cat?' she pleaded. 'Marmalade needs a home. What would you have me do? Toss him out into the street?' She looked over at her scowling cat. Silly question. Of course that's what he'd have her do. In a heartbeat.

The doorbell rang. Both cats stopped yowling and glanced towards the door. Beth went to answer it and discovered, to her pleasure, it was her brother, Harris. She ushered him into the lounge and rushed off to stick the kettle on. Coming back a few minutes later bearing two mugs, she was dumbfounded to see both cats on the couch on either side of him, purring.

'What did you do?' she gasped. 'What magic is this?'

He grinned and produced two catnip mice from his pockets. 'I thought you might need help brokering a peace deal.'

'Thank you, you're the best,' she said with an affectionate smile. 'I owe you one.' Harris hadn't been in her life for long but already she couldn't imagine her life without him. Sitting opposite him she wondered how to broach what was on her mind without annoying him.

'You were at court today, weren't you?' she said casually.

'Yes, I said as much this morning.' His eyes narrowed.

'Did you act for Callum Henderson?'

'You know the score, Beth. I refuse to discuss anything pertaining to my work with you. I'm doing my level best to prove to the Law Society that I have integrity and follow the rules. I've only just started to climb out of the enormous mess my grandfather and father made of things.'

It was true that he was effectively on probation. After a disciplinary hearing resulting from him briefly trying to hide the fact that his grandfather had embezzled money from client funds and dragged his father into the resultant mess, Harris had, eventually, with his mother's blessing called in the Law Society and closed down the family firm. He was now working for another firm but could not become a partner again until his period of probation was over. It had been a difficult time for the family.

'Okay, I totally understand that,' said Beth. 'But surely you can tell me anything that was said in open court? After all, anyone could have been sitting listening in the courtroom. It's a matter of public record.'

'Fine,' he sighed, conceding that she had a point. 'I wasn't duty solicitor, as it happens. He was represented by a solicitor from another firm. The court was informed that Nora Kelly was indeed his biological mother as she'd donated surplus embryos to a woman undergoing fertility treatment who'd been unable to produce her own eggs. Callum Henderson grew up knowing nothing about it until the woman who brought him up died and he came upon the paperwork and a letter from his mother which had been kept and had Nora's address on it. A few months after his mother's death, he travelled to Oban to try and establish contact with his biological mother. Upon discovering her dead body, he was thrown into despair and denial, which is why he was difficult and uncooperative with both you and the police.'

'So, what happened?' asked Beth, agog at this latest development.

'The Procurator Fiscal didn't oppose bail but continued the case for further investigation. I expect you'll read all about it in *The Oban Times*,' he said. 'Their reporter was sitting on the edge of his seat throughout.'

'Poor guy,' said Beth, her sympathies aroused now. 'No wonder he lost the plot. He was still grieving, and to find that his biological mother was still alive must have seemed like such a gift only for it to be snatched cruelly away.'

'That's as may be, Beth, but I want you to promise me you'll steer clear?'

'Hasn't he suffered enough without being ostracised as well?'

'For goodness' sake, Beth, just do it,' he snapped, anger sparking in his eyes. 'You can't rescue every lame duck you come across.'

Beth stared at him, taken aback. The cats both swivelled their heads towards him and then looked at her, their tails twitching. What on earth was with him? He'd no business issuing her orders. The only reason that she could think of for this uncharacteristic behaviour was that he was privy to additional information that he didn't feel comfortable disclosing.

'Fine.' She shrugged, watching the tension leave his eyes and his shoulders come down. She'd only capitulated to stop him worrying about her, but she had no intention of leaving it there. If anything, he'd only whetted her curiosity.

'Did you know that your sister was the police surgeon in the case?' asked Beth.

'Yes,' he said. 'Now can we please talk about something else?'

Beth smiled and switched the chat to other things. It was only after he'd gone and she was locking up before settling the cats back in their respective rooms that she was struck by the fact that she hadn't heard anything from her half-sister, Fiona. They usually met up once a week for coffee or a couple of drinks, but there had been total radio silence from her ever since the body had been discovered. Maybe she'd simply been busy? Or perhaps she was avoiding her…

EIGHT

The following day, Beth was rushing along George Street, trying and failing to get to the chemist and carry out some other chores in her lunch hour. Although she was the boss, she felt it set a bad example to her staff if she was late back, as if she thought she was better than them, which certainly wasn't the case. That said, the sunny weather coupled with Easter approaching had resulted in the main shopping area being filled with meandering tourists, some of whom seemed so ditzy that she was amazed they were allowed out on their own. She became aware that she was grinding her teeth in frustration. She'd just reached the pharmacy when someone bowled out of the door, almost knocking her over.

'Watch it!' she said crossly, almost falling. The man grabbed her by the elbow and drew her inside.

'Sorry,' he said, releasing her. 'I wasn't concentrating on where I was going.'

Beth stared up at him as his eyes flared with recognition.

'You!' he spluttered, taking a step back.

'Hello,' said Beth, feebly waving. 'I didn't get the chance to introduce myself properly the other day. Beth Cunningham, I own the Wild Haggis Bookshop off George Street.'

'Oh!' he said, shuffling awkwardly from one foot to the other.

Beth waited expectantly, assessing him all the while. He was tall and lanky with hazel eyes and looked a bit lost. Hardly surprising in the circumstances.

'I'm Callum,' he offered with an attempt at a smile. 'I suppose I owe you an apology. The other day, I wasn't quite myself,' he blurted out. The blood rushed to his cheeks. He suddenly looked very young, almost endearing, thought Beth.

'Look, we can't talk here,' said Beth, aware of causing an obstacle to people trying to move in and out of the shop. 'Why don't we go for a coffee?'

'A coffee?' he said, his eyes widening. 'Yes, why not?'

They walked out together, and Beth directed him towards a small café which was more off the beaten track up a narrow side street. Once they were seated with steaming mugs and slabs of buttered Bannock, she sat back in her chair and her eyes met his.

'I know it must have been a huge shock for you, what happened the last time we met, the police and everything.'

He scrutinised her as though deciding whether she could be trusted before nodding.

'A few months earlier, I lost my mother, or should I say the woman who brought me up,' he said, his eyes bright with unshed tears.

'She was clearly your mother in every way that mattered,' soothed Beth, reaching across the table to pat his pale, cold hand. He had long fingers, she noticed, the hands of a pianist. 'I lost my own mother only a year ago.'

'Then you know,' he said, his sad eyes meeting hers. 'When I found the correspondence amongst my mother's personal effects telling me that she wasn't my biological mother, I admit that I was completely thrown for a while. I felt angry that she'd lied to me all those years.'

'That's understandable,' said Beth. 'Maybe that anger even helped at first? What about your father?'

'He died when I was six. I didn't know him. He walked out just a few months after I was born. When I found out about my biological mother, it gave me something to cling on to, I suppose.'

'Were you in touch with her before she died?' asked Beth, her voice gentle.

He shook his head. 'I thought if I wrote to her, she might reject me outright, tell me not to come. I decided to go on an ancestry site first – I wondered if I might have some siblings or cousins or something.'

'Did you get any matches?'

'No, but someone did contact me. A policeman from a cold case unit in Glasgow. He said that I was a familial DNA match for an unsolved case in Glasgow. At first, I worried he was trying to pin something on me. I'd been in a bit of bother with the police during the last couple of years, but he said it only meant that a close relative may have been involved.'

'Did he tell you what the crime was?' asked Beth.

'No, he said he wasn't allowed to at this stage. I explained that I had been born through embryo donation and showed him the letter from my mother. After that he left and I never heard from him again.' He shrugged.

'Can you remember his name?' asked Beth.

'Sorry, I can't. I assumed he'd be back in touch if he needed anything else from me.'

Beth felt for him. She really did. But her intuition was telling her that he was still very unstable.

'So, you simply arrived on her doorstep?'

'Not right away. I got DNA tested to see if I had any siblings. I went on an ancestry site, but there weren't any matches. It took a while to work up to it. I thought she might see herself in me. Stupid, really.'

'Did you have time with her before she... passed?' asked Beth.

Abruptly he rose to his feet. 'I need to go now. This is... too much.'

'I'm sorry,' said Beth, genuinely contrite. 'I didn't mean to upset you. Please, take my card, and if I can help in any way...'

'Thanks,' he muttered, stuffing it into his pocket and hurrying out of the café.

Beth slumped in her seat. She'd pushed too hard and he'd shut down. He was more vulnerable than she'd realised. And yet she'd been scared of him that day at the house. He'd admitted he had a criminal record as well. She ground her teeth in frustration that she hadn't managed to get more out of him when he was sat right there across from her.

She'd had one opportunity and she'd blown it big time.

NINE

Arriving back at the shop as the town clock struck two, Beth skidded to a halt and regarded the mess in front of her in horror.

'Chloe, you can't block the entrance to the shop like this. Someone could rush in and trip over some of these boxes and break their neck!'

Chloe popped up from behind the cash desk like a jack in the box. 'Sorry, I was just looking for pins and our double-sided tape – I'm about to tackle the window to set up our Easter display. Morna!' she yelled, her dainty appearance belied by emitting a yell that could be heard on the street. 'Give us a hand to shift this stuff, will you?'

Morna appeared from the stock room, rolling her eyes at Beth after taking in the situation at a glance.

'What on earth possessed you to put them there in the first place?' she moaned.

Chloe flushed. 'We were shut for lunch. I didn't think.'

The bell above the door tinkled and Beth moved to chat with the elderly woman until a safe path was cleared for her to advance into the shop.

'You know what would be great,' the woman said, her face lighting up. 'If you had a display of Easter chicks over there.' She pointed with a quavering finger. 'I remember the department store in town had them when I was a girl. All the children were desperate to go and see them.'

'What? Real ones?' asked Beth, aghast.

Lachlan walked over to join the conversation. 'Afternoon, Sheila.' He smiled. 'I think that's a great idea. I haven't seen anything like that for years. It would be quite the draw. We could have competitions to count the number of chicks for our younger customers. The parents will love it, too. Something different for them to take the kids to.'

Beth held up her hands. 'Okay, I'll think about it, I promise.'

She went to help the girls as the customer wandered over to the crime section. It was a section of the shop she would gladly do without after the events of last year, but it was also one of her biggest sources of revenue. One thing was certain, she would never attempt to start another crime book club. The last one had ended with the murder of one of the participants.

Giving an involuntary shudder she firmly squashed those memories back down. They weren't the only ones she had stuffed down into her psyche like an unseemly pile of dirty washing. Looking for a distraction, she focused on the possibility of an Easter display of chicks. The idea did appeal but the potential for things to go wrong terrified her. She had to stop allowing fear to dictate her actions, she told herself crossly. A shadow crossed in front of her, and she looked up startled into the amused brown eyes of Detective Sergeant Logan Hunter.

'You look like you're having an argument with yourself,' he said.

'Actually, you're not wrong.' Beth grimaced. 'Just weighing up the pros and cons of having a display of live chicks in the shop at Easter.'

'I remember those from when I was a boy,' he said. 'Poppy would love it. You'd probably have to frisk her on the way out of the door.'

Beth laughed at the thought of his very cute six-year-old

daughter sneaking out of the door with a new furry friend in her pocket.

'It is a lovely idea,' admitted Beth, 'very retro. But I'm sure it comes with a whole raft of bureaucracy – that's if it's even allowed these days. I've promised to look into it.'

He handed over a special edition of *Felicity Wishes*.

'I assume this is for your daughter?' she said, tongue in cheek.

'Absolutely not!' he shot back with a twinkle in his eyes. 'I don't know how I'm going to get through my shift till I can get home to read it.'

'I'm not convinced.' She laughed and handed over the paper bag. As she did so, their hands touched and a jolt of electricity shot up her arm. She yanked it back so quickly he almost dropped the book. She could feel the flush bloom in her cheeks. She rubbed the underside of her elbow. 'Ouch! Sorry, got a bit of tendonitis,' she fibbed.

He looked sceptical and confused, as well he might. What on earth was wrong with her? She caught Chloe grinning knowingly at her across the shop. She had to get this encounter back on a proper footing.

'So, I had a coffee with Nora's son,' she announced. It had the desired effect. His expression hardened and his eyes narrowed.

'Why on earth would you want to do that?' he snapped, his voice raised. Everyone in the shop turned to look at them. Aware of this, he lowered his voice, though the animosity remained. 'Is there anywhere quieter we can discuss this?'

Beth led him out of earshot to the back room and motioned him to sit at the table, closing the door to the main part of the shop. Why did she have to goad him by bringing this up? Talk about jumping from the frying pan into the fire. Although, on the other hand, she thought, stiffening her spine, he had no right to dictate to her who she could or couldn't have coffee with.

'Beth, you know nothing about this man,' he said, obviously trying to curb his temper. 'You've led a very sheltered life in some respects. People aren't always who they say they are. I know that you probably meant well but please don't try to insert yourself in this case. I don't want to fall out with you,' he added softly.

Beth felt her defences subside like a pricked balloon. She sensed that the reason he was always on her case was because he cared and didn't want anything bad to happen to her.

'Look,' she said, leaning forward. 'Whether you like it or not, I'm already involved. It was me who discovered poor Nora's body and called you lot out to the house. She was also a good customer of mine and therefore I want to ensure that the truth comes out about what happened to her. As it turns out, I did find out something useful.'

'Go on,' he sighed.

'The killer might have tracked Nora down through one of those ancestry websites. Callum had a visit from someone who said he worked with cold cases and Callum's DNA had thrown up a familial hit.'

'Did he say what unit or what the unsolved crime was?' asked Logan, leaning forward.

'No, unfortunately. He can't remember his name either.'

'It'll be like looking for a needle in a haystack then,' Logan sighed, the light leaving his eyes. 'If it was only a familial match it's likely not even anything to do with this case.'

'I'm still hoping that Nora died from natural causes. Surely you must have the results of the postmortem by now?'

He sighed and shook his head, his lips compressing into a straight line. 'Even if I did, I'm hardly likely to share them with you, am I?' he ground out from between clenched teeth.

Beth softened her voice. 'Look, all I need to know is, was it natural causes? If so, then I'll hold my hands up and walk away, honour satisfied.'

'Stay out of it, Beth, I'm warning you,' he said, rising to his feet and swiftly exiting the shop, his back ramrod straight.

Beth slumped back in her seat feeling bruised by the encounter. She hated confrontation; she always had, ever since her schooldays. Hurriedly, she forced her mind out of that particular cul-de-sac.

As her mind sieved through their conversation, one thing struck her forcibly. It wasn't what he'd said but what he'd not said. If Nora hadn't died of natural causes, that left only one possibility. She had been murdered...

TEN

Beth stretched out her arms luxuriously and snuggled back down in the bed. It was Sunday, the one day of the week where she got to have a proper lie in. The doorbell rang. She groaned and dragged herself out of bed, throwing on her comfy dressing gown before stumbling downstairs, bleary-eyed. Who could possibly be calling on her at this time on a Sunday? Unlocking the door, she cringed at the brightness of the sun as she shaded her eyes and peered at her visitor. A slim, attractive woman who looked to be in her early forties with dark hair pulled back into a bun offered a tentative smile. She looked vaguely familiar, but Beth couldn't place her.

'My name is Maria Sanchez,' she said. 'We met once before. I was Nora's carer. Please, I need to talk to you.'

Recognition flared as Beth's eyes widened, all traces of sleepiness gone in an instant.

'Please, come in,' she said, throwing open the door. She led Maria through to the kitchen and stuck the kettle on. 'Give me two ticks to get changed then we can sit down and talk.'

Five minutes later, she raced back downstairs having washed her face and thrown on jeans and a T-shirt. She was amused to see Marmalade making a fuss of her guest, butting his big head against her hand and purring away, whilst Toby frowned at them from a distance.

'He remembers you.' Beth smiled. Cats weren't a pushover so if Marmalade liked Maria, she couldn't be all that bad, surely?

'It was a nice thing that you did, giving him a home,' Maria said.

Her English was excellent but spoken with a slight accent.

'He's a lovely boy. I couldn't leave him to fend for himself. Coffee?' Beth asked.

'Please, black,' said Maria, clenching her fingers together nervously.

Beth brought over the coffee and a plate of biscuits, then sat down facing Maria who now looked ill at ease.

'I wanted to speak to you in private, not in the shop,' Maria said.

'How did you find out where I lived? Did one of my staff tell you?'

Maria coloured. 'No, I followed you here after work last night. I was going to speak to you then, but I was too afraid.'

Beth froze. The very idea of someone following her out here from town, skulking behind her like some criminal, was more than a little creepy. She forced herself to respond.

'Afraid of what?' asked Beth. 'Why haven't you come forward before now? I'm sure the police would like to speak to you.'

Abruptly Maria stood up, her face turned to stone. 'This was a mistake. I should never have come.'

She turned to flee but Beth caught up with her and grabbed her by the wrist just as she reached for the door.

'Wait! I'm not the police! I won't involve them if you've done nothing wrong, I promise.'

Maria stood still, every sinew poised to flee. Beth let go of her wrist and held her breath, taking a step back.

'I want to help you. Honestly, I do,' said Beth. 'But I also want justice for Nora. Imagine if she was *your* mother?'

'Fine, I will talk,' said Maria with a sigh. They walked back into the kitchen and resumed their seats.

'My visa has expired. I have no right to work in this country,' Maria admitted. 'I want to stay here. I *need* to stay. But it will take time to sort the paperwork out. Until then, I need to stay out of the way.'

'Where are you from?' asked Beth.

'Seville, in Spain.'

'Would it be so very terrible if you had to go back for a while and sort out the paperwork from there?' asked Beth, puzzled.

'Yes, it would!' snapped Maria. 'You don't understand. There is a man there who follows me everywhere I go. Due to freedom of movement in the Schengen area he has even followed me from country to country. Here, he cannot follow without a visa. It is the only place I feel safe.'

'Were you in a relationship with him?' asked Beth, shocked.

'No, he was a customer in a café where I was a barista. I gave him no encouragement, but he became obsessed. The police didn't believe me. He was clever. I came here on a student visa because I needed to put distance between us. I was finally starting to feel safe and that my life was my own again when I got caught up in all this.'

'How did you get the job with Nora?' asked Beth.

'Three months ago, there was an ad in the local newspaper with a box number,' she shrugged. 'I applied and then a man contacted me to arrange an interview.'

Beth was confused. 'A man? You mean her son?'

'Nora did not have a son. No, it was someone else.'

'Who?' asked Beth, leaning forward.

'He said his name was Captain Oliver Saunders. His partner, Nora, had been ill and he needed someone to take care of her for a month or two. He was arranging to leave the army so he could move in with her. He offered cash in hand and didn't seem worried about references. I took the job.'

'Where did you meet him for the interview?'

'The interview was online.'

'What was he like?'

'He was very charming. His accent was different to how people speak around here but still Scottish. He was in army uniform.'

'Goodness,' said Beth, perplexed. 'It seems odd that he was involved enough in her life to arrange for a carer, yet no one seems to have heard anything about him. I don't suppose you have a photo of him by any chance?'

'Yes, I did,' said Maria, flicking through her phone then passing it across to Beth.

The photo showed a man facing into the light in an army uniform with aviator shades obscuring his eyes and an army beret pulled low over his face. He had no tattoos or distinguishing marks that she could see, and the image was blurry and over-exposed. It was a relief to have more information to go on, although it was frustrating that the photo wasn't clearer. A suspicious mind might think that this was deliberate on his part.

'Mind dropping me a copy of that?' asked Beth. 'Just in case it helps in tracking him down.'

Maria hesitated. 'I don't know... What if he is innocent? I don't want to be disloyal. He was good to me.'

'If he *is* innocent, then he has nothing to worry about,' said Beth, trying to keep her body language relaxed so that Maria would not take fright and bolt.

'I suppose you are right.' Maria nodded. A couple of seconds later, Beth's phone pinged and the photo lit up the screen.

Beth smiled her thanks and bent to study the photo. Maybe the police could enhance it somehow?

'Nora told me that they met online six months before,' Maria continued. 'Her face lit up like the sun when she mentioned him.'

'Do you have a contact number or address for him?' asked Beth, her mind spinning as she tried to process this new information.

'I had a phone number,' Maria said, 'but it hasn't been working for a while now.'

'When did it stop working?' asked Beth, dreading the answer.

'When I called him to say that I had returned to find her dead in her chair, he seemed cold, different somehow – maybe it was the shock? I asked him what to do. I was frightened about what this could mean for me.'

'What did he say?' asked Beth.

'He said he would phone the police and take care of everything. He said he knew I had no right to remain here so I should pack and leave immediately.'

'When was this exactly?' asked Beth, feeling sick to her stomach.

'Late on the morning of the first of March. I felt bad running off leaving her there but what choice did I have?' said Maria, her guilt very much evident. 'After that, I was unable to reach him by phone.'

'He didn't call the police,' Beth said flatly. 'I discovered her body that evening when I went to deliver a parcel.'

'What? But he promised me he would. How could he leave her like that?'

You did, Beth almost retorted, but she didn't want to alienate Maria. She had to get her to agree to do the right thing. 'I doubt very much from what you've described that he was a man of his word,' she said instead.

'So, he was a bad man?' Maria asked, her eyes glistening with tears.

'Possibly,' said Beth. 'It's too soon to know. You said that he paid you cash in hand?'

'Yes. I do not have a bank account at the moment. It seemed safer to deal in cash.'

'So, how did he get the cash to you?'

'He paid me for the first three months in advance when he met me to give me the keys at the house.'

'What? He met you in person?'

'Yes, he had left the army by then. He was living at the house. I spoke to Nora at the same time. She was a bit poorly then but still well enough to show me around.'

'When you met him at the house, did he look the same as when you spoke to him online?' asked Beth.

'Yes, of course, why wouldn't he?' said Maria, knitting her brows. 'She was so happy when I arrived. She showed me her engagement ring. They were going to be married once she was better. She thought she only had an infection, nothing that could kill her. It is so cruel that her happiness was snatched away.'

Yes, but by whom? thought Beth. She really didn't know what to think. One thing was clear – she didn't want to be responsible for poor Maria being deported. She'd got in a muddle with her visa, but she seemed decent enough. However, this new development needed to be brought to the attention of the police. But how to do that? Getting in the middle of this investigation was the last thing she wanted to do but neither did she want to let Nora down if she had no one else to advocate for her.

Her first impression from what she had been told by Maria was that Captain Saunders was some kind of catfish or romance scammer, but he had turned up here in the flesh so perhaps he was genuine after all. But, if so, why wasn't he liaising with the police and making himself available to her family. How could he have left Nora just lying like that? Where was he?

ELEVEN

On the way to work, Beth's first port of call was Harris Kincaid's new firm, Edgar and Whitelaw, which was tucked away in a side street near the supermarket. No lofty sandstone here; its façade was white painted brick with a glass door protected by metal shutters which were rolled down at night. With some trepidation she ventured inside. The receptionist was young and a far cry from Miss Pringle at the old place. Heavily kohled eyes looked her over as if to assess whether she posed a threat, and several piercings gave her quite an intimidating air. Beth told herself off for being judgemental. She, of all people, should have learned by now never to judge a book by its cover.

'Can I help you?'

'Yes.' Beth smiled. 'I was wondering if Harris Kincaid is free at the moment? I'm his... er... sister.' It felt like a lie even though it was the truth. She still wasn't used to saying it.

'I'll check,' said the young woman, whose name badge said Ailsa. She picked up the phone and pressed an extension. 'Harris, I have your sister in reception wanting a word. Are you able to see her?'

Then, with a smile that lit up her whole face, she said, 'Just go through. Third door on the left, you can't miss it.'

Beth thanked her and was soon tapping lightly on Harris's door. She guessed that there would be no bone china teacups with shortbread on the side here.

'Come in,' he shouted, and she pushed open the door. His room was small and sparse with a view onto the car park, but he looked happy; his shirt sleeves were rolled up, his desk buried in files and legal aid forms.

'Beth! What brings you here?' He smiled, lifting some files off a seat so she could sit down.

'I need a little advice,' she said, perched on the edge of the chair, 'for a friend. It's about immigration law.'

'Whoa, stop right there,' he said, holding his hand up. 'That is absolutely not my area. There's not much call for it up here. I can give you the name of a good one in Glasgow, however, if that helps?'

'Please,' she said, sitting back as he wrote the details of a lawyer in a firm in Glasgow down on a Post-it.

'Tell him I sent you. He'll give you, or should I say, your friend, mate's rates. He also does legal aid.' He glanced at his watch. 'Is that all?'

Beth was desperate to tell him about what had been going on and get his opinion, but she also didn't want to burden him or cause any problems for him at his new firm. He'd been lucky to land another job in Oban at all after his grandfather's embezzlement had been uncovered.

'I can see you're busy.' She smiled. 'That was all I needed. Don't be a stranger!'

His head had dipped back to his files before she'd even left the room. It was good to see him happy and motivated once more.

Turning up Albany Street, she pondered what to do. How on earth could she get this critical information to the police without causing poor Maria to be deported by the Home Office? She walked by the police station and paused, lost in thought, whilst she stared in the window that faced the street. What if she were to go in and speak to DS Hunter? He was a reasonable man, or so she now believed. Shaking her head, she decided against it. Anything she told him in the station would be seen by him in black and white terms. She didn't want to be sat across the table from him in there. It made her feel vulnerable and powerless, feelings she wasn't keen to experience again. Turning round, she continued down the street, mulling things over in her head, oblivious to her surroundings.

'Beth! Wait up!'

Her heart sank as she turned round to see Logan Hunter jogging towards her, a puzzled expression on his face. He paused before her and she looked up at him, biting her lip.

'I saw you looking in the window. Is there something we need to know?' he asked, turning those gorgeous dark eyes on her. It was an unfair interrogation technique, she thought crossly, aware her cheeks were pinker than they ought to be.

'Maybe,' she muttered, looking away. 'I'm worried it might cause problems for someone else if I tell you. I'm not trying to be difficult.'

'Look, whatever it is, it's probably best if you tell me. I take it this is to do with Nora's death?'

She gave a small nod.

'Come back to the station with me.'

'Not there,' she almost whispered. 'I still have flashbacks from last year. Please don't make me...'

He looked flummoxed. 'Right, well, where then?'

'Come to the cottage tonight at seven. I'll tell you what I can then. Oh, that won't work. Poppy will need you.'

'She's at my mother's tonight for a sleepover,' he said, looking at her so intently she had to fight the urge to visibly squirm.

'Stay for dinner then,' she blurted out. 'Two birds, one stone. We can eat and talk at the same time.'

Beth cringed internally. Why, oh why, hadn't she suggested meeting for coffee? Her default position was always to try and feed people. Still, maybe a more informal atmosphere might soften him up for her request?

He looked at her completely perplexed as though she had suddenly started speaking in a foreign language.

'Fine,' he said, 'it's a date.' Horror gripped his face. 'I mean, I'll see you then. Obviously not a date. Not in that sense.'

'Obviously,' she echoed, trying to look as repulsed as he did at the thought.

Hurriedly, they turned away from each other and started walking in the opposite direction.

'It's not a date,' she muttered. 'The very idea!'

TWELVE

By the time Beth reached the shop it was nearly ten o'clock. She'd stopped by the bakers to get some cream cakes for tea break. Quickly she updated them on Maria's visit.

'I suppose it explains why she didn't hang around,' said Lachlan, a dollop of cream sliding onto his tie, unnoticed, much to the amusement of the girls. 'Have you contacted the police?'

'Yes and no,' said Beth, looking away.

'Which is it?' asked Morna.

'I couldn't face going into the station again, not after last year, so I've invited Detective Sergeant Hunter round for dinner tonight. I'll tell him everything then.' She braced herself for the onslaught. It wasn't long in coming.

'Are you completely mad?' exclaimed Lachlan.

'I knew she had the hots for him,' whispered Chloe in Morna's ear.

'Seriously, Beth, this guy has been trying to lock you up for ages. Are you really planning on giving him enough rope to hang you with?' asked Morna, sounding exasperated.

'Look I get it, really, I do.' Beth winced. 'But if I'd gone through some kind of formal process at the station to tell them about Maria, they would have felt obliged to notify immigration and next thing she'd have been deported. She just needs some breathing space to get her paperwork in order.'

'It's her responsibility to attend to that, Beth,' said Lachlan. 'You can't save everyone.'

'Maria has been through a lot. She has a stalker in Spain who follows her wherever she goes. He has followed her all over Europe due to the freedom of movement there. That's why she's so desperate to stay here.'

The door tinkled and Chloe took a look.

'It's only the post,' she said. 'We're in here, Dad!'

Dave Montgomery came through and passed the mail across to Beth.

'I should have come in earlier,' he laughed, taking in the cake crumbs and the odd smear of cream. 'Have a good day, ladies.' His freckled face exuded uncomplicated good humour. 'Lachlan, you missed a bit,' he added, pointing to the creamy splotch on his tie.

Lachlan dabbed at it ineffectively before giving up and buttoning up his cardigan to cover it.

'Your dad's so lovely,' said Morna wistfully to Chloe, once he had left. 'Mine is so cold, he'd give Darth Vader a run for his money.'

Beth had never met the Abercrombie family but, despite their wealth and status, they sounded horrendous. Morna was still affected by growing up deprived of affection and support. They were doing their best to show her how much they valued her, but the years of feeling worthless continued to exact their toll.

A plaintive miaow sounded. And then another one, a throatier one. Toby strolled in, looking very pleased with himself followed by an anxious looking Marmalade.

Lachlan reached out to stroke him and was met with a hiss as the large cat spiked up to look as threatening as possible.

'Lachlan, you scared him!' scolded Chloe.

'He scared me!' protested Lachlan, who had withdrawn the hand of friendship sharpish.

'Hello, beautiful boy,' cooed Chloe, reaching out a gentle hand for him to sniff. In no time at all she had Marmalade purring ecstatically, his plump sides going in and out like a bellows. Toby looked less than pleased with this development. His fat ginger friend was hoovering up all the attention.

'Come here, Toby,' soothed Beth, pulling him on to her knee and giving him a loose Dreamie that she had found in her pocket. 'You'll always be my number one,' she whispered in his ear. He settled down, looking mollified.

'I can't believe Toby brought him all that way,' Morna marvelled. 'I take it they're getting on better now?'

'They still have their moments,' said Beth. 'Anyway, where were we, before your dad came in, Chloe?'

'Dinner with the delectable detective sergeant,' said Chloe impishly.

'My thinking was that if I told him about Maria in a social setting, it might make him think twice before reporting her to immigration.' Beth shrugged. 'I suppose it depends on how much he wants to solve the mystery of Nora's death. She has information that could help with the investigation, but he would need to offer some guarantee before she'll talk to him.'

'Sounds like she's trying to hold him to ransom which I doubt will go down well,' cautioned Lachlan. 'Please don't allow yourself to be dragged into her mess.'

'You'll have to use all your culinary wiles,' said Chloe, her eyes sparkling with merriment.

'I rather suspect he'll be immune to all my charms, culinary or otherwise,' Beth said, pulling a face at Chloe.

THIRTEEN

Beth was furious with herself for inviting Logan Hunter over for dinner. Why on earth hadn't she simply suggested him popping round for a coffee? The whole thing was going to be fraught with awkwardness, and he was going to think she was an even bigger weirdo than he already did. She'd changed her clothes twice, second guessing herself all the way before settling on jeans and a plain blue T-shirt.

The doorbell rang, causing her heart to jump in her chest. She rushed to open the door.

'DS Hunter, come in,' she said, her mouth struggling to remember how to smile.

'Please, call me Logan. I'm off duty,' he said, dark eyes meeting hers.

He walked past her into the hall leaving a vapour trail of lemon soap with a hint of ginger in his wake. It made her feel quite weak at the knees. Stop that this minute, she scolded herself, suddenly realising that he'd turned to watch her, a smile quirking up at the corner of his mouth.

'You're arguing with yourself again, aren't you?' he said.

'Mind reader now, are you?' she shot back.

'Now, wouldn't that be great?' he sighed. 'It would certainly make my job an awful lot easier.'

'You look tired,' she said, softening. 'Come through to the kitchen. Dinner's nearly ready.'

'I brought you some wine,' he said, fishing it out of a carrier bag and handing it to her. 'You don't need to open it now.'

'Did you drive?' she asked.

'No, I walked. Nice night for it,' he said.

'Then I'll open it,' she declared, reaching up for two wine glasses. 'If you pour the wine, I'll dish up.'

'Smells good, whatever it is,' he said, sniffing appreciatively.

Quickly, she pulled out a tray of hot bubbling lasagna and served up two generous portions to add to the bowl of salad originally on the table.

'Cheers!' she said brightly, as they clinked glasses. 'How's Poppy getting along? Is she looking forward to Easter? You must bring her along to the shop. We're going to have Easter chicks with us for the whole week.'

'You managed to get them, then?'

'Yes, Chloe's parents know a farmer who's letting us have some on loan. The only worry I have is that Toby and Marmalade have taken to visiting the shop. Can you imagine their faces? The display is going to have to resemble a high security prison.'

Logan laughed. 'This is delicious, Beth. Much nicer than anything I could make. I'll definitely bring her along. She'd love to see the chicks.'

'She's such a sweet little girl.' Beth smiled.

'You're very good with children,' he commented.

'I've always found children and animals easier to get along with...'

'Than grumpy police officers?' he suggested.

'Quite!' She laughed. 'It's much nicer talking to you like this than when you're interrogating me at the police station.'

There was an awkward pause. Why, oh, why, did she have to go and spoil things?

'You go through and I'll bring some coffee and tell you what's been happening,' she said, feeling their earlier easy rapport drifting away.

'I'm happy to wash up first,' he offered, rolling up his sleeves.

'No, it's fine,' she said, distracted by the sight of his strong muscular arms and wondering what it would be like to be held by them.

'Are you all right? You're looking really flushed,' he said. 'Maybe I should make the coffee?'

Turning away from his concerned gaze, she waved him away. 'I always get hot when I cook. I'll be through in two ticks.'

She boiled the kettle and poured water into the cafetière then assembled a tray with a plate of cookies she'd made earlier. Glancing through the open doorway she noticed with some amusement that her usually discerning cat was now sitting on Logan's knee being petted and looking very pleased with himself. Marmalade was sulking by the woodburning stove.

'I see you've made a new friend.' She smiled as she walked through with the tray.

'He's a lovely boy,' Logan said, accepting a mug of coffee along with a biscuit. 'Poppy has been begging for a pet but it's a big responsibility and I feel I've got enough on my plate already, raising her on my own.'

'Cats are fairly self-sufficient so they make good pets for people with busy lives,' said Beth.

'How's poor old Marmalade been doing?' he asked.

'I think he still misses Nora. It's horrible when you can't help them to understand why things have changed so much. I don't think he'd have settled as well if Toby hadn't taken him under his wing. He even brings him along to the shop now. We're inadvertently turning into some kind of cat café.'

'I have a feeling you're a collector of waifs and strays,' he said, shaking his head.

'Talking of which,' she said, 'I suppose I'd better get into the reason I invited you here tonight.' She placed her mug on the table.

'Go on,' he said, his dark eyes scrutinising her as he took a sip of coffee.

'Now, before you accuse me of meddling again, I just want to put it out there that this person came to my door, having followed me home from work. I did not deliberately involve myself.'

'What person?' he asked, his voice tight.

'Nora's carer.'

'I see. Go on,' he said, his voice cold now, like he had snapped back into police officer mode.

'Honestly, Logan, she's terrified. She applied to an advert for a carer/home help in *The Oban Times* with a box number. It was an online interview with an army officer who was speaking from somewhere abroad.'

'Some kind of romance scammer?'

'That's what I thought at first but then he met her in person at the house. She saw them together and said that Nora was wearing an engagement ring and seemed really happy.'

'What's this guy's name?'

'Captain Oliver Saunders,' Beth replied. 'The first name of the carer is Maria, but I don't want to give you her second name until I know what's likely to happen to her if she cooperates. She's Spanish, over here on a student visa that has now expired. She's desperate to remain here because she has a persistent stalker in Spain. She wants to do the right thing but not at the expense of her liberty.'

'I can't authorise that, Beth. That's a decision that needs to be taken at a higher level. There's no other evidence of this army officer in Nora's life. She wasn't wearing an engagement ring when we found her. Nor was one lying around anywhere. Have you considered the possibility that Maria might have made him up to evade responsibility for killing her patient, either accidentally or deliberately? Thus far, we've only her word for it that he even exists.'

Could Maria be playing her for a fool? She'd seemed so genuine.

'I suppose time will tell,' Beth sighed. 'But it does seem like either way, you need to talk to her. She did take a screenshot of him at her online interview but it's not very clear.'

'Can you ping it to me?' he said, sitting up straighter, which elicited a cross look from Toby.

'I... er... don't have your number,' muttered Beth, toes curling in embarrassment. What if he thought this was some elaborate ruse on her part?

He held out his hand for her phone and added himself as a contact after which she hurriedly sent it across.

'Interesting,' he said. 'It could have been taken anywhere, and it very much looks like he was attempting to reveal as little as possible about his features without triggering suspicion. It's not enough to identify him or even what country he was calling from.' He peered closer.

'A captain, you say? That doesn't look like a captain's uniform to me. I'm no expert but you can see one chevron on his insignia which to me means this isn't an officer's uniform at all. I'll need to check that though.'

'Of course, none of this would even be relevant, if it was found that Nora died from natural causes,' said Beth, hoping with all her heart that this was true.

'All I can say is that in the eyes of the police it remains a suspicious death,' he said, his voice bleached of emotion. 'We're waiting for the toxicology reports after which we may have a clearer idea of what's gone on.'

'Toxicology,' said Beth slowly, putting down her mug. 'You think she was poisoned?'

'I didn't say that!' he snapped. 'Stop jumping to conclusions!'

Beth froze, stung by his sharp response.

'I'm sorry,' she said, chastened. To her horror she felt her eyes welling up with tears. She jumped to her feet and picked up the tray. 'I'll be back in a second,' she managed, before rushing into the kitchen. In her haste, she tripped over her feet and ended up hitting the tiled floor with an almighty crash, the plate and half full cafetiere smashing around her. It was too much. Mortified, she burst into tears, hurriedly gathering up the broken pieces.

A strong pair of arms lifted her to her feet. 'Beth, you're bleeding,' Logan said in consternation.

'It's just a cut,' she said.

'Where's your first aid box?' he asked, shaking his head. 'That's really quite deep. Might even need stitches.'

'Under the sink,' she muttered.

He strode away to retrieve it and just a few minutes later, she was back in her cosy sitting room with her hand bandaged, sipping a mug of sweet tea with a pair of warm brown eyes watching her every move.

'Thank you, I think I'll live,' she joked, whilst still squirming inside with embarrassment. 'I'll be fine now, honestly, you can go. You probably have plans since Poppy is away.'

As if suddenly remembering, he glanced at his watch and stood up. 'Well, if you're sure. I am supposed to be meeting someone for a drink and it's a bit late to cancel on them.'

Beth felt relieved that this awkward encounter was being brought to an end but, also, weirdly disappointed that he was seeing someone. Hurriedly, she jumped up.

'Absolutely,' she said with a forced smile. She walked ahead of him to the door and, as she opened it and turned back to him, he unexpectedly gave her a hug. It felt so good she wanted to cling to him like a limpet but forced herself to release him. She still had some shred of dignity.

'Good night, Beth,' he said softly, his dark eyes inscrutable. 'Take care of yourself.'

'Good night,' she replied, her heart beating so fast she thought he might hear it.

FOURTEEN

Beth paused outside the butcher's shop, her eye drawn to the three death notices edged in black posted discreetly in the bottom of the window. No one she knew, thankfully. Going inside, she glanced over all the notices pinned to the wall inside, advertising the thrumming community life of her new home. She was exhausted by the deaths that had stalked her since she had arrived in the town. It was high time she found another interest. Zumba or line dancing? Film club or gliding? The choices were endless.

'Can I help you?' asked Glenn, the friendly butcher who was as round as he was tall. 'How are things in that bookshop of yours? I've been hearing good things. My wife is never out of the place.'

Beth laughed. 'Yes, Tamsin's a voracious reader, isn't she? Have you heard that we're having a display of chicks during Easter week? We've also got an Easter egg hunt and story time for the little ones on Easter Saturday.'

'Our little granddaughter would love that,' he said, his kindly face lighting up. 'Get young Chloe to drop off a poster and I'll stick it on our wall of fame,' he said. 'Now what can I do you for today?'

'A pound of mince, a Scots pie and half a dozen pork sausages, please.'

After paying, Beth headed straight into work. She was determined to keep busy today to avoid replaying the events of last night in her brain. It seemed she was completely incapable of acting like a normal person around Logan Hunter. If only she hadn't been dragged into another suspicious death. They always seemed to be on opposing sides. She couldn't stop wondering if the person he had talked of meeting was another woman. *What does it even matter?* she scolded herself. *He's hardly going to look at a scatty mouse like you in that way.* She was so deep in thought that she almost collided with Fiona Kincaid who looked as distracted as she was.

'Fiona! How have you been? I haven't seen you for a proper chat for ages,' Beth exclaimed. She looked at her half-sister more closely. Her eyes were tinged with pink and her face was tight and strained. 'Are you alright?' she asked, taking her by the arm and drawing her to the side of the pavement where they wouldn't be buffeted by tourists. 'Has something happened?'

Fiona tried to smile, pushing her ice-blonde bob back from her face. 'I'm fine,' she said. 'Or at least, I will be. Just having a bit of a bad day.'

'I feel like you might have been avoiding me,' said Beth, with a rueful smile. 'Have I done something to upset you?'

'What? No, of course not!' exclaimed Fiona, giving Beth's arm a squeeze. 'I've just had a lot going on. Look, have you got time now? We could go somewhere for a coffee if you like?'

They settled on a small quiet café near the harbour and sat at a table beside the window. The proprietor, a rotund, cheery woman, brought over their coffees and some warm shortbread fresh out of the oven.

'So, what's been going on?' asked Beth gently, taking a sip of her coffee and nibbling on some shortbread.

'It's silly, really,' Fiona said. 'At my age, I should know better. Did Harris tell you that the reason I moved back here from Edinburgh was because of a rather messy divorce?'

'No, he didn't say a word,' said Beth. 'I'm so sorry, that must have been awful!'

'He cheated on me with my best friend,' Fiona said bluntly. 'So, no great loss when you think about it. Anyway, instead of coming clean and admitting what they'd done I had to endure a year and a half of gaslighting until I finally caught them. In the meantime, he'd been feathering their new nest with money he siphoned off from our joint assets.'

'What a pig!' exclaimed Beth. 'You're better off without either of them in your life.'

'No argument there, I suppose. It's taken me a long time to trust again but I'd finally found someone I was ready to take that leap of faith with. We hadn't been dating long but I felt so comfortable around him and now he's told me he's developed feelings for someone else. It's just put me straight back in that place again. Stupid, I know.'

Beth passed her a tissue. She didn't know Fiona as well as her brother. In fact, if she was honest, she felt a little intimidated by her, even though Fiona was a few years younger. She was tall, blonde, and very much someone who seemed to be in the driving seat of her life.

'None of us are immune from heartbreak,' she said, giving Fiona's hand a brief squeeze. 'Don't beat yourself up for being human. At least he had the decency to tell you and not string you along.'

'Anyway, enough about me,' said Fiona, making an effort to pull herself together. 'How are things with you?'

'A little more complicated than I'd like,' Beth replied. 'You know how I discovered Nora's body?'

'Yes, of course, I was there.' Fiona nodded.

'Well, I just can't stop thinking about it. This woman followed me home one night. It was Nora's carer. It turns out she was hired by some army type who paid her in cash, no questions asked.'

'Have you been to the police?' asked Fiona, raising her eyebrows.

'I told Detective Sergeant Hunter last night.'

'Oh? I thought he was off duty last night?'

Beth had a horrible thought. Could Fiona have been the person he was meeting for a drink?

'He was but I invited him round for dinner so I could get all this off my chest.'

'I see,' said Fiona, raising an immaculately trimmed eyebrow. 'Bribery with lasagna?'

'That's the one.' Beth grinned. 'My signature dish. Anyway, the problem is that Maria, the carer, has a visa but it's expired, and she's desperately trying to sort out the paperwork so she can legally remain here. She doesn't want to go back to Spain and reapply because she's being pursued by a determined stalker over there. I was asking him on her behalf if he could guarantee that immigration wouldn't be notified if she were to come forward but he said it wasn't his decision to make.' She sighed.

'That's a tough one,' Fiona said. 'You do seem to be getting... rather involved. Are you sure that's wise?' Her forehead creased in concern.

'Probably not,' sighed Beth. 'DS Hunter was being cagey as to whether Nora died of natural causes or not. If I knew that was the case, then I could relax and let it all go. Please tell me if you know anything, it's all I can think about right now,' Beth pleaded.

Fiona looked at her then seemed to come to a decision. 'Look, you'll find out soon enough but I'm afraid that her death remains suspicious.'

'You mean, murder?' asked Beth, her mouth dry as a bone.

'I can neither confirm nor deny that,' said Fiona, whilst slowly nodding her head. 'You'd better watch your back, Beth. Leave it to the professionals. Logan is meeting with the family members today to update them on the investigation's change in status. There's going to be something in *The Oban Times* about it tomorrow. No stone will be left unturned. So, if I were you, I'd encourage Maria to come forward.' She stood up to leave.

'I wish I knew what you're not telling me,' said Beth, biting down on her lip.

'Be careful, Beth. Things are about to get very complicated.'

'For me?' she asked, worried now.

'For a lot of people,' Fiona said, turning to leave.

FIFTEEN

Beth entered the shop and immediately sensed a change in energy. There was a beautiful young woman effervescing at a mesmerised Chloe who was hanging on her every word. Even Lachlan was looking slightly pink and starstruck as he rang through some glossy coffee table books that came to an eye-watering amount. It was only when she glanced towards the door to her office and saw a visibly distressed Morna pressed against the inside wall that she realised who their exotic customer must be.

It was Cassandra Abercrombie, model, socialite and, incredibly, Morna's sister. As Morna was estranged from her entire family apart from one uncle, she knew that Cassandra wouldn't have popped in casually. Despite the family having a fabulous estate in Argyll, they tended to shun contact with locals, opting instead for luxury brands and moving in elite social circles that were a combination of old money, iconic artists, and musicians and actors. The woman had her back to her whilst charming Chloe into a melted puddle, so Beth studied her through narrowed eyes. Despite the practised charm and tinkling laugh she couldn't find much of substance about her. She suspected her charms were superficial and underneath lurked something cold and grasping. Clearly, she'd come here with an agenda. She felt a surge of anger and a strong urge to protect Morna from whatever it was her family were cooking up. She gestured to Chloe to wrap it up, seeing her eyes widen in surprise. Cassandra swung round and advanced towards her, tossing her long blonde locks, manicured hand outstretched.

'Hello, you must be Beth, I've heard so much about you,' she gushed. 'I'm Morna's sister.'

'Oh?' said Beth, giving her hand a perfunctory squeeze. 'I didn't know that she had one. If you'll excuse me, I've got an important phone call to make.' With that, she walked smartly into her office, closing the door behind her. Her eyes sought out Morna's then she enfolded her in a hug.

'Has she gone yet?' whispered Morna, white as a sheet.

Beth let her go, opened the door a crack and peered out. 'Yes, she's gone, you can relax now,' she soothed. Morna let out a long breath, ran her hands through her short black hair and together they walked back into the shop. Chloe was chattering away to Lachlan, her voice pitched high with excitement. He, too, looked more animated than normal.

'OMG, Morna. Where were you? Your sister was in and she's desperate to meet up with you. I still can't believe Cassandra Abercrombie was here in our shop. She has, like, a million Insta followers. I've never met someone that cool before. She just oozed style. I swear I almost passed out on the floor. I think Lachlan nearly did, too,' she teased, turning to grin at her colleague.

Morna stood motionless, her skin bleached of colour. She said nothing. Beth, too, remained silent. It wasn't for her to interfere. She wanted to scold Chloe for being so insensitive, but it wasn't her place.

Chloe's face suddenly went bright red and tears sprang to her eyes as she took in Morna's strained expression. She rushed over to her and hugged her immobile body.

'I'm so sorry, babbling on like that, Morna. I'm such an idiot,' she said, contrite. 'Are you okay?'

Morna unfroze enough to give her a hug back. 'Don't sweat it, Chloe. It's called charisma. My family has it in spades, apart from yours truly. The ugly duckling who never made it into a swan.' She gave a bitter laugh.

For the first time, Beth got a glimpse of the pain behind Morna's family estrangement. She'd been under the impression that Morna had rejected her family but now she rather thought the opposite might be true.

'Don't talk about yourself like that, lass,' admonished Lachlan. 'People like your sister turn people's heads because they make you feel like you're the only person in the room but that feeling of connection is ephemeral and disappears like the morning mist. You, on the other hand, are as real as they come and we wouldn't have you any other way.'

The women all looked at him in surprise as he wasn't given to delving into emotional territory.

'Thanks, guys,' said Morna. 'I can't believe she waltzed in here like that. As far as I knew they didn't even know I'm working here. Did she say what she wanted?'

'To meet you for lunch,' said Chloe, fishing a classy business card out of her pocket and passing it across. 'Beyond that, I can't say. Maybe you should meet her, see what it's all about?'

'I really don't want to,' Morna sighed. 'They must want something from me but for the life of me I can't figure out what.'

'Best sleep on it first,' said Beth. 'See how you feel once you've had a chance to weigh things up.'

The doorbell tinkled and a crowd of people poured through the door led by Ruaridh McLean, the cheerful tour guide with his trademark Tam o' Shanter. By now they had their system down to a fine art. Everyone had ordered and paid for their choices from the online catalogue so the books were already waiting in custom paper bags on the table in alphabetical order. This gave them time to browse and chill out in the café area with coffee and a choice of two cakes which Beth had baked specially.

'Morning, everyone!' Ruaridh called, looking even more frazzled than usual. Beth showed him to a small table with a reserved sign and brought him over a coffee and a slab of Victoria sponge cake.

'Just what the doctor ordered,' he said gratefully. 'Some rather strong personalities on this trip,' he then whispered, nodding over to where a group of American tourists were looking around avidly and peering with peculiar intensity at the floor.

'What are they doing?' she whispered back.

'They got wind of the fact there'd been a murder here last year. Don't shoot the messenger,' he said, holding his hands up on noticing her cross expression, 'it wasn't me!'

What was wrong with people? wondered Beth. A woman had lost her life. It wasn't the first time people had shown a macabre interest, but it upset her every time.

Suddenly, one of the women got up and laid down on the floor as her friend took a photo.

'She did not just do that,' muttered Beth, jumping to her feet and rushing over as the woman got back on her chair, an excited gleam in her eyes.

'What on earth do you think you're doing?' she demanded angrily.

A beefy hand was held out for her to shake. 'Marge Peterson,' she said in a Southern drawl. 'Just a little pic for my true crime blog. Real nice to make your acquaintance, Beth, honey. I just love your quaint little shop. Smile!' She whipped up her camera, catching Beth completely unawares. Desperately, her eyes cast around for Ruaridh. Taking the hint, he stood up and blew his whistle, herding all his charges towards the door.

'See you next week,' she said faintly, raising a hand as they all trooped out having scoffed both large cakes and leaving a heap of dirty dishes behind them. The girls quickly loaded up the dishwasher and Beth set about making batches of shortbread and chocolate chip cookies for any afternoon customers. She'd just put the last batches in the oven when she heard two plaintive miaows and looked round to see Toby flanked by Marmalade.

'Hello, boys.' She smiled. 'In for a lunchtime snack?' She walked over to their bowls beside the back door and emptied out some dried food. Marmalade started eating at once, but Toby fixed her with a look as if to say, *Come on, you can do better than that!* Caving under the pressure, she walked over to the fridge and took out a small slice of roast chicken and divided it between them.

'Fine, you win.' She grinned at him.

Leaving them to it she walked back into the main part of the shop. She was standing by the cash desk chatting to Lachlan about some invoices when the door opened. The look of anxiety on Lachlan's face made her turn round to see who had just walked in. At first her heart lifted to see Logan Hunter, but it sank into her boots when he was followed through the door by DC Rhona Quinn. Clearly, they were here on official business.

'Can I help you?' Beth faltered.

'We hope so,' Detective Sergeant Hunter said, his dark eyes inscrutable. She didn't need the smirk from DC Quinn to tell her that she was in trouble. 'We'd like you to come to the station with us voluntarily to answer a few questions to help with our inquiry into the murder of Nora Kelly.' His expression gave nothing away.

'Yes, of course,' she said faintly, looking around at her staff whose shocked expressions she knew mirrored her own. 'Can I follow you down there?' she asked.

'It's best you come with us now,' DS Hunter replied, his tone grave. 'Time is of the essence.'

'Fine, I'll get my coat and bag,' Beth said, knowing when she was beaten.

'I'll phone Harris Kincaid and get him to meet you down there, in case they decide to try any funny business,' said Lachlan, with an angry look at Detective Sergeant Hunter.

Beth had hoped to never again set foot in a police station but that wasn't to be. Walking out to the waiting car, DC Quinn assisted her into the back seat of the car none too gently while Detective Sergeant Hunter walked round to the driver's seat.

Feeling powerless once again she sat back and stared straight ahead as the car made its way through the town centre and turned right towards the police station.

SIXTEEN

Beth felt her heart sink as she entered the police station flanked by the two detectives. There was no one at the front desk and she was taken straight through the back. As the door swung shut behind her and locked automatically, she felt trapped. It was happening again and this time she had no idea why.

'I'll put you in here, meantime,' said DS Hunter.

'I'd like to see my solicitor before the interview,' Beth said, determinedly.

'Harris Kincaid has been notified and is on his way,' DC Quinn said.

Again with the smirk, thought Beth crossly.

'Tea? Coffee?' DC Quinn asked as the two officers prepared to leave.

'Please, tea with milk and two sugars.' She didn't usually take sugar, but she had a feeling she was going to need it.

Twenty minutes later DC Quinn arrived back and deposited a plastic cup on the table along with two rich tea biscuits on a paper plate.

'I wouldn't nick it if you gave me real crockery, you know,' Beth snapped at her.

'It's not about that,' DC Quinn retorted, pulling aside her hair to reveal a scar near her hairline. 'That's what happened the last time I dished out crockery in here.'

'Okay, fair enough,' said Beth. 'And for what it's worth, I'm sorry that happened to you.'

The officer nodded, looking a little less hostile, and left the room again.

Finally, a welcome face in the shape of Harris Kincaid stuck his head around the door. Underneath his smile she could see that he was tense and worried as he sat down beside her and turned to face her.

'What is it? What have they said?' she asked fearfully.

'I'm afraid it's not good, Beth. They got the toxicology report back and it would seem that Nora was poisoned. Traces of a lethal dose of alpha-amanitin were found in her system. Basically, death cap mushrooms. It's quite clear that she was murdered.'

'That's terrible!' said Beth, aghast. 'But wait a minute, what does this have to do with me? Why am I even here?' she asked, trying to read his expression as well as his words.

'This is where it gets tricky,' he said gently, squeezing her arm. 'The police are maintaining that she ingested poison from the contents of your subscription boxes.'

'What? But that's impossible!' she burst out, horrified. 'Why on earth would I do that? In fact, how would I even know *how* to do it?'

Her solicitor shrugged helplessly. 'I don't have any answers for you, Beth. At least not yet. The focus of the investigation is the small items that were in the boxes along with the books. The detective sergeant mentioned a few teabags and some sample chocolates?'

'Those were given to me by other suppliers,' she said. 'I can't imagine how they've come to be contaminated.' A horrible thought occurred to her. 'Nora's wasn't the only box that went out. There are about a dozen others with the same contents. We need to do something. Other people could be in danger. Although, it's odd I haven't heard anything,' she said, puzzled now.

'The police think that it was a localised incident,' he said. 'They're coming now. You know the drill: say nothing until we figure this out.'

The door opened and in strode the two police officers. Now that Beth was aware of what had happened, her heart was beating so fast that she thought she might keel over. How had she managed to find herself in this position again? They sat down in front of her and switched on the recording machine. Knowing what she did, she could expect no mercy or favour from Detective Sergeant Hunter. After they had all identified themselves for the purposes of the tape, he looked her straight in the eye.

'Beth Cunningham, you do not have to say anything. But it may harm your defence if you do not mention when questioned something you later rely on in court. Anything you do say may be given in evidence. Do you understand?'

'Yes,' replied Beth.

'Did you deliver three book subscription boxes to Nora Kelly?'

'Yes, one the day I found her body and the others on the two preceding months.'

'What else was in these boxes apart from books?'

'The content varied according to my suppliers and the differing tastes of my customers.'

Harris was nudging her foot under the table. She paid him no mind. This was too serious to worry about saving her own skin. She had to tell them everything she knew before someone else was hurt in her name.

'Can you give us the names of your suppliers?'

'Like I said, they varied. Basically, I had contacted a number of local suppliers who could, if they wished, let me have small samples of their wares, together with a business card or leaflet, should the customer enjoy it and wish to obtain more. I thought it would be a series of treats for my regulars but also help out local businesses. It could be a small bar of soap, a few herbal teabags, a tiny candle, a couple of artisan chocolates, that sort of thing. If you give me some paper, I'll write down the ones that I used for those three previous deliveries.'

'Interview paused,' the sergeant said, passing across a piece of paper and a pen. Hurriedly she scribbled the names down, feeling guilty for the world of pain she was about to inflict on each and every one of them.

'One of them was a pop-up shop, Time for Tea, that isn't there anymore,' she said, pushing across the list.

DS Hunter held up a hand to stop her. 'Interview resumed. You said just now that one of your suppliers was a pop-up shop that's no longer trading. Was that run by Kathleen Boyle on your list?'

'Yes,' said Beth. 'She wasn't in business long, just a few months.'

'Did she start up before or after you started sending out the subscription boxes?'

'After,' said Beth. 'But I'm sure that she wouldn't... none of them would...'

Another nudge from Harris accompanied by an eye roll. She glowered at him.

'I'm not going to throw someone else under the bus just to get out of a tight spot,' she hissed at him.

He pointed to the recording machine and shook his head at her.

Beth groaned and covered her face with her hands. 'Look. I've been as honest with you as I possibly can. Unless there's anything else I can help you with, I'd really like to go home now.'

The two police officers glanced at each other.

'Nora Kelly left a will,' said DS Hunter, his dark eyes boring into her as though intent on seeing into her very soul.

Beth shrugged helplessly.

DS Hunter opened a folder and removed two copies of a document, passing one copy to Beth and one to her solicitor. Harris snatched it up, his narrowed eyes frantically scanning the text which extended to several pages.

'For the record, copies of the will have now been passed across to Beth Cunningham and to her solicitor, Harris Kincaid. She left you her cat, Marmalade, and her entire estate,' he went on, his voice cold and implacable.

'What?' gasped Beth. 'No, that simply isn't possible. There must be some mistake.' She flipped through the pages helplessly but her brain wouldn't engage with the legal jargon.

'No mistake,' he snapped. 'But in any event, you already knew about the will, didn't you? That's why you waltzed off with Marmalade two mornings after the body was discovered.'

'No, that's not true,' she protested. 'I took him in because that's what anyone halfway decent would have done. This whole will thing is an absolute joke. I don't want anything from Nora. I don't understand any of it.'

DC Quinn leaned forward, her intense grey eyes pinning a distraught Beth to her seat.

'Did you persuade your vulnerable customer to write that will in your favour and then contrive to poison her to get your hands on her estate?' she said, her voice laced with contempt.

'No, I did not!' fired back Beth, her body shaking with fear and anger.

Harris jumped to his feet. 'Unless you're in a position to charge my client,' he said, his voice seething with anger, 'then we're leaving.'

'Interview terminated,' said Sergeant Hunter, the air between them both crackling with hostility. 'You're free to go.'

'For now,' added DC Quinn.

Never one to resist sticking the boot in, Beth thought, glaring back at her. They were shown out of the police station in stony silence. Beth couldn't bear to look at Logan Hunter. Her head knew that he was simply doing his job and following where the evidence led but her heart was bruised by the knowledge that he didn't fully trust her.

SEVENTEEN

Beth sat across from Harris in his small office, her hands wrapped around a mug of hot sweet tea, courtesy of Ailsa the receptionist, who rushed to stick the kettle on when she saw their faces. Beth couldn't stop shaking and her teeth chattered against the rim of the mug each time she took a sip of tea.

'Get that down you,' said Harris. 'It's good for shock. That bastard pulled the will out of his hat like a cheap magician. A heads-up might have been nice.'

'I just don't understand,' said Beth. 'I mean, I knew Nora, I would chat to her when she came in the shop. But it's not as though we were close friends. She always seemed quite lonely, I suppose. She also loved Toby and knew how much I loved cats but that doesn't explain why on earth she would leave me everything in her will, especially when she has a daughter.'

'I have heard of people who leave their estate to their pet so that they will be provided for after their death, but this seems to be such a bizarre decision,' Harris said, leaning back in his seat, a frown on his face.

'I don't want anything from it,' declared Beth. 'Well, apart from Marmalade, that is. I'm too attached to part with him now. The whole thing makes me horribly uncomfortable.'

'That's the least of your worries,' Harris said, his brow furrowed. 'It also gives you a motive for murder.'

Beth's heart banged against her chest then settled back down. This was ridiculous, she thought. It couldn't be happening. It felt like someone was pulling the most elaborate practical joke on her. But it wasn't funny and nobody was laughing. Least of all her. Added to which, the whole thing had put her in the sights of the police again. She tried to reconcile the Logan who had, briefly, held her in his arms last night with the stern unsmiling man who had interviewed her today. She couldn't. It was like they were two different men.

'Beth! Are you even listening to me?' interjected Harris, looking exasperated.

'Sorry, I was miles away.' She grimaced. 'What did you say?'

'The will might be genuine, and Nora was simply more grateful than you knew for what I'm sure were your many kindnesses towards her. Alternatively, someone is using you as a scapegoat and trying to frame you for murder.'

'Wouldn't Nora have to sign it?'

'Yes. It'll need to be compared to other samples of her handwriting. In Scotland, a signature on a will also needs to be witnessed and the place of signing must be stipulated.'

'Who witnessed it?' asked Beth, leaning forward.

'The woman who seems to have been her carer.'

'She never mentioned anything to me about it,' said Beth, folding her arms.

'The will hasn't been prepared by a solicitor, so I'll need to go over it, clause by clause. At first glance, it appears valid, but I'll need to study it in depth and consult a colleague who specialises in that area of law. I don't know much about executry work. I'll make an appointment with the Procurator Fiscal and see if he'll let me examine the principal will. All I have here is a photocopy. I doubt there will be a problem.'

'Can't you get it from the police? Surely, they won't want to withhold evidence?' said Beth.

'Trying to get information out of Logan Hunter is close to impossible. I'm happy to go over his head on this one. I'll also demand to see a copy of the postmortem and toxicology reports. The Fiscal is a fair man. I'm hopeful that he'll consider it in the public interest to make that information available to me at this stage. After the last case, you could have sued them for wrongful arrest but didn't, so I figure he'll be inclined to play ball because you were completely exonerated the last time.'

'In the meantime, I'll arrange to call round on all of the lovely people who donated samples to the subscription boxes,' Beth said, wincing as she thought of how that was likely to go. People would be furious with her if their products were dragged into a police investigation, let alone one in relation to murder. She'd be lucky if they didn't sue her for reputational damage to their businesses. She could lose everything she'd built if the town decided to close ranks against her and effectively starve her out of business.

'Have you still got that list with their names and addresses?' asked Harris.

She fished it out of her satchel for him. 'Here it is.'

Just when she'd thought she was safe and that the locals were starting to treat her like she truly belonged here, the rug was once more being ripped from under her feet.

'It's also entirely possible that the contents of the boxes were doctored by someone in the house who had access to them. Maria the carer, Oliver the fiancé, Jane the daughter and Callum the son, all spring to mind. All could potentially have had access and opportunity. It's possible that both Jane and Callum had made earlier visits without us knowing anything about it. But no obvious motive springs to mind, especially in light of that will,' he sighed. 'You're the sole beneficiary so what would anyone else have to gain by murdering Nora? I'll need to ascertain which firm of solicitors has been instructed to deal with her estate.'

'Honestly, I don't want to even think about that. It feels wrong to me on every level,' said Beth.

'It'll take ages to obtain confirmation through the court,' said

Harris. 'Also, if, by some outside chance, you were found guilty of murder, you wouldn't be allowed to inherit anyway under the Proceeds of Crime Act.'

'It feels a bit weird that our sister Fiona is on the side of the police in all this,' said Beth sadly.

'It might limit how helpful she feels she can be to us, but at the end of the day her role was restricted to police surgeon. Her only involvement has been to declare life extinct, not to determine cause of death. That's all down to the pathologist.'

Beth gathered her things and stood up. She was bone-tired and unsure she had the strength to embark on another fight to clear her name.

'For the first time, I'm starting to wish I'd stayed in Glasgow,' she said quietly. 'I had a small life there but at least I felt safe. I'm not sure I've got enough fight left in me to win this one, Harris.' She looked across at him, her eyes swimming in tears.

Immediately, he jumped to his feet and came across to hug her.

'Beth, no one who knows you thinks for one minute that you have anything to do with this. I think that whoever did this has put you in the frame after learning of your background as a result of the police investigation last year. They are counting on the no-smoke-without-fire theory, but it can only take them so far because you and I both know that you had absolutely nothing to do with Nora's death. I wouldn't be at all surprised if the will is proved in the end to be completely phoney as well, so don't go spending it all at once,' he said with a smile, trying to lighten the atmosphere.

'As if,' Beth scoffed, trying to meet him halfway so he wouldn't worry about her. 'Mind you, with two cats to keep in roast chicken and Dreamies, who knows...?' she added, managing to smile.

EIGHTEEN

Beth padded back to her bedroom with a mug of tea and a slice of buttered toast after feeding the cats. She collapsed back into bed, pulling the folds of the duvet around her like a cocoon, one from which she would prefer not to re-emerge. She'd left a message on the answerphone at work telling them that she wasn't well and wouldn't be coming in as she couldn't bear to speak to anyone. She'd left her curtains open so that if anyone came to the door they would think she was out. A few minutes later she was joined by two cats with fishy breath sitting on either side of the bed staring at her.

'What?' she asked. 'You've been fed and watered and the cat flap's open. Just go about your day and pretend I'm not here.'

This did not go down well. They were creatures of routine, and she was evidently putting a wrinkle in their day. Eventually, they seemed to collectively decide that she needed to be monitored for other signs of aberrant behaviour and plumped down on the bed, one either side of her like bookends, and commenced grooming.

Beth finished her breakfast and snuggled back down in her warm cosy bed. She was glad that she'd done a big shop the day before so she could hide out here indefinitely. She knew that she should be throwing herself into planning and mobilising to defend herself yet again, but she couldn't bring herself to do it. She couldn't even bring herself to care. Perhaps even more surprising was that she had no notion at all to pick up a book and lose herself in it.

Books had always served as a portal to another world, a way to escape the often-unpleasant reality of her own, especially when she was younger. Now, it felt pointless. Everything suddenly felt pointless. It was all just too much, and she couldn't deal with any of it. She turned her phone to silent and put it under the bed. The world could get along without her for a few days. She had nothing left to give.

The doorbell rang, awaking her from a deep and dreamless sleep. She turned on her side and ignored it. Cue more staring from the cats. This was a pattern that was repeated throughout the day. She disconnected the bell. That was better. Her stomach was empty, but she couldn't stand the thought of eating. She gave the cats their tea and continued to lie there immobile, watching as the light faded to darkness.

NINETEEN

Chloe burst through the door of the shop, shaking off the rain like a wet dog. It had been a slow morning, so she'd gone out to Beth's cottage to check on her.

'How is she?' asked Lachlan, coming up to flip the sign to Closed for lunch.

'She wouldn't answer the door,' said Chloe breathlessly, peeling off her sodden waterproof. 'The bell doesn't seem to be working so I hammered on the door but no joy. What are we going to do?'

'It sounds like she's not coping,' said Morna, who had just made a large pot of tea. 'We need to make a plan before all this gets completely away from us.'

'Harris Kincaid came in while you were gone, Chloe,' said Lachlan, producing one of his hardbacked notebooks and a pen as they settled down at the table with their respective packed lunches. 'He's worried about her. She isn't opening the door to him either and she's turned off her phone.'

'Did he tell you what happened at the police station?' asked Morna, while pouring the tea.

'Just the bare bones. She'd been questioned and released

without charge. He said he couldn't tell us more until he'd been authorised by Beth.'

'I got *The Oban Times* when I was out,' said Chloe, pulling a slightly soggy copy out of her shoulder bag. 'It's on the first page. They say that Nora was murdered. Apparently, she was poisoned. I can't believe it. Who would poison a harmless old lady?'

'She wasn't that old, only in her mid-sixties,' protested Lachlan.

'So why have they been questioning Beth?' asked Morna. 'Surely they can't think she did it? That's completely bonkers.'

'There must be more to it than that,' said Lachlan. 'She's apparently been released without charge anyway.'

'Then why is she pulling sickies and hiding away?' asked Chloe. 'Beth's never off sick. At the very least she should be answering her phone. It's her business, after all. It could be burning down right now for all she knows!'

'Do you have to be so dramatic?' scolded Morna. 'Maybe, she's just... you know... sick. Probably got the flu or something.' But her voice lacked conviction.

'I think we should give her space today,' said Lachlan, 'but if she's not in tomorrow we need to...'

'Stage an intervention?' asked Chloe, her eyes huge.

'I was going to say go round and not take no for an answer,' he said. 'She has a spare key in the safe. You girls can go in first and then I can follow once you give me the green light. She has to face this and know that we are on her side.'

'What about the shop?' said Morna. 'Someone will have to stay behind and open up.'

'Then I think that someone should be me,' said Lachlan firmly, never entirely comfortable when the emotional stakes got too high.

'None of us know what's really going on yet,' said Chloe, 'but in the meantime maybe we should do some digging, see what we can find out? The daughter Jane and that lad Callum for starters. It's not exactly happy families, is it?'

'No,' said Lachlan thoughtfully. 'It sounds to me as though

Jane was completely estranged from her mother so why come back now? What changed?'

'Maybe she was more interested in her inheritance than in her mother,' said Morna. 'If she was bitter or angry she might have even had a hand in what happened to her. Don't you think it's strange that she announced her presence here in the shop that first day as if she needed people to know that she had only just arrived? Who's to say she hadn't slipped up here before? Did she come up by train? Do we know if she has a car? A normal person would have called in at the police station first, but she came in here on a fact-finding trip.'

'I didn't take to her,' admitted Chloe. 'She seemed really cold to me, as though she was pretending to be upset to get Beth to feel sorry for her.'

'Hindsight is a wonderful thing,' said Lachlan. 'She could, of course, have had a very good reason to be estranged from her mother. Beth mentioned there wasn't a single photo of her up anywhere.'

'That's not exactly very warm and fuzzy, is it?' said Morna.' Maybe we need to look more into Nora's background. Not every mother is as lovely as yours, Chloe. I doubt my mother would shed any tears if something were to happen to me.'

Chloe hugged her. 'Well, I would! Buckets and buckets of tears. Right, Lachlan?'

'Er... right...' he replied, looking uncomfortable.

'Also, the whole thing about the biological son is super weird,' said Morna. 'I mean, if he's fairly recently lost the woman who gave birth to him and cared for him, why would he come rushing up here the minute he discovered he'd been conceived as a result of embryo donation.'

'And don't forget that he was actually in the house with Nora's dead body,' said Morna. 'How creepy is that? They had to cart him off to the police station to get him calmed down. I mean, it's not the actions of a normal person, is it?'

'Harris's sister, Fiona Kincaid, must have assessed him there, as police surgeon,' added Lachlan. 'I imagine there's no chance Harris will get her to spill the beans meantime. Of course, it's possible he's simply a vulnerable person and finding Nora there like that could have destabilised him.'

'It still doesn't explain how he was actually inside the house though,' said Chloe. 'A dead woman couldn't have let him in.'

'I still think there might be more to the carer than meets the eye,' said Morna. 'I know she's worried about being deported but a woman she was taking care of has died. You'd think she'd be more worried about that than herself, wouldn't you? I mean, I could see the point if she hailed from a really dodgy country where being returned might be unsafe for her, but she's meant to be from Spain. Hardly a million miles away. She was putting Beth under a lot of pressure. Anyway, if the death was by poisoning then surely, as the carer, she'd be best placed to administer any poison or disguise it in food or drink?'

'Maybe Maria and Nora's fiancé were in it together?' suggested Lachlan. 'They could have exploited Nora for financial gain. She has admitted they knew each other. Also, how come she was only interviewed by him for the job and not by Nora herself? That sounds fishy as well.'

'Don't you think it's odd that no one seems to have heard from her so-called fiancé, Oliver Saunders?' said Morna. 'You'd think he would be all over this and the one shouting loudest to the police about finding her murderer. But there's not been a cheep out of him, as far as I can tell. The newspaper article said that they are trying to locate both him and Maria to help them with their enquiries.'

'But with all these potential suspects, why on earth did they come for Beth?' Chloe burst out. 'Surely all these other people are more likely to be involved than her? I hate DS Hunter. He proper has it in for her. it's not fair!'

'I don't think it's that,' said Lachlan thoughtfully. 'He's always struck me as a fair man. As such, he needs to follow the evidence without fear or partiality. He must have taken her in for a good reason. That's what's worrying me. I think we're missing a significant part of the puzzle.'

Glancing at his watch, he walked over to the door and flipped the sign to Open as Chloe and Morna cleared away the remnants of their lunch in troubled silence.

TWENTY

The following evening, Beth woke feeling confused and disorientated. It was dark outside. She stretched out her fingers and made contact with two balls of fur, who started purring. Pulling her phone towards her she could see that she'd missed lots of calls and felt a surge of guilt. It was only 6pm but she hadn't intended to sleep that long without contacting anyone. The cats started stretching, arching their spines and anticipating their next meal. She slipped out of bed and wandered over to the window, about to close the curtains and shut out the darkness. Suddenly, she froze, peering out intently. Who was that? There was someone outside her house staring up at her. It was a man she didn't recognise. Heart thumping, she moved back at once. What to do? She could hardly call the police in the circumstances. Maybe Harris? She picked up her phone and edged back towards the window. False alarm! He'd gone. Sighing in relief, she pulled the curtains shut and threw her comfy dressing gown on. Both cats were now scratching at the door and miaowing, demanding their supper in stereo.

'Keep your fur on, boys, I'm just coming,' she soothed, sliding her feet into her slippers.

Opening the door, she followed them downstairs, each tail

formed into a perfect question mark as they zoomed straight into the kitchen then did their level best to trip her up, winding in and out of her legs as she walked across with their bowls. She left them chomping away side by side then pulled out some leftover shepherd's pie, sticking it in the microwave to warm. Glancing at the work surface while she waited, she noticed the empty bottle of wine that Logan had brought round. The hopes that she had entertained that night seemed laughable now after recent events. It was abundantly clear to her now that her developing feelings for him would never be reciprocated, she'd been a fool to hope otherwise. Happy endings only happened in fairy tales.

Lighting the woodburning stove, she carried through her supper and sat by the crackling flames, feeling the heat seep into her bones. Today had been a setback but it was time to regroup and get on with things. Hiding away would solve nothing. Problems had a way of multiplying behind your back. She carried her empty plate back through to the kitchen then brought through a mug of peppermint tea and a notebook and pen. She would make a list, she decided. Thing always felt more under control with a list.

The first item had to be contacting her staff. She felt a pang of guilt as she realised that they'd most likely been worried about her. Hurriedly she sent them a group text letting them know she was feeling much better and would be in bright and early tomorrow. Now that it seemed inevitable that she was going to be dragged into the investigation into Nora's death, she hoped they would continue to have her back. The police had obviously had to question her if something in one of her boxes was implicated but that didn't mean that they really thought she had murdered Nora. It was simply a line of enquiry they had to follow, right?

Yes, but what about the will, though? Panic fluttered like the wings of a bird in her chest. How on earth had that happened? It made absolutely no sense whatsoever. She'd known Nora as a customer, and well enough to have a chat with should she bump into her in the street, but that was as far as it went. Admittedly, she often tended to be drawn to women of that age due to having recently lost her own mum, but Nora had never acted in a remotely maternal way towards her. Plus, she had her own daughter as well. A daughter she had never seen fit to once mention when they were together. It surely couldn't all be about Marmalade, could it? She'd have gladly taken him in anyway. In fact, she had done. She reached out to the big furry cat wedged in beside her on the chair and stroked his head, causing a flurry of purring and a venomous look from Toby lying on the rug in front of the stove.

No, the way she had been implicated was suggestive of a diabolical amount of planning. She was being set up as a convenient scapegoat by a puppeteer who was masterfully working all the strings. Nothing and no one were what they seemed. She was going to have to be smarter to outwit a cunning adversary in a battle that was not of her choosing.

TWENTY-ONE

After she locked the door to the cottage behind her, Beth walked slowly around her house, checking for anything amiss. The sight of the man staring up at her last night had made her uneasy. It was probably nothing but, still... A loud banging drew her attention to the bottom of the back garden, and she cautiously approached to investigate. The wind had got up, and she soon established it was the door to her wooden shed banging against the fence. She wasn't much of a gardener and hadn't had her lawnmower out since well before Nora's death. However, even though she might conceivably have forgotten to lock it, she knew that the heavy padlock should still be attached to the door. It was missing. She looked inside but nothing appeared to have been taken. If someone had broken in undetected then why hadn't they taken her lawnmower or garden tools? What else were they expecting to find?

Unsettled, she secured it with some gardening twine until she could replace the padlock and continued on her way to work, her earlier positive mindset struggling against this new information.

'You're blowing it all out of proportion,' she muttered, then smiled self-consciously at a startled neighbour who crossed over to the other side of the road.

Probably just kids, looking for somewhere to hang out in the rain, she told herself, although she would have expected to see some cans and other litter had that been the case. Oh well, it would all come out in the wash, as her mother would say. She put it from her mind and focused on the stunning views of the scudding clouds and foaming waves of the bay. Seagulls glided on the myriad currents of the wind, their haunting cries borne away. A rainbow appeared above McCaig's Tower which she paused to admire before it disintegrated. Nothing was permanent and nor were her current troubles. She would find a way through the maze. She always had before. This time would be no different.

Striding alongside the bay, she was forced to slow down as she hit George Street where the tourists were meandering about as though they'd completely forgotten how to walk in a straight line. Rounding a corner, she sighed with relief to reach the sanctuary of the bookshop, the repository of all that she held dear. As she pushed open the green wooden door, the smell of warm scones baking and fresh coffee brewing felt like coming home. Inhaling deeply, she pinned on a bright smile.

'Someone's been in early,' she said. 'I thought my first job today would be making a batch of scones, but I see one of you has beaten me to it.'

'Beth, you're back,' said Chloe, beaming. 'I made them. Mum taught me to bake years ago. I made a Victoria sponge cake, too.'

'How are you feeling?' asked Lachlan, wandering through clutching his morning coffee.

'Much better,' she declared. 'I'm sorry I bailed on you guys but I'm back now.'

Morna came through from the back carrying two mugs of coffee. 'Figured you'd need a pick me up.'

'You're not wrong.' Beth glanced up at the cuckoo clock. 'Still half an hour until we open. Can I catch you all up on what's been going on?'

They settled round the large table. Beth took a deep breath and began.

'The reason the police wanted to speak to me is that there's been some rather alarming developments in Nora's case.'

'It was in *The Oban Times*,' said Chloe, dashing behind the counter to retrieve her now well-thumbed copy. 'It says she was poisoned.'

'Yes,' said Beth. 'What I doubt it mentioned is that she was poisoned by something in our subscription boxes.'

'You mean one of the samples?' queried Lachlan.

'Yes, it was the mushroom tea, apparently,' Beth said with a grimace.

'That's terrible,' said Morna, 'but it's hardly your fault? It was a pop-up shop and Kathleen cleared out a couple of days after Nora died. I popped up to see what else she had and the shop was completely empty. I didn't think anything of it at the time. Do you think that she knew?'

'Wait a minute,' said Lachlan, his voice rising. 'What about all the other boxes? Didn't those contain the tea, too? We need to contact the recipients immediately!'

'Already done,' said Beth. 'The police attended to it. They've sent everything in the boxes off for testing apart from the books.'

'We did have a lot of subscription cancellations yesterday,' said Chloe. 'Nearly all of them, in fact. This totally sucks. Poor Nora.'

'I don't see how we can ever start it up again. Word will have got round and no one will trust the samples anymore,' said Beth. 'What's more, I can't honestly say that I blame them. I should have taken more care. The others were well-established businesses. I popped round to see them on the way in here this morning. They've been pretty decent about it, all things considered. The mushroom tea sachets were just so attractively packaged. I thought it would be a real treat for our customers. I should have been more wary and looked into them properly. A mistake I'm never going to make again.'

'You weren't to know,' said Lachlan, reaching across and patting her hand. 'Nora had a carer. She'd been unwell. There was probably some underlying condition that made her particularly vulnerable.'

'I'm afraid there's more.' Beth grimaced.

Her staff glanced at each other, looking worried.

'You're not going to believe this, but Nora had apparently named me as sole beneficiary to her estate, which estate specifically includes Marmalade the cat.'

'I don't know what to say,' said Morna. 'That's... so weird.'

'I can see where this is going,' said Lachlan, his face creased in a frown. 'And I don't like it. Not one little bit.'

'Wait, what do you mean?' asked Chloe. 'I don't get it.'

'Don't you see?' Morna rounded on her. 'It gives Beth a motive to have murdered Nora.'

'But that's ridiculous,' said Chloe. 'Beth would never...'

'We know that,' said Morna. 'The police, on the other hand...'

'To be fair, they can hardly ignore the evidence,' said Beth with a tight smile. 'I just don't know what to think.'

'It's a stitch-up. It's got to be,' said Lachlan. 'Someone has planned all this in cold blood, including finding someone to take the rap for them. Unfortunately, that will be you if we can't uncover the truth in time.'

TWENTY-TWO

Someone banged at the front door, making them all jump. Beth glanced at the clock. It was gone nine. She rushed to the door but by the time she'd opened it, the person had gone. One of her subscription boxes was lying there. Glancing all around, she picked it up and headed back inside, flipping the sign to open.

Carrying it through to the table she opened it, jumping back in horror when an angry snake reared up and hissed at her. Everyone screamed and jumped back, including Lachlan who then looked mortified.

'What the holy heck is that?' whispered Chloe, pointing a long quivering nail in its direction.

At that moment, the doorbell tinkled and everyone yelled, 'Get out!' in unison. A face poked round the door, eyebrows raised comically.

'Dad!' yelled Chloe and rushed over to the door, throwing herself into his outstretched arms, as if she were five years old again.

'Any room for the rest of us in there, Dave?' asked Beth with a wan smile.

Lachlan stepped forward, trying to assert some belated control over the situation.

'There's a snake in that box,' he explained. 'It was left outside. Beth had no idea and picked it up.'

'Let's have a butcher's,' said Dave, disentangling himself from Chloe and approaching cautiously.

The door tinkled as Mike, a regular customer, walked in accompanied by two cats. Morna swiftly ushered him to one side, explaining what was going on. Toby and Marmalade strode confidently towards Beth, dispenser of Dreamies, then comically skidded to a halt and arched their backs, puffing themselves up sideways on and letting out demonic howls that would put the fear of God in anyone. It certainly worked on the snake who reared up and flicked out its tongue.

'Blimey, it's like being in a David Attenborough show,' said Mike, pressing himself against the bookshelves he'd retreated to.

Beth rushed forward and chased the cats into the kitchen by bribing them with Dreamies. She suspected they were happy to avoid the confrontation but still save face. She hurried back out in time to see Dave gently holding the snake in both hands, talking to it in a soothing voice. Everyone else was transfixed with horror. He gently settled the snake back in the box and slid the lid on, placing a heavy book, handed over by Morna, on top.

'Relax, folks, it was only a corn snake, they're harmless,' he said. 'It was probably more scared of us than we were of it.'

'I highly doubt that,' said Beth, plumping down heavily on a chair.

'How come you know about snakes, anyway, Dad?' asked Chloe.

'I kept a few as pets until I met your mother.' He grinned. 'She made me get rid of them. I still think they're pretty cool though.'

'But why was it here?' protested Beth. 'I don't understand.'

'It's a warning,' said Lachlan. 'What else could it be? We're a bookshop, not a reptile house.'

'Best call the police,' was Dave's parting shot as he gathered up his mail bag. 'Never a dull moment with you lot. Watch yourself, love,' he said to Chloe, giving her a hug and sending a stern look over her head to Beth.

Message received loud and clear, she thought, nodding back to him. She called the police, tapping in the number from memory. That's what it had come to, she thought glumly. After a brief conversation, they announced they would send a team across to recover it.

Mike wandered over to join them. 'I read the paper this morning. I heard it was Beth who found Nora's body. Poisoning, eh? I take it another investigation is underway?' he asked, looking worried. No doubt he remembered being caught up in the last one.

'Only because DS Hunter has already hauled me in for questioning,' Beth said bitterly. 'Mind you,' she continued with characteristic fairness, 'I can see why. I found the body, the poison may have been in my subscription box, *and* she appears to have left me her cat and all her money.'

'A series of unfortunate events,' he said, wiggling his fingers, 'as Lemony Snicket might say.'

'Did you know Nora?' asked Beth.

'Yes, a bit. We taught together until she retired about five years back. Nice enough woman, kept herself to herself. Heavily involved in Victim Support, I seem to remember. She'd no enemies amongst the staff but no real friends either, which was a bit sad. She was strangely... colourless, as though she didn't want to draw attention to herself. I believe that the kids she taught got good results though, so respect for that.'

'Interesting,' said Beth. 'Almost as though she was hiding from someone or something.'

'Well, shout if you need me. I owe you guys everything, I'm never going to forget that.'

'How's life as a *Sunday Times* bestselling author treating you?' asked Beth.

'Loving the makeover,' said Chloe impishly, taking in the trendy new clothes and haircut.

'Beats teaching unruly teenagers.' He grinned.

'I can't thank you enough for having your inaugural launch here,' said Beth. 'It really put us on the bookshop map.'

'All those bright young things up from London looked like they'd beamed up from another planet.' Morna laughed. 'I offered one a haggis bonbon and she looked at me with such horror I thought she was going to drop at my feet.'

'It's been surreal at times, alright. I'm tempted to start another blog, about the publishing world this time...' Mike winked.

'I'd pay good money to read that,' Lachlan said wryly. 'But best not to bite the hand that feeds you.'

Mike laughed and walked up to Morna to ring through his purchase. As he was leaving, two constables entered and she heaved a sigh of relief that it wasn't DS Hunter and the implacable DC Quinn.

'PC Jenny Clark,' the younger of the two said to Beth, before turning to smile at Chloe. 'I understand you have a snake for us?'

'Hey, Jenny, it's in that box,' said Chloe, pointing. 'My dad says it's a harmless corn snake, but I wouldn't take any chances.'

PC Clark looked where she was pointing. 'That box isn't really substantial enough for transport. Fortunately, we brought a more secure one with us that it should fit inside. Ewan, could you get it from the boot, please?' she asked, passing the even younger constable the keys.

'Don't worry, we'll find a good home for it.' She smiled at Beth.

'I think it was sent to threaten me,' said Beth quietly. 'I've recently been questioned in relation to the murder of Nora Kelly. Whoever left it for me was most likely wearing gloves when handling the box, but you never know.'

'Oh!' said PC Clark, her eyes widening as her colleague came in and carefully placed the box in another, more robust, container. 'I'll be sure to pass that on. In the meantime, I'll get this snake out of your way.'

'Thank you,' said Beth.

'See you, Jen,' said Chloe with a small smile.

'You know her?' said Beth, once she was out of earshot.

'We were in the same class at school,' said Chloe. 'We hang out with the same people at the weekend sometimes. She's pretty cool.'

Beth remembered the cats and rushed to let them out of the kitchen. They stalked out, heads swivelling to and fro, then marched to the front door, miaowing to be let out.

More customers appeared and the normal hustle and hum of the bookshop resumed. However, all Beth could think about was those red eyes glaring at her as the snake hissed and rattled its tail. Someone had wanted to intimidate her. It had worked. But how on earth could she possibly begin to extricate herself from this mess when she didn't have a clue what was going on?

TWENTY-THREE

Harris Kincaid looked up from the typewritten will he'd been studying. The Procurator Fiscal, Tom Reid, stared back at him over steepled fingers, raising an eyebrow.

'It's clearly not valid,' said Harris, exhaling. 'It's not signed by the testator on every page, which is a legal necessity in Scots' law. It's got all the clauses you would expect to find but it can't be implemented. If you ask me, someone has knocked this up as a smokescreen to try and make it seem like my client has a motive for murder.'

'Well, you would take that view,' said Tom Reid, a small smile tugging at the corners of his moustache, his grey eyes giving nothing away. 'Once again, your client has found herself in the eye of the storm. Even if the will is invalid, she may well have been unaware of that fact, therefore, it hardly matters in that regard whether it stands or not. The motive remains, I'm afraid, as far as the Crown is concerned.'

Harris sighed. At most it might sow a seed of doubt in the mind of the jury. He picked up the forensic report that was passed across to him next.

'As you will see, the primary cause of death is liver and kidney failure,' the Fiscal said. 'Nora Kelly's body appears to have been exposed to an amatoxin, known as alpha-amanitin. In other words, she appears to have been systematically poisoned over a few weeks with death cap mushrooms, most likely from drinking mushroom tea, the very same tea that was in your client's subscription boxes.'

'Then why did no one else get sick?' snapped Harris. 'The tea came from free samples, and the proprietor has now disappeared. Unlikely to be a coincidence, wouldn't you say?'

'Your client could have tampered with one of the sachets after it had been handed over,' the Fiscal fired back.

'The box she was delivering when the body was discovered. Did you think to test the tea in that?' asked Harris.

The Fiscal grimaced. 'We did and it was negative for death cap mushroom. There was a teabag remaining in each of the preceding two boxes which, however, did test positive. Look, your client isn't off the hook for this yet but I'm striving to keep an open mind, particularly given the fact that a number of key people have disappeared. I'm not sure what's been going on, but mark my words, we'll get to the bottom of it.'

Harris got to his feet and the two men shook hands.

'Thanks, Tom. I appreciate this early disclosure.'

'I thought it was only fair in the circumstances,' the Fiscal said, walking him to the door.

TWENTY-FOUR

Beth was trudging home after a long tiring day when she stiffened to see Jane entering Aulay's Lounge Bar alone. Should she go in after her and speak to her about what had been going on, or was that inviting a whole heap of trouble? The bigger part of her just wanted to head home and block out the rest of the world but she knew if she missed this opportunity, it might be hard to engineer another meeting. She presumed that by now Jane had heard about the will. She must surely be raging. Beth had no desire to profit financially from Nora's death, but she needed to be sure that the person she gave the money to was entirely innocent of her murder. She owed Nora that.

Her heart thumping at the potential awkwardness of what might be to come, Beth pushed open the stained-glass door into the pub and stood there self-consciously before heading towards the bar. She wasn't used to going into pubs on her own and it made her feel uncomfortably conspicuous. As she perched on a stool waiting to be served, she noticed Jane coming out of the ladies' toilet to her left and heading to a table in the far corner. With a start she realised that the young man with his back to her was Callum. Immediately, Jane engaged him in conversation. His shoulders came up about his ears and he suddenly looked very young, defensive and ill at ease, as if he wasn't wholly on board with what was being said. This wasn't good. If only she could hear what they were saying without revealing herself. She ground her teeth in frustration.

The cheerful young barman deposited a large glass of red wine in front of her. Gratefully, she took a gulp. Her eyes met the amused gaze of the man sitting next to her in the mirror beneath the gantry.

'Rough day?' he asked.

'You could say that,' she replied with a cautious smile. Her eyes floated back to the mirror where she could see the conversation heating up between those in the corner. Fortunately, they hadn't clocked her yet as she had her back to them and they were too fixated on each other.

Her neighbour at the bar was a few years older than her, wearing a rumpled suit and looked vaguely familiar but she couldn't place him.

'Shall we grab a couple of the comfy seats?' he asked, turning to face her. 'I'm Grant, by the way.' He offered his hand and she tentatively shook it, feeling slightly unnerved. Navigating the opposite sex wasn't exactly her speciality subject and she was floundering already.

'Beth.' She smiled shyly.

He leaned closer and whispered in her ear, 'Plus, if we sit on the other side of that wooden partition, you'll be able to hear what those two over there are saying.'

'Pardon?' asked Beth, startled. 'I don't know what you mean...'

'Relax.' He grinned, his brown eyes crinkling at the corners. It was a face that looked like it laughed a lot. 'I kind of want to know what they're saying myself. They look like they're planning to rob a bank or something.'

Beth dithered but then decided to follow him across to the table. She really did want to know what Jane and Callum were up to. They were in a public place. What could go wrong?

'Are you from Oban or just visiting?' she asked.

'I'm from here, originally, but I'm up for the weekend visiting family. I work in Glasgow so I'm just off the train, hence the suit.'

'I work here now but I used to live in Glasgow,' she offered. 'I own a bookshop in town.'

'Oh, you're *that* Beth,' he said. 'I've heard a lot about you.'

'From who?' asked Beth, startled.

'Oh, here and there,' he said enigmatically.

The voices through the partition grew louder. Grant laughed and took his phone out.

'Knock yourself out,' he said, inclining his head towards the partition.

Beth grabbed her phone, following his lead, pretending to scroll so that she didn't look to a casual observer as though she was listening, although in reality she was straining every sinew trying to pick it up.

'I can't believe how she pulled the wool over our eyes with that "I just want to help" bullshit,' snapped Jane, her voice hard as flint. 'She had me falling for it as well. I blame my grief over my poor defenceless mother.'

'What grief?' snorted Callum. 'No one even knew she had a daughter, by all accounts. She had to actually die before you deigned to visit her, you hypocrite.'

'Don't you dare presume to point a finger at me. My mother didn't even want you. She gave you away,' snapped Jane. 'This family has nothing to do with you. I don't even know why you're here!'

The voices subsided to a low angry murmur after that. Beth's body relaxed, unshed tears stinging her eyes. She took another large gulp of wine. It wasn't the first time she'd had people hate her, but it still hurt.

After a few minutes the two of them left, their faces hard and angry. Beth hid her face behind a menu and thankfully neither of them spotted her. Suddenly she remembered her companion. Her face flushed as she realized that she'd been terribly rude. What must he think of her?

'Your face is a picture,' he laughed. 'Look, don't mind me. It's clear you're going through some stuff.'

'I'm so sorry, I'm not normally this rude,' Beth said, mortified now. 'Please, let me make it up to you. Can I buy you another drink and this time I promise to give you my full attention? What will you have?'

He glanced at his watch. 'I suppose I've time for one,' he said with a smile. 'But, honestly, it's not necessary.'

Beth rushed to the bar and obtained a pint for him and another wine for herself. She shouldn't be drinking on an empty stomach but one more would be fine. She liked this man. There was something about him that she trusted, a faint but comforting feeling of familiarity that she instinctively wanted to lean in to.

'So, what do you do in Glasgow?' she asked, noting he'd already removed his tie and stuffed it into his bag.

'I'm a vet,' he said. 'Running a bookshop sounds like fun.'

'It is.' She smiled. 'I've dreamed of nothing else since I was a small child.'

'What, no poofy dress and retinue of bridesmaids?' he teased.

'Ugh, definitely not.' She grimaced. 'I absolutely hate being the centre of attention. I'm perfectly happy on my own.'

'You want to become a crazy cat lady,' he laughed.

'I'm already halfway there,' she joked. 'Two and counting. What about you? Wife and kids?'

A shadow passed over his face and for a moment she wished she hadn't asked.

'I'm sorry, you don't need to answer that,' she said hurriedly.

'No, it's fine.' He smiled, though there was sadness behind it. 'I've never been married. Nobody will have me,' he joked. 'My friends keep setting me up on pity dates. It's excruciating!'

'That must be so hard,' said Beth, feeling for him.

'Anyway, sorry to be such a buzzkill,' he said with a rueful smile.

'Hey,' said Beth, 'given how our evening started, I think your social skills have far exceeded mine.'

'That's true, I suppose,' he said in mock seriousness.

She smiled back at him, hoping the warmth of her smile would soothe the wounded part of him that he'd allowed her to glimpse.

The door opened and in walked Detective Sergeant Hunter. He scanned the bar and when his eyes alighted on her they widened in surprise.

'I'm so sorry,' she said to Grant. 'I really have to go. If you're at a loose end you know where to find me.'

'Beth...' he said, half rising, but she was already marching out of the bar, giving Logan Hunter a curt nod on the way past, her cheeks burning. He put out a hand to detain her, but she swatted it away as though he was a troublesome fly.

TWENTY-FIVE

Beth was feeling lightheaded. The wine had really gone to her head. She needed to eat something. She backtracked until she came to the fish and chip shop, ordering a fish supper with lots of salt and vinegar, then took herself off to a quiet bench in front of the harbour to eat it before walking home. It was already pitch dark and the moon was skulking behind clouds swollen with rain drifting slowly across the bay. She felt thoroughly rattled by the events of the day, her thoughts whirling round her head like some macabre carousel.

The snake had been meant to frighten her into backing off from the case. What did someone not want her to find out, apart from the obvious, of course – who murdered Nora? At least it hadn't been a venomous snake, more of a warning than an attempt to harm her. Well, she wasn't going to just sit there and take it like a passive victim. Why did they have to involve her subscription boxes? Word had evidently got out that they had been implicated, hence the swathe of cancelled orders. After the events of last year, it hardly seemed fair that she had once again come under suspicion for something that she hadn't done.

'Beth?' Nora's son, Callum, stepped out of the shadows and stood in front of her. 'Can I talk to you?'

Wordlessly, she gestured to him to sit, her nerves jangling.

'Chip?' she asked.

'No, thanks. Look, I saw you there, in the pub,' he said. 'I didn't let on to Jane. For what it's worth, I don't think you killed my biological mother.'

'What was the woman who raised you like?' Beth asked.

'She was everything you could want in a mother,' he said, his voice hollowed out with loss. 'She showed up. Whatever I was doing, she was there, on the sidelines, cheering me on. She loathed sports but every Saturday morning she rocked up and stood in the freezing cold to cheer me on playing football as a kid. Then, later on, when I got more into music and drama, she was at every performance, clapping and cheering her head off. I went pretty rogue as a teenager, staying out all night, but we had got past all that. I got tangled up in a bit of bother in a pub two years ago, got charged with assault and breach of the peace. When the police released me on bail and I saw her waiting for me, like she'd been there for hours, I felt about an inch tall. I vowed there and then never to put her through anything like that ever again. Then she had to go and get sick.'

'What about your dad?' Beth asked.

'What dad?' he snorted angrily. 'He took one look at me and bailed, the bastard. Good riddance. Said I looked nothing like him and everyone would know I wasn't his.'

'Your mum told you that?' said Beth, horrified.

'No, her sister did when I was giving Mum a hard time. She said I shouldn't as she was the one who stayed.'

Beth could see how emotionally fragile he was. She didn't dare to push him for fear he might explode but she needed information. Who knew when she would get this opportunity again?

'Sure you don't want a chip?' Beth said with a smile, shuffling along the bench to make room for him.

'Fine, go on then,' he said, sitting down beside her and helping himself to a couple. 'These are good!'

'Help yourself,' she said, putting the box down between them. They ate in silence for a few minutes.

'What's Jane's deal with her mum?' she asked casually, sliding another chip into her mouth.

'I'm not sure,' he said. 'She's all up in arms about you stealing her inheritance from under her but from what I can gather they hadn't even spoken in a very long time.'

'No one up here even seemed to know that she had a daughter,' mused Beth. 'I'm assuming the police have checked that she is who she says she is?'

Callum shrugged. 'I assume so. They certainly chased down what I told them. The IVF clinic contacted me to say they'd been in touch and to get my permission to release the information to them as Mum's next of kin. So, they wouldn't have just taken her word for it.'

'That day I came to the house,' Beth said delicately, 'you were understandably upset...'

Callum went very still. She was worried he might explode and lash out but she had to try.

'Did you get a chance to speak to Nora... before she passed?'

He jumped up and started pacing, his fingers flexing. Beth remained seated, not wanting to rile him up further.

'I know what you're really asking,' he said, his expression suddenly hostile and threatening.

It was Beth's turn to freeze. It was cold and dark. There were very few people on the streets, and none at all in this dark corner of the bay. He'd already admitted he had an assault charge against him.

'You're asking if I killed her?'

'And did you?' Beth almost whispered.

'I'd have had every right to kill her,' he said, the rage she sensed, simmering below the surface, now rising up in a wave. 'She robbed me of my birthright, giving me away to some random woman like I was garbage. I needed her to see that I was worth something, that she'd made a mistake throwing me away. I mean, she already had one kid, why couldn't she have had me, too? Was the very idea of me so abhorrent to her? Why would you throw away an innocent baby? I needed to hold her to account for what she had done.'

Beth was completely out of her depth. She should never have started this. Callum wasn't thinking clearly. He was plainly unstable and should only be questioned by a professional. But, regardless of that, she had to take the risk. It was now or never.

'So, did you? Hold her to account?' she said, her voice as non-confrontational as possible. 'Did she let you in when you went to see her?'

'No. I got there late in the morning and saw her carer run off in a hurry. She didn't even lock the door, just ran clean out of the house like she was being chased or something. She looked upset. Once she'd gone, I rang the bell. I'd brought flowers. Despite every-thing, I wanted to make a good impression, wanted her to regret not having had me in her life.'

'Did she answer the door?' asked Beth, holding her breath.

'NO!' he shouted. 'She bloody didn't. I pushed the door open and went looking for her. She was sitting in the chair. She wouldn't look at me. I showed her the flowers, but she wouldn't even turn her head. I'd come all that way, but it was as if I didn't exist for her, like I was a fricking ghost or something. I got angry. I grabbed her arm and shook her. I realised there was a bad smell coming from her. I thought maybe I'd scared her or maybe she was embarrassed and trying to hide it. I lit some candles that were dotted around to make her feel better, more like talking. I went upstairs and looked around. I lay down on one of the beds. I thought if I had a sleep and let her rest we could maybe talk later when she was feeling more up to it. Then you came. You ruined everything!'

Beth froze. He obviously believed that what he was describing amounted to rational behaviour, which it patently did not.

'She was already gone, Callum. Nothing you could have said or done would have changed that,' said Beth softly. 'I know that part of you realises that. What you've gone through, it's terrible. But the only person to blame is the person who poisoned her.'

He sat back down, the air hissing from him like a pricked balloon. He looked completely lost, as if the ground under him had undergone a seismic shift. She realised that what she had previously mistaken for aggression was no more than fear and confusion as he struggled to orient himself in a world where he had to now stand alone, without the love and support he had previously known. It was a feeling she could identify with. He was clearly vulnerable, and his actions in Nora's house had been far from rational.

'Do you have any idea who your biological father was?' she asked, trying to head the conversation into less stormy waters.

He shrugged. 'The paperwork I found at home had a photocopy of a letter he'd sent to the clinic through his lawyer. It said he would consent to the embryo being donated to someone unable to have their own children as their marriage had broken down irretrievably. Both he and Nora had to give their consent for it to go ahead.'

'What was his name?' she asked.

'Darragh Brennan. He's some professor who lives over on Mull.'

'I don't suppose you have his address?' she asked.

Callum pulled a business card out of his pocket. 'Jane gave me this.'

Beth took a photo with her phone and handed it back to him.

'Thanks, Callum. I'm really not your enemy, you know,' she said quietly as she stood to go.

He shrugged. 'Time will tell.'

She walked away from him. After a while she glanced back. He was still sat there, staring over the bay, his face shrouded in darkness. Beth sighed and continued on with a heavy heart.

TWENTY-SIX

Beth had no sooner got home, fed the cats and jumped into her jammies when the doorbell rang. Groaning, she paused the TV and padded to the door, put the chain on, and opened it a crack. As if she hadn't had a bad enough day, Logan Hunter's face glowered at her through the gap.

'Do we have to do whatever this is now?' she sighed.

'I would prefer to speak to you now,' he said stiffly. 'But if you'd rather, you can come down to the station in the morning?'

That was no choice at all, she thought crossly, as she opened the door and stood aside to let him come in. As he clocked her pyjamas, he halted, looking taken aback.

'I'm sorry, I didn't realise you would be ready for bed, I mean... I hadn't realised it was so late.'

She took pity on him. 'It's not really. I just wanted to get comfy to chill out in front of the telly. I don't actually go to bed at half past eight, believe it or not. Tea?'

'Please,' he said, still looking uncomfortable. The two cats ran over to see him, competing for his attention.

'Traitors,' she muttered, shooting them a dark glance as she walked into the kitchen.

As she came through carrying a tray, she noticed that he was still standing to attention.

'Sit, for goodness' sake,' she said, pointing to the comfortable sofa. 'You might as well take off your coat as well. But maybe not the stab vest,' she added with a wicked grin.

'Very droll,' he said, doing as she asked.

They perched at either end as she poured the tea and offered him a biscuit. 'So, what did you want to speak to me about?' she asked, looking at him from over the rim of her mug.

He cleared his throat. 'Well, first of all, I want to apologise for not getting into the shop today after that snake business. PC Clark told me all about it. You must have all been quite shaken up?'

'You could say that.' She shuddered. 'I felt a lot better once Chloe's dad told me it wasn't venomous. I hope someone's looking after it? I might not be a huge fan of snakes, but I wouldn't want it to be harmed.'

'I've handed it off to someone who'll be able to find it a good home,' he said. 'It's disturbing that it turned up in one of your subscription boxes.'

'It means it's directly connected to whoever killed Nora,' she said. Her voice hardened. 'Of course, if that person is me then the smart thing would have been for me to send it to myself, right?'

'Beth, I'm not your enemy,' he said softly.

'You say that, but the opposite feels true at times,' she fired back. 'Haven't you managed to work out by now that I'm not the type of person to murder someone?'

'I think, given the right circumstances, anyone can be that person.'

'What? Even you?' she scoffed.

'You'd be surprised,' he said grimly. 'And no, for the avoidance of doubt, I never have. I might have been tempted once or twice...'

Something about the way his jaw tightened and the expression in his eyes made her think he might not be joking. A shudder travelled up her spine. How well did she really know him, after all?

'I take it there were no useful prints?' she asked.

'No. I was wondering where they could have got the box from? Obviously, we still have Nora's in evidence.'

'I got them off Amazon,' Beth replied. 'So, very easy for someone to track them down. Have you managed to find Kathleen from the pop-up shop yet?'

'No, we've put feelers out to the other forces, but she's disappeared without a trace.' He sighed, settling back onto the couch and stretching his feet out. He really did look utterly exhausted. Was there something else bothering him apart from work?

A terrible thought struck her. What if they were looking at this all wrong? It looked like the poison had been in the tea supplied by Kathleen, but what if it wasn't? What if whoever did it had instead emptied out the supplied tea and substituted it for the one laced with poison. Kathleen was a convenient scapegoat.

'I assume you tested all the other boxes for poison?' she asked.

'Yes, of course, as soon as the toxicology report came back, we gathered them all up immediately. We were a bit panicked in case there were going to be additional deaths.'

'But Nora's was the only one who tested positive,' Beth said.

'Thankfully,' he said, turning to stare at her. 'What are you saying?'

'I'm saying that far from being part of the plot, I think Kathleen is innocent. I'm worried that someone has killed her to make it look like she is guilty.'

'There's no evidence to suggest that,' he said, beginning to look worried, nevertheless.

'Kathleen merely handed the sachets of teabags to me. She had absolutely no control over what was placed in each box. For her to be implicated, the poison would have had to be in every box. Something has happened to her. Something bad. I'm sure of it,' she said, turning anguished eyes towards him.

He slapped his forehead angrily and stood up.

'Dammit, Beth. You could be right. How did I miss this? The trail will have gone completely cold.'

He was pacing up and down, looking increasingly agitated. She should have kept her mouth shut. It could have waited until the morning.

'Look, you can't be everywhere. You work in a tiny under-resourced police station in the Highlands with next to no manpower. Go home and rest. There's nothing you can do about it at this time of night. If I'm right about this, and I sincerely hope that I'm not, then nothing can be done to save her. All you can do is catch whoever's responsible and bring them to justice.'

Muttering, 'Hang on a sec,' Beth darted into the kitchen, returning with one plastic tub containing two slabs of lasagna and another with some chocolate chip cookies.

'Take these home with you. You need to look after yourself,' she said.

Logan nodded gruffly, looking emotional as though he couldn't quite trust himself to speak.

'Thanks, Beth. Goodnight.'

With that, he pulled open the door as though he couldn't get out fast enough and disappeared into the night. She closed the door after him, confused as ever about her feelings for this prickly, complicated man that could never seem to coalesce into one settled emotion.

TWENTY-SEVEN

Beth stood outside the empty shop. All traces of the previous occupant had been erased. A blank canvas for the next hopeful person to paint their dream on. She'd borrowed the keys from the estate agent letting the property on the pretext of looking for premises for a cat café. Her staff had all been upset when she explained her theory about what had happened to Kathleen. Like her, they'd felt guilty that they'd assumed the worst of her so easily.

With a quick glimpse behind her she opened the door, locking it once she was inside. The wooden floors echoed as she walked around the forlorn empty space, poking into every little nook and cranny for some hint of a clue. There was nothing on the ground floor. If there had been anything, it would have been cleared away by the estate agent readying the place to be let out again. This was probably a complete waste of time, but she had to try. She owed Kathleen that, at least. Walking through to the back, she unlocked the door to the one-bedroomed flat above the shop. Again, it had been professionally cleaned. This time, though, she discovered two boxes in an airing cupboard, obviously ready to be uplifted. Feeling it was a bit of a violation but desperate for answers, she carried them over to the simple wooden table. The first one contained clothes and as she pulled out Kathleen's signature jewel-coloured scarves, she felt a lump in her throat as she recalled her whirling in and out of the bookshop wearing them, professing a weakness for her Victoria sponge.

The next box was more interesting as it contained paperwork in relation to her business. Locating the order books, she ran her fingers down the neat columns of figures until she came to the tea in question. She had sourced multiple brands in small quantities. The one that she recognised as the same type as her samples came from an organic speciality mushroom farm in the Borders. She googled it on her phone and it appeared to be legitimate. The packaging was distinct and ornamental and Kathleen had bought in quite a lot of it. Possibly, that was why she'd donated the samples. Perhaps it hadn't been selling as well as she'd hoped? Momentarily stumped, she sat back and thought hard. The sample couldn't just have been selected randomly. Nora's murder had evidently been planned with great precision. Nothing had been left to chance and the police, from what she could gather, were no further forward in catching her killer. Yet it was more than likely that one of the people she had already met was entirely responsible.

Sighing, she rustled about in the box until she came upon the rolls of till receipts at the bottom. She started with the date the subscription boxes were first advertised in the local paper and worked forward until the day she had realised that Kathleen had left the shop. There had been a clear uptick in sales of the tea, not just the mushroom but other varieties as well. Beth felt sick to the stomach as she realised that during that time someone must have been experimenting on the tea, working out how to combine it with a poison that would not be easily detected by the person it was intended for. Kathleen must have been so buzzed to see her business turnover increasing, not realising that she was an unwitting pawn in a murder plot.

Someone was banging on the door downstairs. Someone who apparently wasn't going to take no for an answer. She ran lightly down the stairs and saw DS Hunter standing outside in the pouring rain looking very grumpy alongside DC Quinn who was, of course, standing smugly beneath an umbrella. Hurriedly she let them in. The detective sergeant looked far from pleased to see her.

'Beth, what are you doing here?' he growled. DC Quinn looked at her like she was something stuck to the bottom of her shoe.

'Got these from the estate agent,' she said, jangling the keys and smiling sweetly, which she knew would infuriate him even more. 'You can hand them back for me when you're done if you like.'

He swiped them from her hand. 'What's that you've got there?' he asked, staring suspiciously into the box.

'I was going to drop it all off at the station,' she explained. 'I was wondering why Kathleen chose that particular kind of tea to give me for her samples. I found her till rolls in here,' she said, pointing to the box at her feet. 'It showed me that sales of the decorative sachets of tea had really increased in the four months or so since I started the subscription service. I think someone was buying up her supplies and experimenting on which flavours could be successfully combined with an extract of poisonous mushroom without making the taste unappealing.'

'But how would that even work?' chimed in DC Quinn. 'The killer had no way of knowing that the right samples would end up in your subscription box.'

'Don't you see?' said Beth. 'It didn't matter which ones were included. It was all about plausibly pinning the blame elsewhere.'

'And isn't that exactly what you're doing now?' said DC Quinn, her eyes narrowed.

Beth drew herself up to her full height, which regrettably fell several inches below that of DC Quinn.

'My reason for coming here was to see if I could find any clue about what happened to Kathleen,' she said coldly. 'Having discovered this link, I felt obliged to share it with the police. Now, if you'll excuse me, I have a shop to run.'

She marched past them both, her chin held high.

'Beth, wait!' she heard DS Hunter call after her, but she ignored him and kept walking.

He could have stood up for her when DC Quinn started in on her. She was annoyed with herself as well. It was time she stopped allowing that infuriating man house room in her head let alone her heart. She was done with him.

TWENTY-EIGHT

Beth was still fuming when she reached the shop. She decided not to burden her team with what had happened meantime. As she headed into the office to deal with some outstanding invoices, she was frustrated about how little knowledge she had gained. The main question she wanted answered was whether Kathleen had been in on the plot to murder Nora, or whether she was merely a useful pawn who had moved on to pastures new. Remembering the vivacious young woman with her bright clothes and sparkling eyes, Beth desperately hoped it had been the latter. However, she wouldn't rest until she located her whereabouts and could ascertain that she was, in fact, safe. Her biggest fear was that if Kathleen was innocent, whoever had devised this diabolical plot might have seen her as a loose end that needed to be cauterised. She shuddered and a headache began to throb at her temple. Trying to ignore it she bent herself to her task until she became aware of raised voices through in the shop.

Jumping up, she opened the door and walked through. Morna was standing behind the cash desk with Chloe standing nearby wringing her hands. She immediately recognised Cassandra Abercrombie. She assumed that the other two were Morna's parents by the way they were dressed and their braying upper class voices that demanded to be heard. Clearly tempers were becoming frayed. One of her customers, Harriet Brown, a retired headteacher, raised an eyebrow at her from the crime section.

'Just what seems to be the problem here?' demanded Beth crisply.

Morna looked shut down and smaller somehow. Beth felt a wave of fury grip her, but she managed to rein it in.

The man turned to her and approached with his hand outstretched. He had a full head of charcoal hair and an imposing build. His suit fitted him like a glove and she'd warrant his shoes were handmade. He oozed old money. Despite his warm smile, his eyes were cold and calculating. Reluctantly, she shook the proffered hand, getting a whiff of expensive cologne as she did so. Morna looked like she wanted the ground to open up and swallow her whole.

'Maxwell Abercrombie,' he said, 'and this is my wife, Hilary. I believe you've already met my daughter, Cassandra.'

His wife was one of those women with timeless elegance, her caramel hair swept up in a chignon. She looked chic yet unreachable. Her eyes were slightly glassy as though she'd had a drink or two.

'A pleasure to meet you both,' said Beth, surreptitiously wiping her hand down the side of her skirt.

'I was just explaining to them that I've already had my break so I can't go out for lunch,' Morna ground out.

A queue was starting to form behind them. It was obvious that Morna didn't want to go with them so her first duty was to her employee.

'Yes, I'm afraid that's right,' she said, hardening her voice and pointing to the growing queue. 'This is our busiest time, I'm afraid. I'm sure she can call you to arrange lunch another time.'

She knew that Morna would do no such thing. She just wanted them out of the shop.

'Can we get a move on, please?' called out Harriet, brandishing her crime novel and winking at Beth.

'We don't have all day,' complained Tamsin, the butcher's wife, also with a wink.

Evidently, they had the measure of the Abercrombie's.

'Look, how about we sweeten the deal, make it worth your while?' said Maxwell, in the manner of someone who was accustomed to being obeyed. 'We just want to have lunch with our daughter. Why don't I buy some books, eh?' He randomly picked up half a dozen books within his reach and placed them on the counter.

Beth was at a loss. She locked eyes with Chloe. The situation was getting out of hand. It appeared they weren't willing to take no for an answer. She could threaten to call the police if they didn't leave but that would only make matters worse for Morna and she'd make a powerful enemy in the process. In the end, it was Morna who made the decision for her.

'Fine, if you want to talk to me that badly, I'll come with you,' she snapped at them. Angrily she rang up the books. 'Beth, can I take an hour now, please?'

Beth nodded. 'If you're sure,' she said, knowing that talking to her awful parents was the last thing her assistant needed.

'Let's go,' said Morna, leading them briskly out of the shop.

Chloe quickly slid behind the desk and made short work of the queue. Harriet Brown was last and when she arrived at the cash desk, she nodded at Beth.

'Watch out for that lot,' she said in a low voice. 'Morna did well to get away from them. Whatever they want with her now, I guarantee it won't be to her advantage. Despite their enormous wealth, they're known for never giving a penny to local causes unless there's something in it for them. Mark my words, they're up to something.'

'Thanks for the heads up, Harriet,' Beth replied. Harriet, now retired, had been a headteacher for years and was a pillar of the local community. 'My only concern is for Morna. Enjoy the book!'

Harriet had turned to walk away when something occurred to Beth. 'Actually, there's something I want to ask you about. Fancy a cuppa?' She jerked her head towards the door to the café.

'I'd love one,' Harriet said, smiling. 'It'll be a welcome respite. My feet are killing me in these new shoes.'

Once they were settled with coffee and inviting slabs of cake, Harriet looked over the rim of her coffee cup with her usual penetrating gaze. 'What can I do for you, Beth?' Incisive and to the point as usual.

'I was wondering if you knew a customer of mine, Nora Kelly? I thought perhaps you might have overlapped at Oban High School before she retired?'

'Yes, she was a gifted maths teacher. No interest in advancing into management. She died recently in rather suspicious circumstances, but I'm guessing that you knew that,' she said shrewdly, turning those piercing eyes on Beth again.

'Was she close to anyone in particular at the school? Another teacher, perhaps? Someone in whom she might have confided?'

Harriet thought hard then shook her head. 'I'm sorry, no one in particular stands out. Although we were about the same age, I had my own problems back then, as you know. My circumstances didn't really allow space for friendships to develop. She was polite and accommodating but there was a reserve about her that wasn't easily breached. It was only in teaching a class that I saw her spark into life. Her pass rates were second to none. She was truly dedicated to her pupils.'

'When was the last time you saw her?' asked Beth.

'Let me see, it would have been early January. I bumped into her in Tesco's. I must say, it was the happiest I'd ever seen her. Just as well she didn't know what lay ahead of her, poor woman,' she sighed.

'Thanks anyway, Harriet,' Beth said, taking a sip of coffee. Nora Kelly had been an enigma to everyone she came across, it seemed.

'I hope you're not getting too involved, Beth,' said Harriet, her sharp eyes narrowed. 'These things are best left to the professionals.'

'I'm already involved,' said Beth with a sigh. 'It was me who found the body.'

They finished drinking their coffee in reflective silence.

TWENTY-NINE

Once order was restored and the last customer had left the shop, they closed for lunch. As Chloe and Lachlan sat at the table, Beth brought through a tray of tea, and poured it from the large pot adorned with a purple and pink tea cosy that her mum had knitted.

'I hope Morna's alright,' said Chloe, fretting about her friend. 'I get it now, why she hates them. I can't believe I was taken in by Cassandra. She's all style but hollow inside.'

'Hate is a rather strong word,' chided Lachlan, reaching for a sandwich. 'But I agree that they're rather hard to like. I can only imagine what life was like for Morna as a child growing up with those sorts of values.'

'They treated her like a total reject,' said Chloe angrily. 'Like she was some sort of lumpen throwback and was damaging their brand. She's worth ten of them.'

'She may not want to talk about it when she gets back,' said Beth. 'We'll have to take our cue from her. In the meantime, there's someone else I'm rather worried about.'

'Who?' asked Chloe, leaning forward.

'Kathleen, the girl who gave us the tea samples for our boxes.'

'But wasn't she only a pop-up shop?' asked Lachlan, puzzled. 'She'll have long gone. Isn't that what they do?'

'Yes,' conceded Beth. 'Although, I did get the impression when I talked to her that she would have liked to stay up here if the pop-up was successful. Otherwise, why would she even have been interested in donating samples?'

'You don't think she was directly involved in what happened to Nora, do you?' asked Lachlan, looking worried.

'I really don't know,' said Beth. 'But I was in her shop this morning having a nosey around and I found till rolls for the months before Nora's death. She sold quite an extraordinary amount of tea on four separate occasions, always paid for in cash. I mean, who's walking around shopping with large amounts of cash these days?'

'Unless they don't want it to be traced back to them,' said Lachlan.

'Exactly,' said Beth.

'But wouldn't that mean that she'd be able to identify who made those purchases?' asked Lachlan.

'Very possibly,' said Beth. 'That's why I'm worried that she may have come to harm. The timing seems suspicious to say the least.'

'Have you mentioned your concerns to the police?' Lachlan asked.

'Yes, last night.' She turned to Chloe whose thumbs were flying over her phone as normal. 'Earth calling Chloe?'

'I was listening,' said Chloe. 'I've been digging around for information. I wish I'd got to know her better. She looked like fun. Her business has a Facebook page where she posts where she's going to be next. She seems to have done a lot of craft fairs in the central belt and down in the Borders as well. There's been no postings since she disappeared though.'

'Apparently, her mushroom tea was sourced in the Borders,' said Beth. 'It was that one someone laced with poison.'

'It must have been targeted, or other people would have died or become seriously ill,' said Lachlan.

'Only someone who had access to Nora's house could have laced the tea,' said Beth. 'One slightly disturbing development is that I noticed Callum and Jane having a drink together in Aulay's Bar last night. Later on, Callum came upon me eating some chips in front of the bay and sat with me for a while.'

'You think they might be in it together?' asked Lachlan.

Beth shook her head. 'No, there seemed to be little love lost between them. From what I overheard, Jane can be quite cruel.'

'It all makes no sense,' said Lachlan, frustrated. 'I mean, no offence but why would Nora leave you her whole estate in the first place? I know that you like cats so that could have been a factor but from what I can gather you weren't all that close to her.'

'None taken. I've asked myself that self-same question many times,' Beth sighed. 'We were only slightly more than acquaintances. If we'd been true friends, I wouldn't be stumbling around in the dark like this. The only thing I can think of is that her rift with her daughter was so profound that she would go to any lengths to disinherit her.'

'Given that Callum didn't arrive on the scene until she was already dead, she wouldn't have left him anything,' said Chloe. 'But didn't you say that Nora sent his mother a letter with her address on it? Perhaps they kept in touch so she would have known all about him?'

'The whole will thing muddies the waters,' said Beth. 'It removes the motive of financial gain from everyone but me.'

'There's other motives though, it's not necessarily about money,' said Lachlan. 'What about her former husband? Maybe he couldn't handle seeing her waltz off into the sunset with someone else?'

'Maybe a pupil with a grudge who blames her for the way his life turned out?' contributed Chloe.

'You're right. It's important to keep an open mind and, hopefully, the police will too,' replied Beth. 'I can't help thinking we're only seeing a couple of fragments of the puzzle. We still have to track down this Captain Saunders. I mean, if she was engaged to him then why didn't she change her will in his favour?'

'People often forget about their wills until it's too late,' said

Lachlan. 'No one likes to comprehend their own mortality. She wasn't all that old. Probably thought she had plenty of time.'

'Maria has vanished off the face of the earth as well,' said Chloe. 'And she's the only one who knows what this Captain Saunders really looks like. It's hard to tell anything from that dodgy photo.'

'She could work with a police sketch artist so people could actually look for him. We need to find her and to convince the police not to turn her over to immigration,' said Beth.

'If he's in the army, I don't see how the police haven't been able to track him down,' said Lachlan.

'Trying to get information out of Detective Sergeant Hunter is like trying to get blood out of a stone. He's the most exasperating man!'

Lachlan and Chloe glanced at each other and hid smiles.

'What?' demanded Beth. 'You know I'm right.'

She glanced at her watch and began loading the cups back on the tray as it was already past time to reopen after lunch.

Chloe's phone pinged. She read the message, looking concerned. 'That was Morna,' she said, looking worried. 'She's said she's sorry, but she won't be back today and will explain tomorrow. Her horrible family are up to something. I just know it!'

'Tell her it's fine and I'll see her tomorrow,' said Beth. Privately, though, she thought that this time Chloe might be right.

THIRTY

That evening, Beth let herself into the cottage and looked longingly at her couch. Both cats jumped down to greet her, then firmly escorted her into the kitchen to deliver their supper. On the way home from work, she'd received an email in the shop's inbox from Grant, the man she'd met in Aulay's last night. He'd asked her to meet him for drinks followed by dinner as he'd enjoyed her company the night before. Her first reaction had been to refuse. She barely knew him. He lived in Glasgow. *And he's not Logan Hunter*, a voice had piped up from the depths of her psyche which she'd squashed firmly back down. If she was brave enough to take a chance this could be her very first date.

After she was released from the secure home she'd been sent to – following a conviction for culpable homicide – she had left Aberdeen with her mother for a secluded life in Glasgow. The stress had worsened her mother's illness and Beth had retreated further into herself, too frightened to engage with a world that had moved on without her. Dating had been the furthest thing from her mind. Until now. Dare she?

They were meeting in a public place and, if it was terrible, he'd be off back to Glasgow in no time. If she didn't want to spend the rest of her life alone, this was a good first step. Feeling the acid creep up her throat with nerves, she hastily emailed him back agreeing to meet before she managed to talk herself out of it. This led to another quandary. What on earth was she going to wear? Groaning, she rushed off to inspect the meagre contents of her wardrobe. This was all happening too soon, she fretted.

By the time she'd walked into the town centre, her nerves were more under control.

'It's only drinks and dinner,' she muttered under her breath. She could leave whenever she wanted to.

As she arrived at The Oban Inn and fought her way upstairs through the throng, she spied Grant talking to her sister, Fiona, at the bar. They looked relaxed, as though they'd known each other for a while. Could he be the mystery man who had broken Fiona's heart by calling it off between them? She didn't look broken-hearted. Walking up to them with a tentative smile, she stood until they noticed her.

'Beth!' exclaimed Fiona, with a smile that lit her up from inside. 'Sorry to crash your date. I know Grant from my university days. I can confirm he's one of the good guys.' With that, she gave Beth a quick hug and rushed off with two glasses borne aloft, disappearing into the crowd. Leaning over, Grant kissed her on the cheek in greeting.

'I got you the same as you were drinking last night if that's okay?' he said.

'Perfect.' She smiled.

A couple got up to leave right by them and they scooted into the empty space. Grant was entertaining company and regaled her with outrageous stories of his time as a veterinary student. She in turn gave him edited highlights of her life to date, trying to keep the tone light.

There was an awkward pause. She'd obviously blown it by being too honest but her life up to now had been difficult. There was no getting away from that. She shifted uncomfortably and looked away from him, but he took her hand and pulled her into a quick hug.

'I can't believe you've managed to navigate through all that and come out the other side such a lovely person,' he said.

He finished off his drink at the same time as she did. 'Hungry?'

'Starving,' she replied with a smile.

He pulled her to her feet and led her back out of the busy pub. As they reached the bottom of the stairs, she peered into the bar and came face to face with a startled Logan Hunter who looked anything but pleased to see her. Turning away from him she continued out of the door, feeling his eyes burning into her back.

They headed to the local Chinese restaurant and ordered a sharing platter of starters followed by Kung Po chicken and beef satay with fried rice and prawn crackers on the side. There was a mix of ages in tonight and everyone seemed set on having a good time. The décor was oriental in style with red lanterns and colourful decorations adding to the atmosphere. They'd agreed to share a bottle of white wine and as Beth sipped slowly, she felt the tension leaving her body. Grant was great company and full of tales of his animal patients.

'The patients are the easiest part,' he said. 'It's handling the owners that's the biggest challenge. Of course, most of their stroppy behaviour is borne out of love for their pet but one wealthy woman with three Corgis actually gets her chef to drop off tasty morsels for the little tykes. He hates them with a passion. She even insists they sleep on their own luxury beds in a private room with soft classical music playing.'

Beth let out a snort of laughter. 'Don't tell my cats, they'll expect me to up my game. They've enough delusions of grandeur as it is!'

Beth excused herself to go to the toilet. She was having a great time. Grant was such a lovely person. As she was walking past the entrance to the kitchen, the door swung back to admit a waitress laden with dishes. Beth's mouth dropped open in shock as she glanced across and spied Maria to one side of the kitchen, chopping vegetables. Fortunately, the Spanish woman didn't see her.

Returning to the table in a daze, she wondered what to do for the best. She could either hang about and try to catch her as she came out of work, or she could contact the police and get them to do it.

'Hey, what's up?' asked Grant in concern as she returned to the table, all jollity gone. She knew that it wasn't exactly first-date material, but this was her life right now. She had to be honest with him.

'I've got a bit of a situation going on,' she said. Hurriedly, she caught him up on some of what had been happening since she'd discovered Nora's body. She hadn't planned on mentioning it but given her immediate dilemma she felt she had to say something.

'So that was what you were up to in Aulay's?' he said, sounding intrigued. 'I did wonder!'

'It's the most awful mess and I seem to be slap bang in the middle of it,' she groaned. 'Like I said, I've just spotted Maria working in the kitchen, no doubt being paid in cash. If I confront her myself, she'll probably just push past me and disappear again. But, if I bring in the police then she'll clam up completely, they'll contact immigration and she'll be deported. I don't know what to do for the best.' She wrung her hands. 'Sorry to lay all of this on you.'

Grant sat back in his chair thinking. There was something solid and reassuring about him, Beth thought. It felt good to unload what was worrying her, but she wouldn't blame him for running for the hills. It was a lot for a first date.

'Rock and hard place.' He frowned. 'But it seems to me you've already given her the chance to step up and do the right thing. We're talking murder here, not a broken plant pot. If she's withholding information for purely selfish reasons, then she has to be made to share it. She was the woman's carer, after all.'

'You're right, I'm going to call them.'

She took out her phone and debated whether to call the office number or Logan Hunter's mobile. She had spotted him in the pub which was just two minutes away. If he turned up on his own in casual clothes, that might well take the heat out of the situation. Decided now, she called up his number.

'Logan...? It's Beth... I'm at the Chinese... I've just seen Maria working in the kitchen... Can you come? On your own? Okay! See you soon.' She ended the call. 'He's out with another police officer, as luck would have it, so they're both coming. We've to stay put for now. The other officer is going to cover the rear door while he comes in the front, so she can't get away.'

The conversation dried up between them as they waited in silence. Beth felt bad for Grant. All he'd been looking for was a fun night out and she'd turned it into a stakeout. No wonder she was single. Startled, she jumped as he covered his hand with hers and gave it a gentle squeeze.

'None of this is your fault, Beth. I can hardly blame you for trying to do the right thing. Most people would just take the inheritance and run without a backward glance. All you're after is the truth of what happened to Nora even if it means having to relinquish it.'

'I'm happy to keep Marmalade but the rest makes me feel so guilty. She had a daughter, for goodness' sake.'

'A daughter she pretended didn't exist, from what you said. There must have been a reason for that.'

'I suppose,' Beth said. 'I can't honestly say that I took to Jane.'

'And I imagine that you take to most people,' he said, his eyes crinkling as he smiled at her.

'I try,' she admitted.

At that moment a very bad-tempered looking Logan Hunter arrived with DC Quinn at his heels. He approached their table, taking it all in at a glance. Beth snatched back her hand causing Grant to raise his eyebrows in surprise. Logan was obviously off-duty and he was wearing his scuffed brown leather jacket and worn jeans.

'Just stay there until it's all over,' he said, before taking out his warrant card and marching into the kitchen.

Everyone stopped talking. You could have heard a pin drop.

Beth swallowed, her mouth dry as parchment. There were the sounds of raised voices, then a scuffle and finally a draft of cold air as the back door banged shut behind them. Everyone started talking at once looking around them, wide-eyed. The owner, a dignified woman in her sixties, came out from behind the counter and cleared her throat.

'Police say all over now. Please, enjoy your food. One free drink on the house.'

'Another glass of wine?' asked Grant, searching her eyes.

Regretfully she shook her head. The earlier rapport she had felt building between them had collapsed. She felt tense and on edge. All she wanted was the security of her own four walls.

'I'm sorry, it's been a lovely evening. Well, until five minutes ago, but I have work tomorrow and need to get home.'

'Fair enough,' he said, trying to hide his disappointment behind a generous smile. 'Can I walk you home?'

'Honestly, it's fine,' she said. 'I'm out of your way anyway. Is it tomorrow you're heading back to Glasgow?'

'First thing. It's been so great meeting you, Beth. I hope you find the answers you're looking for. Don't let that brother of mine throw his weight around too much. His bark is worse than his bite.'

'Your brother?'

All of a sudden, she had it. The reason for that nagging familiarity.

'You're Logan's brother,' she said.

'The very same,' he said with a small smile, helping her on with her coat. 'I realised from that night in Aulay's Bar that you knew him and weren't his biggest fan. I wanted to get to know you better before confessing we were brothers, so you didn't take fright and run for the hills.' His eyes were unreadable.

It made sense now why Logan had looked so angry when he arrived at the restaurant. Probably thought I was seeing his brother just to put a wrinkle in his day, she thought bitterly.

'Your brother hates me,' she confided, after she'd insisted on splitting the bill and left the restaurant.

'I doubt that very much,' he said, turning to face her at the bottom of Albany Street where they would go their separate ways. 'I suspect that the reverse is true.'

They hugged goodbye and Beth set off alone. What had Grant meant by that last remark? Logan Hunter had made it clear that she was nothing but a thorn in his side. Grant had simply misread the situation.

As she passed the police station, she glanced in the window but there was no one at the front desk. She was desperate to know what was happening with Maria.

It was going to be a long night.

The next morning, Beth arrived at the bookshop early. She'd tossed and turned all night so decided she might as well be productive. By the time Lachlan and Chloe came in, she was several batches into the day's home baking, and a wonderful aroma of baking scones and fresh coffee filled the air. The bell tinkled once more, and jaws dropped as a self-conscious Morna arrived rather sheepishly in the kitchen.

'Morna, what happened to you?' exclaimed Chloe. 'You look... er... you look...' She couldn't go on.

She plainly had no words for the drastic transformation before them. Gone was the heavy makeup, the piercings and black combat trousers and T-shirt. Instead, Morna's barely there makeup accentuated her features and revealed a delicacy they hadn't suspected was there. She wore an expensive black pinafore and white blouse together with small gold hoop earrings. Her hair was smooth and silky. Her black suede ankle boots completed the look. Quite frankly, Beth would have walked past her in the street.

'Morna, you look amazing!' Beth managed with a bright smile. 'Coffee?'

'Yes, please,' her colleague mumbled.

She did look stunning after her makeover, but Beth was

concerned that it hadn't been of Morna's own choosing. What on earth were her dreadful family up to? And how had they managed to persuade Morna to get on board with it? She looked softer and more vulnerable now that her habitual armour had been stripped away. Like a newly hatched chick.

Chick? Beth slapped her hand to her forehead. Easter was fast approaching, and she'd put it to the back of her mind with everything else that had been going on.

'Chloe, where are we with the Easter chicks?' she asked.

'They're coming on Monday,' Chloe announced. 'Joe, the farmer's son, took me out to see them. They're super cute. He's not too bad either.' She fanned her face with her notebook.

Morna rolled her eyes. She hadn't changed completely then.

'I've got all the instructions on how to care for them,' Chloe went on. 'Joe's going to set the enclosure up and bring a supply of food, straw and a powerful heat lamp. Basically, everything we'll need to look after them properly.'

'Someone will need to sit by them at all times to make sure the kids don't get carried away. Some of the adults, too, no doubt.' Lachlan said.

'I'm going to get started on the Easter decorations today. The window's looking good, but we really need to jazz up the shop as well,' said Chloe. 'I'll need a bit of a hand at times.'

'I'll help.' Morna shrugged.

Lachlan looked relieved. Tissue paper and sticky back plastic were so not his thing. His contribution was going to be making a guest appearance as the Easter Bunny to hand out Easter eggs and prizes to the children.

There was much more Beth needed to say to them, but the first customer was already knocking at the door as if life would come to an end if it wasn't opened at that precise minute. Hurriedly, she ran to let them in.

'Hello, Valerie.' She smiled. 'You're bright and early this morning.'

'I can't stop long,' the older woman said, glancing around

nervously. 'It's just that I remembered something after the last time I was in. Something about poor Nora.'

Beth led her through to the café and poured them both some tea. They settled down on two wingback chairs with a small round table between them.

'So, what was it you wanted to tell me?' she asked gently.

'A while ago, I lent Nora a book. Not long before she died, I went round to see her. She was in bed and seemed rather poorly. A dose of the flu, I thought. The book was on her bedside table, and she insisted on giving it back to me. Her poor hand was shaking like a leaf. I wasn't bothered about the book. I had another copy so, actually, didn't need it back.'

'Who was there at the time?' asked Beth. 'Did you meet Captain Saunders then?'

'No, dear, I never met him. The carer, Maria, was in the corner putting laundry away in the drawers. I remember Nora's eyes following her about the room rather than looking at me. She seemed on edge. But I put it down to not liking the carer bossing her about when she was ill, even if it was for her own good. I thought she might even be a bit embarrassed at being caught at a disadvantage in bed during the day.'

Beth was perplexed by where all this was going but Valerie did seem worried so she forced back her impatience. Valerie fished around in her handbag and produced an old hardback copy of *Marjorie Morningstar* by Herman Wouk.

'Oh, that's one of my favourites!' exclaimed Beth. 'My mother had a copy, too.'

Valerie opened it and a cream sheet of paper fell out. With a shaking hand, she scooped it up and passed it across to Beth. In a spidery sprawl she read the words:

HELP ME!!

Beth went hot and cold all over. Nora must have been aware

that someone was trying to harm her, rather than being oblivious to her impending fate, as she had hoped.

'I took it off the shelf this morning to pass to a neighbour of mine. When that fell out, I nearly dropped where I stood. Nora needed me and I let her down.'

'Without meaning to, I think we all let her down,' said Beth sadly. 'I think you should take this to the police. They need to see it.'

'Could you take it for me, dear?' asked Valerie. 'I think my old legs have had enough of an outing for one day.'

Beth's heart sank but she couldn't very well refuse in the circumstances. Once she'd walked Valerie to the door, she placed the book in the safe until closing time. Why hadn't Nora said anything to anyone? She could have told Maria when Saunders wasn't around. Unless, of course, Saunders and Maria had been working together all this time. With a heavy sigh she returned to the shop floor.

All of them were run off their feet until lunchtime. During the course of the morning, Toby and Marmalade arrived and amused the customers no end by chasing each other all over the shop, trailing some of Chloe's crepe paper behind them before collapsing onto two comfy armchairs in the military history section where no one was likely to disturb them.

'The shop's looking great, Chloe,' Beth said as they gathered round the table for lunch. 'Have we had many RSVPs for the children's Easter egg hunt and story time?'

Chloe's expressive face lit up. 'Loads! I think practically every kid in Oban is coming here on Saturday.'

'You'd better order more Easter eggs then,' said Beth. 'We can always eat the leftovers.'

'Now you're talking,' said Morna, with a slight smile. She'd been subdued all morning.

'Is everything all right?' asked Beth. 'You don't need to tell us if you'd rather not. It's just that we couldn't help noticing...'

'That you've turned into some kind of a Stepford daughter...' added Chloe.

Beth glared at her youngest member of staff who shrugged her shoulders, unrepentant.

'Well, it's true, isn't it? What I want to know is, why?' She stared at Morna, waiting for an explanation.

'My father is trying to get elected to parliament,' Morna sighed. 'They begged me to toe the line to support him, saying if I didn't, some vicious journalist hack will dig me up and parade me in the national media as some kind of weapon to hurt them. My anonymity will be blown, and I won't be able to lead the life I've made for myself anymore. My only option will be to disappear into some anonymous city.'

'But that's not fair!' exclaimed Chloe. 'They were happy enough leaving you to rot before and now they want to play happy families?'

'I know all that,' said Morna, downcast, 'but it's not as black and white as you think. Even though at times I've hated them, deep down, I kind of love them a bit as well. I like my life as it is. It's all mine, something I've created through hard work and determination. But, if I'm honest, a teeny tiny part of me has always longed for them to love and accept me. I know that's totally tragic.'

'They're your parents, lass,' said Lachlan. 'You don't get any more powerful attachment than that.'

'I'd feel a bit happier if they wanted you by their side as who you really are,' said Chloe, her eyes bright with tears. 'Cos that's amazing. Cassandra might have star quality, and I admit I was blinded by that when I first met her.' She held up her hands in surrender.

'Yeah, you were.' Morna grinned. 'You did everything but roll over and ask her to tickle your tummy, you were so into her.'

'True,' said Chloe sheepishly. 'But you're a way cooler person than she is.'

'I think we can all agree on that.' Beth smiled. 'But be careful,

Morna. There's only so much of yourself you can offer up to another person, if they're not willing to meet you halfway.'

Personally, she felt furious at the Abercrombies for treating their youngest daughter so shabbily. She knew it had taken years of struggle for Morna to make her peace with their rejection and gain her current equilibrium. Now, they'd swanned in to take her up into their midst again, not because they loved her and wanted to put things right but to satisfy their venal desire for power and status. Despite not being aggressive by nature, quite frankly, it made her feel like punching someone to see poor Morna so ill used.

Deciding a change of subject was called for, she regaled them all with news of her date last night, her discovery of Maria in the kitchen of the Chinese restaurant and subsequent call to the police. She kept the upsetting note from Valerie to herself in the meantime as she knew it would weigh heavily on them.

'Imagine my horror,' she said dramatically, playing it for laughs to cheer them up, 'to discover that the man I'd just been out with was none other than Detective Sergeant Hunter's brother. He caught us together before I even knew.' She groaned.

'That is SO cringe!' said Chloe, covering her eyes. Morna was hiding a laugh behind her hands.

'It rather killed the vibe,' said Beth, wiggling her fingers.

'Who needs soaps when I've got all this drama unfolding before my eyes at work?' declared Lachlan, getting into the spirit of things.

Beth smiled at them, pleased to see they all looked more cheerful. Glancing at the clock, she started gathering up the lunch things onto the tray.

There was a frantic banging at the door.

'For goodness' sake, this is a bookshop, not A&E. What could be so urgent?' grumbled Lachlan.

Beth walked over and opened the door, only to stand back in surprise when it revealed Maria who was white as a sheet with dark circles under her eyes.

THIRTY-TWO

'I need to speak to you,' Maria said, pushing past Beth into the shop.

Lachlan took a few paces forward, but Beth motioned to him to stay back.

'We can go into the office,' she said. 'Chloe, would you be kind enough to bring Maria and I some coffee?'

Chloe's eyes widened but she went quietly off to the kitchen.

Once they were in her office with the door closed, Maria sat across from her, clearly struggling to contain her anger. Beth wondered if she'd been too hasty closing the door behind them.

'You had me arrested,' Maria said flatly.

Her nails were bitten down to the quick and she looked as if she hadn't slept or been able to wash or change her clothes. Beth remembered how that had felt, as though she'd been denied her basic human dignity.

'I'm sorry,' she said quietly. 'You left me no choice. I was out for a meal last night and saw you there. What else was I meant to do? I need answers and you're the only one who can provide them. Nora was *murdered*. I can't just walk away and pretend it has nothing to do with me. I owe it to her to find out the truth. Someone else has gone missing, too. They may have been harmed or be in terrible danger.'

Maria's body relaxed and she slumped down in the chair. 'I know that you tried to help me earlier, but I was too afraid when I realised what I had got mixed up in.'

'What happened at the police station?' *And how come they let you go?* Beth wanted to ask.

'I was interviewed by Detective Sergeant Hunter. At first, I was terrified. I thought he would make me tell him everything then hold me in a cell until immigration came for me. The other one, the woman, she is even more fierce. She tricks you, tries to make lies out of everything you say. She was annoyed because I had interrupted her evening with her boyfriend.'

Beth felt her spirits sink like a stone. Rhona Quinn must have been out with Logan. They had arrived together and were both clearly off-duty at the time. She pushed that thought aside to mull over later. *Focus, Beth!*

'I need to know what happened to Nora. It seems clear that she was poisoned using the mushroom tea sample in my prescription box laced with poison. I want to know how that could have happened on your watch, if you're as innocent as you claim? Nora had only had two boxes before she died. The day I found her I was dropping off a third box. You might not have been in the house then, but you were certainly there beforehand as Nora got weaker and weaker. Were you feeding her the tea?'

'Yes,' Maria burst out, tears spurting. 'I fed her the bloody tea. Oliver told me to. He said it would help her. He showed me all these articles about the nutritious properties of mushroom tea. He seemed so determined to make her better. And it was only tea. I couldn't see the harm in it. It wasn't just the few teabags in your box. He had a big jar of it as well in the pantry.'

'I take it you mean Captain Saunders?' Beth said. 'You know that he's completely disappeared. No one but you has ever seen him. Did he live at the house with Nora? How often was he around?'

'Please, stop with the questions. It's too much. I've been up half the night answering questions from the police. I need to think.'

Beth was reluctant to ease up on her but there was a knock on the door and Chloe walked in bearing a tray of coffee, a chicken salad roll, and shortbread fresh out of the oven.

'Thanks, Chloe.' Beth smiled, resisting the urge to run her hands through her hair in frustration.

She poured Maria some coffee and placed the plate in front of her, guessing she'd be hungry after her ordeal last night. Maria fell upon it, using both hands to stuff food in her mouth. Despite the urgency of the situation, Beth felt guilty for putting her under so much pressure. Was that how Logan Hunter had felt when she was the one being interrogated? *Haha, not a chance*, she thought, suppressing a wry smile at the very idea.

Beth held her tongue until Maria had polished off all the food and pushed back in her seat, nodding for her to continue.

'Did Nora ever confide in you?' Beth asked. 'I don't know, maybe ask for help or state that she felt threatened by Saunders?'

'No, of course not! I would have done something. Despite what you seem to think of me, I am not a bad person,' Maria snapped.

'Have you managed to give the police a good description of Oliver Saunders?' she asked.

'I did my best,' Maria sighed. 'They want me to go in and work with a sketch artist who'll come up from Glasgow.'

'I take it he hasn't been in touch?' asked Beth.

'No, the mobile number I had for him is still not working. I don't understand it. I thought he really cared for Nora. The police say that they've no record of him even existing. He was never in the army.'

'That sounds bad,' said Beth, her heart sinking. 'But if it was a simple romance scam then how come he didn't get Nora to make her will in *his* favour? What does he stand to gain from all this. If he's a scammer, then he's really bad at it.'

'I hear that Nora left you her whole estate,' said Maria, with a hard stare of her own. 'You are the person who benefits most from her death, no?'

'Yes, so it would seem,' said Beth. 'I can't work out why she did that. It makes no sense to me. Apart from Marmalade, that is. I already love him to bits. I can't help feeling there's a lot more going on than meets the eye in this case.'

'That is why I have come. I want to help.'

'What did the police say about your immigration status?' asked Beth, warily. She had no idea if Maria was now being straight with either her or the police. Her recent behaviour hadn't exactly inspired confidence. She also felt she couldn't mention Nora's note to Valerie before she had run it by the police.

'It turns out they have some discretion to report me or not. They said as long as I continue to cooperate with the investigation, they can justify doing nothing. Hopefully, by then my paperwork will be in order. In the meantime, I agreed to check in with them once a day.'

'But how will you live while this goes on?' asked Beth.

'I'll find some cash-in-hand job and stay in a cheap backpacker hostel,' Maria replied. 'Detective Sergeant Hunter also gave me the name of a local church which helps people like me, no questions asked. He gave me a cheap phone with ten pounds of credit. This is the number.' She scribbled it down on a Post-it from the table.

'You seem to have it all figured out,' said Beth with a faint smile, writing her own personal mobile on a business card and handing it across.

'I'm getting there,' Maria sighed. 'Look, I want to get on, so I'll answer your questions since you've been dragged into this mess. Saunders stayed at the house but in the spare room. In fact, he never went out at all while I was there, now I think about it. The shopping was delivered to the house by Tesco and for anything local, he would give me the money to nip out and get it, saying it would be a chance for me to take a break. He would tell me to go for a coffee or do something for myself while I was out. I thought he was being kind and caring and that he must be devoted to Nora.

He would tell me the doctor had been while I was out sometimes or that one of Nora's friends had called round to see her.'

'And now you think that none of that was true?' asked Beth.

'I don't know what to think. He has disappeared without a trace but then so did I,' she said with a defiant tilt of her head.

'Do you remember acting as a witness when Nora signed her will?' asked Beth.

'I do remember being asked to witness her signature,' Maria admitted. 'I don't know what the document was as they had placed a blank piece of paper on top of the page. I was just asked to watch Nora signing and then sign my name alongside hers. I don't think they wanted me to know what it was all about.'

'So, Oliver Saunders was present at the time?'

'Yes.'

'How was Nora at that time? Did she seem to know what she was signing?'

Maria frowned. 'She was alert and seemed willing. I wouldn't have added my name otherwise.'

'Callum said when he arrived at the house you fled past him, seeming upset. When exactly did you find Nora dead? Was Captain Saunders there at the time?'

Maria ran her fingers through hair that was already standing on end. Beth felt like a heel for continuing to push her but who knew when she would get another chance?

'She was alive that morning when I got up but drifting in and out of consciousness. I was worried and asked Oliver whether we should be calling an ambulance? You have to understand, I was hired as an unskilled carer. I have no nursing experience. I was quite clear about that when I was hired. Her deterioration over the time that I worked there worried me.'

'So how did he reply?' asked Beth.

'He said I had just missed the doctor and that he had confirmed it was simply a urinary tract infection. He said that it looked a lot worse than it was. She'd been prescribed antibiotics, and he had already decanted them into her pill box.'

'So, you didn't see the box which would have confirmed the prescription?'

'No, but I had no reason to doubt him. I know that UTIs can appear alarming; people can become confused and disorientated. It had happened to my grandmother. So, although Nora looked bad, I thought it would soon clear up now that she had the correct treatment. He asked me to dress her and help her downstairs to sit in her chair. He thought a change of scenery would encourage her, make her feel brighter. I had my reservations, but I did as he asked.'

A pained look twisted her face.

'What happened next?' prompted Beth, feeling sick to the stomach that she was effectively hearing Nora's last moments alive described.

'I helped her to dress and switched on Radio Four for her as she would normally listen to it at that time. She seemed feverish and confused. I had to call Oliver to help me get her downstairs as her legs kept giving way. In the end, he carried her down himself. There were tears running down his cheeks. How could I doubt him?'

'And then?' prompted Beth.

'He produced a long shopping list. It took me all over town. I left him spooning that damn mushroom tea into her mouth. She tried so hard to swallow it. She wanted to please him,' Maria said, her voice breaking, tears glistening in her eyes. 'I can't stop thinking about it.'

'How was she when you got back?' asked Beth.

'She was sitting in her chair. I called out to her and popped my head in the door to tell her I was back and would be in once I'd put the shopping away. The radio was still playing when I went back in. I stopped in front of her and that's when I knew. I knew completely. She was gone.'

'You didn't think to call an ambulance?' asked Beth, trying to keep the censure out of her voice.

'What would be the point? She had no pulse and was already cooling. There was nothing more to be done for her. I called out for

Oliver, ran all over the house shouting his name, but he'd gone. I went into his room. All his clothes and toiletries were gone. It was as though he was never there. I knew that was not right. I knew something was very wrong. I phoned him. He said he would handle things. I thought about how it would look to everyone. How it would look to the police. I had overstayed my visa. I had no formal qualifications. A woman had died in my care. I ran, rushed out the door in a panic, just as a man arrived at the house. I did not know him. I thought he might hurt me. So, I ran, and kept running. Until now.'

Beth stood in front of the police station, took a deep breath, and pushed open the door. She instantly felt better when she saw that it was PC Jenny Clark behind the desk.

'Hi, Beth,' the young officer said with a welcoming smile. 'What can I do for you? Got any more weird and wonderful creatures for us?'

'Hi, Jenny, I'm afraid not. I was wondering if Detective Sergeant Hunter was in? I have something for him in relation to an active investigation.'

'Hang on a sec and I'll check,' PC Clark said. 'You can have a seat if you like.' She then disappeared from sight.

Beth reluctantly sat on one of the shiny plastic seats yet again. Only a couple of minutes passed before DS Hunter opened the door and motioned for her to come through to the back. They walked along the corridor in silence.

Beth was relieved when she was shown into the comfortable room rather than the one for formal interviews. The detective motioned for her to sit opposite him. He didn't offer her a drink and she was glad of it. She wanted to be out of there as fast as possible.

'What's this about?' he asked, without further ado.

She extracted the book from her handbag, letting it fall open to the piece of paper. 'Valerie Bole, a friend of Nora Kelly's, brought this in to show me today. She was very distressed having just found the note inside it this morning. Nora had pressed the book on her the last time they'd met at her house, but Valerie had already read it so didn't see the note until now. She didn't feel up to coming in so asked me to pass it across instead.'

DS Hunter took it from her then secured it in an evidence bag.

'This case gets more baffling by the minute,' he said, sounding as frustrated as she felt. 'Do you happen to know where Valerie Bole lives?'

'Yes, I wrote it down for you,' she said, handing across a piece of paper torn from her notebook. 'Maria also came in to see me today. I'm so glad you didn't tell immigration. That was really kind of you.'

'I don't do kind,' he sighed. 'I uphold the law. Sometimes those things clash. When they do, I apply the law. In Maria's case, I applied to exercise a discretion. I felt it was more beneficial to keep her around to assist in the identification of Captain Saunders, should he ever be found.'

Beth glared at him. He really was the most impossible man. There she was trying to pay him a compliment. He clearly wasn't in the best of moods, but she decided to press on regardless while she had the chance.

'I've been thinking...' she said.

'Here comes trouble,' he muttered.

'Excuse me?'

'Sorry, that was unprofessional,' he admitted. 'Please, go on. I shouldn't be taking my bad day out on you.'

Beth stared at him. He looked exhausted, like he hadn't slept in a while. His skin was greasy and there was a dark shadow where normally he was clean shaven. This case must be really getting to him. Unless, of course, the reason he hadn't slept was due to the charms of his date last night, the delectable Rhona Quinn. The mere thought caused heat to rush to her face. He raised his eyebrows at her prolonged silence. Hurriedly, she continued.

'It occurred to me on my way here that maybe we've been looking at things all wrong,' she blurted out.

'What? There is no "we". The police are the ones doing the investigating, not you.' The frown was back.

'I assume that most cases like Nora's involve a vulnerable person being exploited for monetary gain. The driver is money.'

'The only person who appears to have profited financially from Nora's death is you,' DS Hunter said bluntly. 'How do you explain that?'

'Well, exactly, that's my point,' Beth said, raising her own eyebrows.

'I'm not following,' he said, rubbing his hand over his stubble.

'Well, why would someone go to such incredible lengths to orchestrate a successful murder by poisoning, disappear without trace, yet make no monetary gain whatsoever? It's like Nora's money was completely irrelevant to the killer. In fact, the killer may even have convinced Nora to make her will out to me as a diversionary tactic. Especially if they were aware of my background and the likelihood that I would fall under suspicion.' She paused, then added, 'And it worked!' She sent him an accusing look.

He sat back in his seat. She could practically hear the cogs turning.

'Let's say you're right,' he said at last. 'What other possible motives could there be?'

Beth opened her mouth to reply but the detective sergeant glanced at the clock and suddenly jumped to his feet.

'Hold that thought. I have to pick up Poppy from after-school club. If you don't mind walking there with me, we could continue this conversation on the way? Besides, I can't really be caught spitballing about a case with a potential suspect, can I?' he said with a small smile to take away the sting of his words.

Beth waited for him at the bottom of Albany Street and fell

into step with him as he came alongside her. It felt a little strange to be walking to the school with him to collect his daughter, but it was true that they'd be able to speak more candidly outside the police station.

'Well, obviously,' she began, trying to match her stride to his long one and failing, 'the motive isn't passion. It appears from what Maria said that, despite his proposal, Saunders and Nora didn't share a bedroom. He may have proposed but there's no sense of a grand passion about it by all accounts. There also appears to be no suggestion of Nora having been involved with anyone else over the years. She parted ways with her husband decades ago. None of her friends appear to have known about any man friend until now.'

'So, what does that leave?' he asked, thinking aloud.

'Revenge,' they both said at once.

'That's got to be it,' said Beth excitedly. 'It's the only thing that makes sense. We need to look into Nora's past.'

'Again, with the "we",' he said, shooting her an exasperated glance.

'If we find out what she did then we'd find out who wanted her dead,' said Beth. She suddenly felt a bit faint. Didn't the same rationale also apply to her? She had killed someone when she was no more than a child. It may have been unintended and acting in self-defence but if her theory held good for Nora, then maybe one day someone would come knocking at the door for her. A life for a life. Was that it? Had Nora killed someone?

'Beth? Are you alright?'

She saw Logan's worried face staring at her from what seemed a long way away. Darkness bled around the edges of her vision. By now they'd reached the primary school. Her knees buckled and she felt a pair of strong arms supporting her to a bench under a tree outside the playground. The darkness receded.

'You look like a corpse,' Logan said in a low voice, his arm still around her.

'You say the nicest things,' she huffed.

'I meant, white with a touch of blue around the lips,' he said, as if that made it alright. Just as well he was a policeman and not a diplomat, she thought.

'I'm fine now, honestly. I just felt a bit faint. You go and collect Poppy. You don't want to be late.'

He looked conflicted.

'Go!' she said more strongly.

'Fine, I will! But wait here until I get back,' he said with a cross look. 'You've been overdoing it.'

'You're one to talk,' she managed with a small smile, as he strode off across the playground and into the school.

Beth concentrated on taking deep breaths and after a few minutes she got to her feet and swung her arms about, aiming to get some colour back into her cheeks and stop him fussing. She really didn't want to gatecrash his precious time with his daughter, so her plan was simply to bid them farewell and head off back home. She'd reckoned without Poppy.

'Beth!' the little girl exclaimed, rushing up and throwing her arms around her. 'I haven't seen you for *ages*. You read us that story about the naughty Jelly Monster. And guess what? We had jelly for school lunch last week, but I gobbled it down quickly and watched everyone else's so it didn't escape!'

Beth bent down and hugged her back, her face splitting wide in a smile.

'Yes, we missed you at story time on Saturday. Toby was wondering where you'd got to.'

'He's such a sweet cat.' Poppy smiled. 'I love Marmalade, too, but Toby's my favourite. Daaad, when can I have a kitten? I'll look after it and be really, really good, I *promise!*'

'*Sorry,*' Beth mouthed at Logan over the top of Poppy's head.

'Maybe when you're older,' her dad said, ruffling her hair.

Poppy looked disappointed but soon brightened up. 'Is Beth coming for tea?'

'What? Er, I hadn't thought that far ahead,' he said, looking mortified.

'Please, Dad, you said I can have my friends over for tea whenever I want. It would make up for not getting a kitten, *please*, Dad,' she implored.

Beth laughed at his discomfiture. It felt good seeing the intrepid detective being outmanoeuvred by a six-year-old.

Logan laughed and squeezed his daughter to him. 'You'd be very welcome to join us, if you'd like,' he said with a smile. 'I need to pay you back for the other night anyway. It's only a chicken curry, nothing fancy. We'll drive you home afterwards.'

'In that case,' she said, smiling at Poppy, 'I gratefully accept!'

THIRTY-FOUR

After a few minutes' walk, they arrived at an immaculate semi-detached house in Park Road with a small enclosed front garden filled with daffodils and a central rose garden.

'You're a gardener, then?' she asked, surprised as she spotted the glass greenhouse round the back.

'It helps me unwind from the pressures of the job,' he said, as he unlocked the front door. Inside, it was bright and welcoming with wooden floorboards and cheerful scatter rugs.

There was a lot of pink and purple. On the wall were photos of a beautiful smiling woman who Beth realised must be his late wife, Joanna.

'You can blame the colour scheme on Poppy,' he said under his breath, as he headed to the large open-plan kitchen to get Poppy a snack. Once she was curled up on the sofa, watching her favourite cartoons, he took Beth through to the kitchen and started dinner. She offered to help but he wouldn't hear of it, so she sat down on a comfy sofa and watched him instead. It occurred to her belatedly that it was probably a big deal for him to have invited her into his home. It was a sign of trust. After about twenty minutes, he came over to join her as the kitchen was filled with a delicious aroma of cooking spices.

'Smells good.' She smiled up at him.

'It's a recipe my... wife, Joanna, used to make,' he said, a hitch in his voice. 'She was an amazing cook.'

'I'm sure she'd be happy that you're honouring her memory by making it,' she said, patting his arm. He was still grieving. She knew from experience that grief could catch you unawares when you were least expecting it.

'I try to keep her memory alive for Poppy. Every day it becomes harder and harder to feel her presence. But I owe it to both her and Poppy to do everything in my power to keep it with us.'

'My mum was the centre of my world,' Beth said quietly. 'When I lost her, all I wanted to do was cloak myself in memories. I even wore some of her clothes, determined to hoard her very essence. But no matter how hard I try, day by day she drifts further out of my reach. Poppy will find her own way of navigating the loss. You've made space for her memories in your home. She'll know that she was cherished by both of you. Children are more resilient than we give them credit for sometimes.'

'It breaks my heart that Poppy has to grow up without her mother,' he said, looking away from her while he composed himself, then rising from the sofa to give the pot another stir.

'So,' he said, changing the subject and rejoining her on the comfortable couch, 'are you feeling better now? Not so faint?'

Beth groaned. 'I'm fine, honestly. It can happen sometimes, particularly when I'm feeling overwhelmed. I think I must breathe really shallowly or forget to breathe at all. It's embarrassing more than anything. It makes me feel like some Victorian maiden having an attack of the vapours.'

'Maybe I'd better start carrying a phial of smelling salts with my standard kit,' he said, his mouth quirking up in amusement.

A sudden shadow passed across his face. 'I gather you've been spending a bit of time with my brother,' he said, his voice studiedly neutral. 'Grant is a great guy.'

'Yes, he is.' She smiled. *But he's not you*, she thought sadly, increasingly sure now that no one else would do.

'Are you planning to see him again?' he asked. 'Sorry, don't answer that, it's none of my business.'

Beth bit her lip. This was all getting rather intense and her feelings were all over the place. However, she felt that she owed him an honest response.

'I really liked him as a person, but I've made no plans to see him again,' she replied.

He turned and looked at her. She held his gaze, her heart beating faster. She felt like she was drowning in his eyes and his head moved almost imperceptibly closer to hers. Her mouth felt dry and she could feel the heat coming off him.

'Daddy, I'm starving! Is tea ready yet?'

Startled, they both looked up to find an oblivious Poppy skipping into the kitchen. Logan jumped up like he'd been electrocuted and Beth followed suit.

'Just about to dish up,' he said, smiling manically at his daughter.

'Poppy, shall we set the table?' Beth smiled at the little girl, covering her confusion with action.

They were treated to all the school gossip as Poppy chattered away during the meal. Apparently, the school dinner lady was now going out with the janitor. Also, her group of friends had been asked if they could look after a little girl who was being bullied.

'Her name's Jodie, Dad. Can I have her over to play on Saturday? She's been really sad and lonely, and I want to make her happy again.'

'I'll get her mum's number and give her a ring,' he said, reaching out to give Poppy a hug. 'I'm off that day so if she's allowed to come, we can maybe go to the beach at Ganavan, after we've been to see the Easter chicks?'

'Yay!' Poppy clapped. 'Daddy, I've finished. Can I get down from the table, please?'

'Sure, off you go,' he replied. 'We'll be taking Beth home in a little while, remember.'

They carried their coffee outside to the decking. It was still sunny but cold, so they threw a couple of blankets around their shoulders to ward off the chill. The earlier tension had dissipated, and Beth felt relaxed as she stared out into the garden.

'You must be very proud,' Beth said quietly.

'Yeah,' he said with a quick grin. 'She's a pretty cool kid.'

They chatted idly whilst they drank their coffee, neither wishing to return to their previous intensity, although Beth felt that a genuine, yet fragile connection had been established between them. She'd glimpsed a different side of him tonight.

Once their coffee was finished, Logan drove her back to the cottage. Beth's heart was full as she hugged Poppy goodbye and waved them both off into the night until only their receding tail-lights were still visible.

THIRTY-FIVE

Beth fed the cats, lit the stove, then settled herself on the couch with the cats on either side of her like bookends. She fired up her laptop and got to work.

'Who were you, Nora Kelly?' she murmured. She'd assumed that her customer was local, but the funeral home had recently posted an obituary. This would give her something to get her teeth into at least. She felt a burning certainty that Nora had been killed because of something she had done in her past.

Nora May Kelly was born in Inverness on 13th January 1960. She graduated from Aberdeen University with first class honours in mathematics in 1982. For a number of years, she taught in Glasgow schools before moving up to Oban in the Western Highlands in 1995, where she continued to teach until her retirement in 2020.

The funeral will be private and take place on Saturday 26th April 2025.

No flowers. If desired, donations in her memory can be made to the local branch of the Cats Protection League.

Beth looked up from the computer, frowning. This wasn't right? Why didn't it mention her daughter, Jane, for one thing? And why was it private? Surely her local friends should be allowed to go and pay their respects? Although it did give her some things to go on.

She figured that if revenge was the motive, it was unlikely to be for something small like a private grievance. No, for someone to harbour a grudge for years like this it must have been for a major transgression and therefore most likely had been reported on some years ago, before she moved to Oban. If she started with Nora's year of graduation in 1982 and finished with when she moved to Oban in 1995, that should give her a window for research.

Eagerly, she started typing away on her laptop before grinding to a halt with a groan. She was an idiot. It wasn't going to be as easy as she thought. The internet didn't become widely available until 1993, social media didn't explode until the 2000s, and even LinkedIn didn't start to get properly going until 2004.

It looked like her research was going to have to be old school. She could see long boring days in the library in her future. In the meantime, it wouldn't do any harm to launch a few Google searches just in case. She decided to start by typing in the name of Nora's daughter, Jane. The divorce must have happened after Jane was born so she typed Jane Brennan into the search engine. There were no relevant hits. Jane had indicated that her surname was Guthrie which she had assumed was her married name. Just for completeness she typed it in anyway. Her jaw dropped as she saw the huge number of hits loading.

This changed everything. She clicked on a leading article in *The Herald* newspaper, dated 13th March 1992.

Bittersweet Reunion for Baby Jane

A happy ending tinged with sadness for Glasgow father, Jim Guthrie, who has finally been reunited with his little girl three long years after she was snatched from her pram late on sunny afternoon in June 1989.

Tragically, Jane's mother died last year from complications arising from pneumonia. However, despite the diagnosis, Jim's theory is that she effectively died from a broken heart, 'She had no fight left in her,' he explained, as he held his child close...

So, Nora *really* didn't have a daughter, thought Beth, horrified by her discovery. She clicked on another article, this time in a law journal.

Mad or Bad? 4th December 1994

The Baby Jane case has stimulated intense debate on sentencing policy in relation to women who steal other women's babies after suffering multiple miscarriages or even the trauma of a stillbirth, as was the case here. Some have argued that Nora Brennan was severely unwell and a prison sentence would have been too harsh. Others maintain that a hospital order, which ended after two years, was unduly lenient.

It could be argued that the extent of planning that went into the execution of this crime distinguishes it from other cases where a woman gives in to a momentary impulse, having temporarily taken leave of her senses.

Ironically, having flawlessly executed a plan many months in the making, she was unable to bond with the baby. Her psychiatrist maintained in court that the guilt ate away at her until she unravelled completely and it all came pouring out...

Has justice been served? Have your say below…

Stunned, Beth closed her laptop. A complete and utter tragedy for all concerned. Now that she was settled and happy, Beth herself was beginning to yearn for a child of her own. Having experienced the closest of maternal bonds with her own mother, she longed to experience that again with a child of her own. She couldn't even imagine how awful Nora must have felt after losing her babies. The stillbirth, in particular, was probably the most harrowing thing a woman could ever have to face.

Clearly, moving up to Oban and reverting to her maiden name had been an effort to break with Nora's tragic past and start over, even if she could never really outrun the torment of her own mind. Beth and her mother had also tried to reinvent themselves once Beth was released from detention, changing their names and moving from Aberdeen to lose themselves in the anonymity of Glasgow. Even when she realised that she was dying, her mother had moved heaven and earth to arrange a whole new life for her in Oban, forcing her out into the world in a small town where she hoped she would thrive. As she thought of everything her beloved mother had done for her so unselfishly over the years, a sob hiccoughed out of her, which she hurriedly swallowed back down. If she was going to climb out from under this, she needed to be strong.

She would share the news with her staff tomorrow, but she wasn't going to share it with the police just yet. Jane had suffered greatly as a result of the actions taken by Nora Kelly. She needed to be completely satisfied she was implicated in Nora's death before heaping any more anguish on either her or her real family.

THIRTY-SIX

The next morning, once everyone was in the shop, including Morna, who still disconcertingly looked like another person, Beth updated them all on her big discovery over mugs of freshly brewed coffee.

'That's terrible,' said Chloe, tearing up. 'I want to be furious at Nora, but she has suffered so much, too.'

'A terrible mess, every which way you look at it,' said Morna, shaking her head. 'But Jane has surely known about this her entire life. What could have prompted her to come looking for Nora now, let alone murder her?'

'Possibly, Nora simply disappeared. You said she lived and worked in Glasgow,' said Lachlan, pushing his glasses up his nose. 'People didn't have an online trail to follow back then. Once she was divorced, she reverted to her maiden name which wouldn't have helped either.'

'Yes, she kept a very low profile up here,' said Beth. 'I think her only social contact was her monthly book club with Valerie and popping along to the shops.'

'Maybe her victim support work was her way of trying to make amends for what she'd done?' said Chloe.

'A rather lonely life,' said Lachlan. 'It can't have been easy.'

'What happened to her when it came out?' asked Morna. 'I mean, I assume she went to prison?'

'No,' said Beth. 'She'd already had a severe breakdown by then, so she was given a hospital order. When they deemed her to be sufficiently recovered, she was released.'

'Are you going to tell the police?' asked Lachlan. 'It'll take the pressure off you if they've got someone else to focus on.'

Beth felt the heat rush to her face as she recalled how it had felt to be the focus of a certain policeman's attention last night.

'Why's she gone all red?' Chloe whispered to Morna.

Morna shrugged, looking at Beth with interest.

'Not at the moment,' she said, gathering herself together. 'I want to wait until I'm sure she had a hand in Nora's death. For all we know, she just heard about her death and came up to ascertain for herself if it was true. We still haven't accounted for Captain Oliver Saunders in the mix either.'

'So, what's the plan then?' asked Lachlan.

'Well, I think I'm going to go over to Mull tomorrow to speak to Professor Darragh Brennan. He must know a lot more about Nora's early life than anyone else. I think they married when she was in her early twenties and then divorced after the whole thing came out about stealing the baby.'

'Shouldn't you take someone with you?' asked Lachlan. 'You don't know what you'll be walking into. I've heard a bit about him. Bit of a recluse now, they reckon. Hardly ever comes over to the mainland. I can come, if you like?' he offered valiantly.

'Thanks, Lachlan, but he's a retired professor. He might not agree to speak to me, but I doubt I have anything to worry about. At the very least, it'll give me a chance to jump on the ferry and get one of these gorgeous islands under my belt.'

'You'll need to hire a car for the day as it's a bit hard to get round the island otherwise,' said Lachlan, ever practical. 'You can drive, can't you?'

'Yes, my mother made me learn when I was seventeen,' Beth replied. 'I'm a bit rusty though.'

'As long as you don't miss the ferry and end up in the harbour,' joked Chloe.

'Maybe I should wear a life jacket, just in case,' Beth laughed. She turned to Morna.

'How's the electioneering going?'

'It's pretty dire. It's exhausting playing happy families. Can you believe they're doing a big photo spread in *Argyll Country Life* magazine? How embarrassing is that? Shoot me now. And that's not even the worst of it. We're going to be interviewed live on STV just before the elections.'

'You know,' said Lachlan thoughtfully, 'I think your family's got this all wrong, the way they're trying to make you over into something you're not.'

'But I'm obviously unpalatable as myself,' Morna said in a small voice.

Beth wanted to give her a huge hug. She refrained, knowing that Morna didn't cope well with displays of affection.

'Your father is a rich Tory, part of the landed gentry. How are locals going to be able to relate to that? Think about it, you could be their secret weapon, Morna. It would make them look less out of touch with the electorate if you turn up as yourself. It makes them look more inclusive and broadminded,' said Lachlan.

'Which they're not.' Morna grimaced. 'I've had friends walk past me in the street when I'm dressed like this. The one good thing about it is that after the election, I can go back to being me again and most people will be none the wiser. If I show up as myself for all the publicity events, then my cover will be blown and everyone will know I'm related to them.'

'Would that be so bad?' asked Beth gently. 'It would force them to accept you for who you are. They wouldn't keep trying to change you then because what would be the point?'

'You've met them, haven't you!' Morna shouted. 'Sorry, it's just stressing me out at the moment.'

Time to change the subject, thought Beth.

'Obviously, Jane has a strong motive to have murdered Nora,' she said. 'She was removed from her home as a baby and had no further contact with her family until she was nearly four, by which time her poor mother had died. That motive is revenge. But Nora also gave away her remaining frozen embryos after her marriage broke down. What if Callum didn't come up here looking for a mother figure but to berate her for giving him away as though he was "just garbage". His words, not mine. He might have gone to see her for the purpose of having an angry confrontation. Maybe it got out of hand? I've seen his temper firsthand. Also, he has at least one previous conviction for assault.'

'Still doesn't explain the poisoning,' said Lachlan. 'I could see it if he'd pushed her over and she'd fallen and hurt her head. It's a whole other thing to coldly poison someone day after day knowing you could stop and save them at any moment. That is a cold fury, not a hot temper. Also, Jane's not been up here long enough to have orchestrated that. Well, as far as we know, anyway.'

'It must be someone remorseless,' said Beth. 'Someone who believes they are executing justice for a terrible wrong.'

'What, like some sort of vigilante?' asked Lachlan, looking worried.

'I don't think we'll ever really know what happened until we locate Captain Oliver Saunders,' sighed Beth. 'There seems to be no record of him in the army. It's probably not even his real name. Maybe he had some prior contact with Callum that we don't know about under his real name. Callum seems to have been the only one that knew about Nora's current whereabouts. How terrible if, despite his desire to meet his biological mother, he revealed her address to the wrong person and was the unwitting catalyst to her murder.'

THIRTY-SEVEN

Beth clasped the steering wheel with sweating palms like it was the only thing standing between her and falling off a cliff. Or at least, into the actual harbour. As the queue of traffic inched forward towards the huge ferry, she felt like she and her tiny car were being swallowed into the belly of a big black whale. She didn't relax until she was parked in an echoing chamber with clanging noises reverberating all around her.

As she tried not to breathe in all the petrol and diesel fumes, she made for the stairs as the rear door was closing. The huge anchor rattled noisily as its chains were mechanically wound up. Grabbing a coffee and a pastry, she headed up to the top deck. With a deep burp, the funnel belched steam as it slowly started to pull away from the harbour, moving cumbersomely across the bay then circling round to head past Kerrera and Lismore to the Isle of Mull. Beth sat on a bench, feeling the sea breeze lift her hair off her neck, and sipped her coffee as she drank in the beauty of the morning light on the bay with the sun rising behind them. Seagulls wheeled above them, their plaintive calls lingering like notes from a forgotten melody after they'd flown by.

Last night she'd done some research into the reclusive professor, Darragh Brennan. He and Nora had got together at university.

Reading between the lines, she had been a gifted student and he had been her professor, as there seemed to be a ten-year age gap between them and they were attached to the same faculty. That was a big discrepancy in age and power. She found a graduation picture of Nora, no doubt placed in the local paper by her proud parents. It showed a young woman full of vitality with a smile that could light up a room. Try as she might, she couldn't marry that image with the one of the quiet, rather diffident, grey-haired woman that she had become. Nora Kelly's smile had long since been extinguished by the traumas of her past. It had become a frail, fluttering thing.

After those early years, Darragh Brennan had turned down the path of academia whilst Nora's ambitions, despite her earlier promise, seemed to have become more modest. She had taught in a secondary school in Glasgow. Then, around the early 1990s, Nora had quietly disappeared until the later flurry of newspaper reports about the baby snatching case. After she was released from hospital, she then faded once more into a life of obscurity. There was no further mention that she could find of Darragh Brennan's name coupled with hers. Evidently, their marriage hadn't survived the strain caused by what she did. Beth had fallen asleep in front of her laptop and been plagued by horrible dreams until she woke with a start when her alarm went off.

The journey to Craignure on Mull only took forty-five minutes and it was soon time to disembark. After another white-knuckle ride, Beth heaved a sigh of relief to be off the pier and took the turning for Tobermory. The scenery was spectacular, and she felt the tension she'd been carrying around with her leave her body as the beauty of the island wrapped her in its embrace.

Twenty-one miles and another forty-five minutes later her eyes widened with pleasure as she took in the brightly coloured houses facing the harbour in Tobermory. It was a joy to behold. Parking at the harbour she went for a wander round the quirky local shops before getting a panini and some coffee from The Tobermory Bakery, then settling down on the harbour wall to eat them whilst enjoying the stunning views. She wished she were here only as a tourist and not to try and obtain insight into a murder. Sighing, she disposed of her leftovers and went in search of Professor Darragh Brennan, armed with his last address from the electoral roll.

After a steep climb, she came to a whitewashed cottage surrounded by a lawn filled with daffodils and spectacular red camelias growing against a painted white wall. She'd decided against alerting him to her visit in advance so he couldn't put her off coming. Of course, that meant that he might not even be in and she'd have come all this way for nothing. Mind you, she could hardly call her experience of Mull's beauty nothing, she consoled herself.

Opening the small wooden gate, she walked up the path and rang the doorbell. As she did so, she noticed that someone had sprayed red graffiti on the wall to her left. The large 'V' looked decidedly familiar. With a feeling akin to an electric shock travelling the length of her body she remembered where she had seen it before. It had been sprayed onto Nora's garden wall, too. Back then she'd paid it no mind, thinking it was just kids mucking about and totally random. What did it mean? There had to be a connection. She whipped out her phone and had just taken a photo of it when the door was flung open and she found herself gazing down the barrel of a shotgun.

'Don't shoot!' she squealed, reflexively holding up her hands and backing away.

The man holding the gun was tall and lean, despite his advanced age, and wearing denim jeans and a checked shirt. His tanned face was weathered and his blue eyes hard and unwavering. The hands that held the gun were steady.

'Who are you and what do you want?' he asked, his voice cultured but menacing, like he wouldn't hesitate to pull the trigger should he not like her answer.

'My name's Beth Cunningham and I own a bookshop in Oban,' she said, her voice an octave higher than usual, courtesy of the gun being pointed at her face.

He didn't look impressed. The gun stayed where it was.

'I knew Nora,' she said in a more normal voice. 'She was a customer of mine. I've been looking into her murder. I hoped you could help me with some information about her past.'

He lowered the gun and gave her such a searching look she felt he'd be able to see what she'd had for lunch, then dropped it to his side with a sigh. He walked to the end of the path and peered intensely up and down the road before coming back to her.

'You weren't followed here?'

'Er, no?' said Beth, slightly alarmed. She hadn't thought to check.

'You'd better come in, I suppose,' he said, turning to lead the way.

As she entered the cool interior of the cottage, he locked the door behind her and laid the shotgun propped up against it. The lock looked new and there was a bolt and chain as well. As far as she knew, crime wasn't an issue on the island. It looked like he was expecting trouble. She didn't want it to arrive when she was here and declined coffee, accepting a glass of water instead.

Even now, at the age of seventy-five, she could feel this man's magnetism. When he was younger, he must have been incredibly compelling. No wonder Nora had fallen for him. The cottage was very masculine but clean. The sitting room had floor to ceiling bookshelves on two walls and an eclectic mix of books piled up on a side table by his comfortable armchair. A laptop sat on a desk covered in papers against a third wall.

Clearing her throat nervously, she began.

'I know that you were divorced a long time ago. Nora was murdered. Someone poisoned her.'

'I'm aware,' he said, picking up last week's *Oban Times* and flapping it at her.

'She was poisoned using mushroom tea which she got samples of in book subscription boxes from my shop,' she said in a rush.

'That I did not know,' he said, raising his eyebrows.

'They were just included as free samples and came from a pop-up shop which has now closed down and the girl, Kathleen Boyle, who ran it, has disappeared off the face of the earth. I don't know if she's part of the plot or a victim herself.'

'Anyway, what does all this have to do with me? Nora and I parted company decades ago.'

'That's the thing. I think that her murder might be a way of settling old scores. I've been dragged into it as, on the face of it, my book subscription service has been the delivery mechanism. I want justice for Nora and also to protect my own reputation, if I'm being wholly honest.' She shrugged helplessly.

'I see,' he said, his face giving nothing away.

He was making her work for it. *Here goes nothing*, thought Beth, hoping that her next words wouldn't have him reaching for the shotgun again.

'A young woman arrived in Oban the day after Nora died,' Beth said. 'She claimed to be Nora's estranged daughter. She satisfied the police as to her identity by producing a birth certificate.'

'Nora and I had no children,' he growled.

Beth glanced around the room. There were a number of photos around of a baby girl with the latest photo showing a smiling younger version of Darragh with a beaming little girl in his arms.

'I know what she did,' Beth said gently. 'It must have been terrible for you.'

'You have no idea,' he ground out, his face twisted in remembered grief. 'We'd desperately wanted a family. All that loss, culminating in a stillbirth. It drove Nora almost insane. It wasn't easy on me either. When I had to go off on sabbatical, it felt like such a relief not to have to deal with it for a while. Cowardly, I know. Then, I got the news that she was pregnant. She said it would be different this time. She had a good feeling. I was away for most of the pregnancy teaching in Washington but whenever I flew back, she seemed to be blooming. I didn't suspect a thing,' he said bitterly. 'Then, the final time I flew back, I discovered she'd had the baby prematurely, or so she said.'

'You registered the birth?' asked Beth.

She'd wondered how Jane had managed to convince the police that she was Nora's daughter.

'Yes. Things were a lot more fluid back then. No one questioned it. I was told that the baby had arrived prematurely at home.'

'You didn't suspect anything at the time?' asked Beth.

'No, why would I?' he said, getting up to pace around. 'It was the furthest thing from my mind. I couldn't believe it when Nora didn't seem to bond with the baby. It was the last thing I'd imagined happening. I turned down career opportunities so I could be at home with her more. Nothing helped. She was unravelling before me. Even then, I didn't suspect anything was amiss. It wasn't until she was sectioned and locked up in a mental health unit that it all poured out of her.'

'It must have been a shock,' said Beth, her voice thick with sympathy as he sat back down opposite her.

'I loved that kid,' he said, his voice bleak. 'By then she was three years old and the centre of my world. Having to give her to that social worker was the worst day of my life. They had to pull her out of my arms, she was clinging on that tightly, screaming in distress. I don't mind admitting it broke me for years. Still, shit happens. What can you do?'

He picked up one of the photographs and stared at it, his eyes soft with remembering. Then he raised his eyes to meet hers.

'So, is that what this is about? You think someone tracked Nora down after all these years and murdered her for what she did back then?' he asked.

'Honestly, I'm not sure,' Beth admitted. 'There's something else I need to ask you. I couldn't help but notice the graffiti sprayed on the wall of your house. I noticed that exact same "V" sprayed on the wall of Nora's garden. Do you know what it represents?'

His face tightened immediately. 'I have a fair idea, hence the shotgun. You've just confirmed my suspicions. I woke up to find it this morning. I'll ask again. Could you have been followed?'

Beth shook her head. 'I honestly couldn't say. It never even occurred to me. Please, tell me what's going on,' she begged.

'This is something I've never spoken about before,' he sighed. 'But I suppose there's no time like the present.'

Beth had the feeling she was about to hear something terrible. She wasn't wrong.

'Nora and I met at university a million years ago. I was a young professor and she was one of my students. I was also married at the time. She had a brilliant mind for maths. I suppose I was flattered by her adulation. It started off as a fling then quickly developed into something more serious. A meeting of the minds as well as a physical attraction. I flew around her like a moth to a flame, knowing she had the potential to destroy everything I had worked so hard to achieve, yet I was powerless to resist.'

Beth thought that was a bit rich given that Nora had been a teenager and his student whereas he had been a grown man knocking thirty and in a position of trust, to boot. He was making it sound like he was some hapless victim rather than a married lecherous professor. She bit back her retort though, wanting him to keep talking.

'But why is this person now targeting you specifically?' she demanded. 'I get why they went after Nora. She did a terrible thing. But why target you if you were unaware of what she had done at the time? It doesn't make sense.'

'No, I suppose it doesn't,' he said wearily, running a hand through his hair.

'There's more, isn't there?' Beth asked, steeling herself. 'You may as well tell me. I'm involved in this now, whether I like it or not.'

Darragh froze, his eyes locked on hers. Beth stared right back at him, refusing to flinch. Suddenly, as if he'd been having an internal battle with himself, his face relaxed and he slumped in his chair.

'I swore to Nora that I'd take this secret to the grave but now that she's gone, well, I suppose it's time to come clean about what happened. I'm an old man. It's time to set the record straight, I guess.'

Beth waited, scarce daring to breathe in case he changed his mind.

'When I first met Nora, I was completely enchanted with her. Nora was so full of life and energy. I, on the other hand was settling into a premature middle age with a wife who was pushing me to succeed in academia and liked to spend more money than I earned. It felt like I was bound in chains. Nora set me free. Although, perhaps, looking back, I merely exchanged one cage for another. The folly of youth,' he said with a wry grimace.

Beth furtively glanced at the clock behind him. Time was getting on. She needed to get out of here. Fear fluttered in her chest, yet she forced herself to remain outwardly composed.

'Sorry, I know I'm wittering on. I've kept this secret for so long, it's hard just to blurt it out. I needed to work up to it, give it some context, I suppose.'

Beth nodded with a tight smile.

'It was June 1979. We were both living in Aberdeen. I hadn't left my wife yet. Nora's exams were over and we'd been out celebrating. We'd both been drinking but I somehow figured I was still good to drive. The arrogance of youth, I suppose. Back then I thought I was invincible.'

'What happened?' asked Beth, unable to restrain herself any longer.

Darragh sprang out of his seat, avoiding her eyes and began to pace up and down, agitation evident in his jerky movements.

'We were having an argument. Nora wanted us to get a taxi. She wasn't happy about me driving. She was begging me to stop. I was angry with her for ruining what had been a great night. She tugged on my arm and I lost control of the car. A woman was crossing the road at a pedestrian crossing. I ploughed right into her. I'll never forget that sickening thud. It played over and over in my dreams for years.'

'You killed her?' asked Beth, eyes wide with horror, picturing it vividly.

'Not just her but her unborn child as well,' he said, his voice breaking. 'We didn't realise she was four months pregnant until the press coverage afterwards. She also had an eight-year-old son.'

'I take it you were charged?' said Beth.

Wordlessly, he shook his head, shame covering his face. 'We didn't stop. Nora wanted to. Her first instinct was to get out of the car and try to help her. But... I panicked. All I could think about was that our affair would cause a scandal and taint my career in academia, not to mention the fallout from my wife discovering our affair. Nora reached for the door, but I threw the car into reverse, did a U-turn and drove off, tyres screeching on the wet pavement. It was a split-second decision. I wasn't thinking straight. All I could think about was getting away from there. Before then, I'd laboured under the impression that I was a decent enough person. It was a shock to discover such an immense fault line in my character.'

Beth was stunned. She hadn't expected anything of this magnitude.

'I don't know what to say...' she said, her voice low and quiet.

'We got away with it. But never for one moment did we forget or forgive ourselves for what we'd done.'

'That might be more convincing if you'd turned yourselves in to the police,' said Beth, her voice scathing.

'I stopped the car two streets away, long enough for Nora to dash out to a phone box and dial 999. She was covered in blood by this time after banging her nose in the crash. Nora begged me to go to the police, but I refused. I promised to leave my wife for her if she agreed to never reveal what I'd done. She was torn but she loved me and back then I could be very persuasive. I figured what was done was done. What good would it have done to ruin our lives as well?'

'How about justice? Some form of closure for the family?' snapped Beth.

'Nora was convinced that every baby we lost was punishment

for what we did. It ate away at her all these years. It was why I stayed with her as long as I did.'

Beth stood up to go. He might be seeking absolution, but he wasn't going to get it from her.

'Wait, did you see the graffiti? I suspect the "V" stands for vengeance. It would make sense. Someone wants to avenge the poor woman that we mowed down. Nora was murdered. It's probably my turn next.'

'You can still turn yourself in to the police. Give the woman's family the opportunity to see you belatedly brought to justice? You can tell them what you know and get taken into protective custody. It's never too late to do the right thing,' Beth urged. 'Whoever is behind this is no more righteous than you were, whatever they may think. You have the power to stop them in their tracks.'

'I'll think about it,' he said, suddenly looking every one of his seventy-five years. 'You'd better get going.' He got to his feet. 'I don't want you here when they come for me. I've got a letter for Jane. I'm begging you to give it to her, if you get the chance.'

He walked over to his desk and pulled an envelope from a drawer, holding it out to her, beseeching her to take it.

'I wonder why her father never changed her name back when she went home?' asked Beth. 'I take it you and Nora gave her that name?'

'Yes, we did and registered her birth accordingly. The social worker told me that as she was already three when her real father got her back, he thought it would confuse her even more. Obviously, she got her family name of Guthrie back though.'

Beth glanced at her watch. The time had flown by and she would need to hurry to make the ferry. She had a strong feeling she wouldn't see Darragh Brennan again. There were no words for the magnitude of what she had just learned. Beth reluctantly took the letter from him.

'Goodbye,' she said simply, and walked out of the door without looking back. She'd thought about telling him about Callum but decided nothing good could come of it. Darragh Brennan was no kind of role model. It was up to Callum to contact him if he saw fit.

She turned the key in her car with shaking fingers and set off for the ferry. She hadn't gone far when she heard a loud bang. Beth jumped but kept driving, tears running down her face, not quite sure who she was crying for. She couldn't say for sure that it had been a gunshot, but she suspected that Darragh Brannagh had ran out of time. Either that or he had shot himself. Trembling, she pulled over when it was safe to do so, took out her phone and dialled 999. Once she had explained the situation, she started the engine once more and drove on towards the ferry with a heavy heart.

THIRTY-EIGHT

By the time the ferry drew back into the harbour, the sun was setting over the bay in fiery splendour and there was a definite chill in the air. Beth wanted nothing more than to head home and bury herself under the duvet, but she had to take this new information straight to the police. She drove there directly from the ferry, having decided to hang on to the car for another day.

'I need to speak to Detective Sergeant Hunter, please,' she said to the young policeman manning the desk, feeling like she had aged ten years since that morning.

Seconds later, DS Hunter was buzzing her through, looking worried. He opened the door into the comfortable room, but Beth shook her head.

'I think you need to interview me on tape. What I have to tell you is important. Maybe you should get DC Quinn as well?'

He looked alarmed but nodded acquiescence and showed her into the interview room she had become all too familiar with. DC Quinn was summoned by radio and they took their seats across from her.

'Would you like to have your solicitor present?' DS Hunter asked her.

'That won't be necessary,' said Beth.

As soon as the recording began, in a flat and emotionless voice, she told them all about what her investigations had revealed.

Eventually the recording device was switched off and Beth sat there silent, completely spent.

'Thank you,' DS Hunter said formally. 'I need to alert the Specialist Crime Division in Gartcosh as to what's been going on up here as well as liaise with our colleagues on Mull. You're sure that Professor Darragh Brennan is dead?'

'I can't be sure,' she snapped. 'I wasn't about to go back and check.'

'No, of course not,' said DC Quinn, on her side for once. 'You dialled 999 and there's an accident and emergency department on Mull. If he could be saved, they would have done so.'

'We did know about what Nora Kelly did in relation to snatching the baby. We've been keeping a close eye on Jane Guthrie, though her alibi seems to check out,' said DS Hunter. 'Leave it with us.' He pushed back his chair to stand. 'Rhona, can you please drive Beth home?'

'No need,' she protested weakly, 'I have a hire car.'

The two detectives looked at each other.

'No way,' said DC Quinn. 'You're dead on your feet after all that. Come on, let's get you home. I'll meet you out front.'

Five minutes later Rhona Quinn pulled up in a small white car. Beth got in, her teeth beginning to chatter as the events of the day caught up with her. The detective glanced at her then turned up the heater before pulling smoothly away.

As they reached her cottage Beth turned to her.

'Thanks for the lift. Can I offer you a coffee?'

'Another time, perhaps. I'm needed back at the station. I took the liberty of phoning your brother. I don't think you should be alone right now.'

She nodded towards the front door and Beth saw the familiar shape of Harris Kincaid detach himself from the wall he'd been leaning against. Her eyes filled with tears of relief. Finally, she felt safe.

'Thank you, you've been very kind,' she said with a watery smile, before leaving the car and slowly walking towards him, as the car turned round and headed back into town.

Harris gave her a hug and unlocked the door for her as her hands were still shaking so much. He cast a worried glance at her once they were inside. Both cats made a beeline for them, miaowing plaintively.

'Go sit on the couch and I'll light the stove and bring you some tea,' he said, pulling the curtains and rushing off to feed the cats.

A few minutes later, the flames were licking around the edges of the logs and Beth was cupping a mug of warm sweet tea, wrapped in a comfy throw and with two cats purring away on either side of her.

'I don't know what's happened today, but Rhona said you'd had a rough time of it,' he said, sitting across from her, looking worried.

'It was nice of her to phone you,' Beth said.

She'd glimpsed a different side to DC Rhona Quinn today. She hadn't seemed as hostile as she normally was. Mind you, if she was dating Logan Hunter, she probably had plenty to smile about, she thought, with a twinge of jealousy.

'You don't have to talk about it if you don't want to,' he said. 'We can just chill or watch TV, no pressure.'

'I want to talk,' she said. 'I need to get it all out of my head.'

Haltingly, she explained about her research into Nora Kelly's past and all that had transpired that day on Mull.

'Beth! That was an insane risk to take. You could have been killed! Are you trying to give me grey hairs?'

'I know it sounds bad now, but as far as I was concerned, I was just going to speak to a crusty old academic who might have been a bit crotchety and given me short shrift. I never imagined anything so insane.'

'You heard a gun go off. Do you think he took matters into his own hands, or do you think that Nora's killer caught up with him?'

'I think I'd rather not know,' she said, weary to her very bones. 'DS Hunter said that they'd be sending a Major Investigation

Team up from Glasgow in the morning. I've done all that I can. It's time to let it go.'

'I wonder what will happen to Jane Guthrie now?' Harris wondered. 'She's got no right to live in Nora's house, now it's been established that they're not related. I wonder why she even came up here in the first place? Maybe her motive was financial? I can see why she felt that Nora Kelly owed her. She robbed her of precious years with her own mother. The fact that Nora didn't bond with her makes it even worse. That could have caused all sorts of psychological damage.'

Beth shrugged. Her eyes were so heavy she was in danger of nodding off.

'You get off to bed,' said Harris. 'I'll sleep on the couch, just in case. Things will look brighter in the morning.'

On Monday, Beth woke to the sun streaming in through her curtains and Marmalade's weight across her feet. She wiggled her toes to get rid of the pins and needles, causing Toby to pounce. Whilst the events of yesterday weighed heavily upon her, she felt a sense of relief that additional officers were going to be flooding into the town to help mop up the mess. She didn't know how she felt about Nora in light of recent revelations. How could one woman have created so many different ripples in her lifetime? One thing she was sure of: the killer was no better than the people against whom they were seeking revenge. They had appointed themselves judge, jury and executioner.

Walking downstairs, she noticed that Harris had already left, leaving the blankets neatly folded on the top of the pillow. He'd clearly fed the cats but that didn't stop them trying to extort a second breakfast from her with pitiful wails. She decided to have breakfast in the garden and sat at her small table, sipping coffee and eyeing the antics of the robin as he went about his business, thankfully undetected by the cats who were busy grooming themselves.

Her first job was to return the hire car then she walked into town, along the bay. Seeing the Calmac ferry setting off for Mull, her stomach clenched. She wondered how many police officers were now on the island, unravelling the events of yesterday. She did worry that perhaps she'd led the killer to Darragh Brennan's door, but reasoned that in any event he'd have been easy enough to find for someone sufficiently determined. Besides, to have sprayed the graffiti on his wall, they must have gone over to Mull the day before she'd got there.

She arrived in the shop to find scenes of chaos. The chicks had arrived before her and her staff were beside themselves with delight, peering in at the spacious, high-sided enclosure with transparent plastic so the little kids could see in, too. Strong netting stretched across the top, which should thwart the cats and anyone else who might be tempted to run away with one. A tall, handsome young man in jeans and a rugby shirt was giving them all instructions on their care. This must be Joe, then, she thought, given Chloe's doe-eyed demeanour as she smiled up at him through her lashes. Poor lad didn't stand a chance. Beth rushed over to introduce herself.

'Thanks for doing this, Joe.' She smiled. 'The chicks are going to be a big hit with the kids, and the rest of us.' She could see that even Lachlan was smitten by the yellow balls of fluff with their tiny orange beaks.

'No bother, Beth. My dad was glad to help,' he replied with an easy smile. 'I've left all the instructions with Chloe. The most important thing is to remember to switch the heat lamp on or they'll be too cold. The food and dishes are in that bag. Make sure they have water at all times. That's it really. Any questions, just give me a call.' He looked directly at Chloe as he said it, who blushed and nodded. On that parting shot he left and the rest of them stood gazing at their furry charges in awe.

'I want one of us to have eyes on them at all times,' said Beth, bringing over a bucket seat and putting it next to the display.

'Six days is a long time to have responsibility for all these furry bundles,' said Morna. 'How many are there?'

'Twenty-four,' piped up Chloe. 'We should do a head count at the end of each day.'

'Not so easy when they keep running around and shifting position,' said Lachlan, who still looked charmed, nevertheless.

'The Easter decorations are stunning, Chloe,' said Beth. 'Did you come in yesterday and finish them off when the shop was closed?'

'Yes, it was the only time I could get enough peace to do it. Morna came in and helped.'

'I did the donkey work,' said Morna. 'As usual, the creative vision was all her.' She jerked a thumb at Chloe.

'Well, it looks amazing.' Beth smiled. 'I think that deserves an Easter bonus. You've all been going above and beyond recently. Right, everyone, ready for the onslaught? I have a feeling it's going to be a busy day.'

Beth was nonetheless surprised to discover a queue snaking down the street when she opened the door, comprised of senior citizens, young mums and pre-schoolers all chattering excitedly. Lachlan manned the cash desk, and Chloe and Morna fielded questions about the chicks while watching that no one became too boisterous around them. Beth meanwhile did a roaring trade in the café as people then drifted through there to chat with their friends over coffee and cake. She'd laid on lots of little treats for the kids as well.

As expected, Toby and Marmalade arrived mid-morning, doing a double take when they saw the chicks, and very cross when they realised that they couldn't get in amongst them. They finally perched on top of the nearest bookcase to gain a bird's eye view.

'Do you ever get the feeling that Marmalade is Toby's apprentice in the dark arts?' asked Lachlan during a momentary lull.

'Definitely,' laughed Beth. 'Marmalade was a big softie when I first got him and now he struts about like a Glasgow gangster. I think Toby quite likes having a sidekick. It makes him feel powerful.'

Eventually, it was time for lunch and they all sank gratefully into their usual seats around the table. Beth looked round at them all. She knew that she needed to tell them everything that had happened the day before, but it was a lot to drop on them. She hadn't even fully processed it herself yet. However, the deciding factor was that she had to warn them to be on guard until the police tracked the killer down. It was too big not to share.

FORTY

Beth became aware that they were all staring at her. She'd been lost in her own thoughts for too long.

'There's been a number of developments since I saw you all on Saturday,' she said. 'Nora Kelly wasn't who we thought she was. She had done things in her past. Terrible things.'

'Like what?' asked Lachlan, frowning at her.

'Well, for a start, Jane isn't her daughter.'

'I knew there was something phoney about her,' said Morna. 'She didn't seem to have any feelings for Nora at all.'

'It's a bit more complicated than that,' said Beth. 'Jane was snatched from her birth mother as a young baby. No one figured it out until Nora confessed when Jane was three years old. In the interim, her birth mother had died.'

'That's awful,' said Chloe, her hand over her mouth in shock.

'I don't condone what she did but there were extenuating circumstances,' said Beth. 'She'd experienced a number of failed pregnancies culminating in a stillbirth. It seems she wasn't quite in her right mind. Her husband thought the child was his.'

'A tragedy for all concerned then,' said Lachlan. 'So, you think this Jane murdered Nora as some kind of payback?'

'I'm afraid there's more,' said Beth, feeling sick to the stomach as it all came back to her. 'When Nora and Darragh Brennan were young, they were involved in a hit and run.'

'What? Nora?' said Morna in disbelief. 'I can't believe what I'm hearing.'

'Darragh Brennan was driving. They'd both had a fair bit to drink. He was married and they were having an affair. He was a good bit older and also her tutor,' continued Beth. 'They mowed down a pregnant woman at a zebra crossing in Aberdeen. She died along with her unborn child.'

Everyone started talking at once and Beth held up her hand to quiet them.

'How come we've never heard about this?' said Lachlan.

'It happened back in 1979. Nora and Darragh were never caught. They fled from Aberdeen to Glasgow and kept a low profile. I heard it all from the mouth of Darragh Brennan on Mull yesterday.'

'So, what? Nora's death was payback for all those years ago?' asked Morna.

'The police believe that the killer finally tracked them both down, determined to exact their revenge. Darragh Brennan is now dead,' she said flatly, trying to close the door in her mind.

'Have they got any leads on Captain Oliver Saunders yet?' asked Lachlan. 'By the sounds of things, he's the one who's been pulling the strings.'

'Not yet but I know that Maria is going to be working with a sketch artist so once his image is released to the public it'll be harder for him to hide,' Beth said. 'It's likely that he is someone who knew or was related to the original victim.'

'It's scary to think that he might even have been in the book-shop and we wouldn't have known it.' Chloe shuddered.

'If only we could locate Kathleen,' said Beth. 'She must have met him several times. I'm really worried that because of that some-thing bad may have happened to her.'

'If the killer's whole purpose is to avenge wrongful deaths, then how could they justify killing someone who was innocent?' said Morna, folding her arms.

'That's a good point,' said Beth. 'Unless, of course, she's been working with them all along and Kathleen Boyle isn't even her real name.'

'She's not got any personal socials,' said Chloe. 'All I could find was her business accounts on Insta and Facebook. I thought that was unusual for someone her age.'

'Does anything mention what town she's from?' asked Beth. 'If we knew that, we could maybe track her down via an old classmate from school, or find someone who knew her parents. I wonder if they've reported her missing?'

'I doubt it,' said Morna. 'As this is the last place that she worked, it is bound to have been mentioned on the news or featured in the paper. Surely her parents would have arrived asking all sorts of questions?'

'For sure,' said Chloe. 'Maybe something spooked her and she's gone into hiding? She might still be in touch with her parents so they're oblivious to there being a problem. Can't say as I blame her with everything that's been going on. I'll have another dig around. There must be some trail we can follow.'

'I can't exactly report her as a missing person because it was only a pop-up shop and we've no information to suggest that she hasn't simply left of her own accord. It was only ever meant to be temporary,' said Beth. She started to gather together the lunch things on a tray.

'Chloe, can you check on the chicks before we open back up?' she said.

'On it,' her youngest employee said with alacrity, before going off to check on her feathered friends. Toby and Marmalade followed her to cast their eyes over this exciting new development, too. Beth deposited the tray in the kitchen and left Lachlan to stack the dishwasher and Morna to wipe down the surfaces in the café.

With some trepidation she went to turn the sign to Open. Normally she would be happy for the shop to be inundated with customers but today she had an irrational desire to keep the door locked and shut them all out. Who knew who she was inviting into their midst at the moment?

Pasting on a smile, she opened the door, a feeling of dread settling in the pit of her stomach. The rest of the afternoon flew by. Everyone, young and old alike, was charmed by the chicks which brought a much-needed positive vibe to the bookshop. There was a table where the youngsters could sit with Chloe and make a chick picture, whilst their worn-out parent collapsed in the café with a cup of coffee for a few minutes. The cats, of course, had their own fan club so some of the children opted to do pictures of them instead. It all looked so cosy and wholesome that Beth felt like bursting into tears. Everything she held dear was being stalked by a shadowy presence that could decide to extinguish her in a flip of a coin.

<h1 style="text-align:center">FORTY-ONE</h1>

Beth was exhausted by the time she made it home. After a relaxing bubble bath, all she wanted was to veg out with some comfort food in front of the TV and a large glass of wine. The cats were exhausted from all the excitement in the shop and had crashed out in front of the lit stove once they'd been fed. Shutting out the darkness with the heavy burgundy drapes, she curled up on the couch and switched on the TV.

As she'd walked past the police station on her way home, she'd glanced in the window and noticed about a dozen unsmiling officers standing around the small space. DS Logan was in the thick of them, a large map spread out on the desk. He didn't notice her as she walked quietly by. Hopefully, this whole big mess would be mopped up and the person responsible placed safely behind bars. She wondered whether Jane herself was part of it or whether she had simply been circling to try and obtain financial recompense for the damage inflicted on her as a young child. Sighing, she forced her mind back to her soap opera. Normally, she regarded them as a form of escapism but tonight she found the shrill voices and manufactured animosity set her on edge.

Switching off the TV, the house was wrapped in silence. A silence she usually enjoyed but tonight it made her feel vulnerable.

For the first time she wished that she didn't live alone. Well, apart from two cats who would escape out of the cat flap at the first sign of trouble. Disconsolate, she wandered over to her bookshelves running a finger gently along the spines. Crime thrillers were definitely out. She pulled out a worn hardback copy of Little Women, still in its original paper jacket. That would do nicely.

She'd no sooner settled down on the sofa and opened the book reverently to the first page when the doorbell rang, making her jump. With a sigh she looked out the sitting room window to see a uniformed officer outside. What now? Hastily she opened the door. A young woman with a pristine blonde bob and a friendly dimpled smile stood there. She wore trendy purple glasses and carried a clipboard and pen.

'Beth Cunningham?'

'Yes.' Beth smiled back. 'Can I help you?'

'I'm PC Townsend. Detective Sergeant Hunter asked me to pop round and check out the security on your home. He's become increasingly concerned that you might be targeted as a witness in the Nora Kelly murder case.'

'Oh, I see,' said Beth. 'Well, you'd better come in then. I don't think we've met before, have we? I recognise your Aberdonian accent. You're a fair way from home.'

'Well spotted,' said PC Townsend with a quick smile. 'I only transferred up here a couple of weeks ago. My partner got a new job up at the hospital.'

'Can I offer you a cup of tea before you get started?' asked Beth, glancing longingly at her opened book on the sofa.

'Thanks, but I'll just get on. It's been a long day,' she said, whipping out a notepad and pen from her jacket. 'I'll start with upstairs, if that's okay?'

'Sure, help yourself.' Beth smiled, returning to the sofa, but it was hard to concentrate when a stranger was prowling around her house opening and closing windows. Beth thought of the piles of laundry spread over her bed and the state of her bathroom and wished she'd had advance notice. After about twenty minutes she heard her feet on the stairs. As she entered the sitting room, Marmalade puffed up and hissed at her. Toby did a double take, glancing from one to the other, then decided to follow suit.

'I'm so sorry.' Beth smiled. 'I don't know what's got into them.'

'Not really a cat person,' the young police officer laughed, unfazed. 'I do have three dogs, though, which is probably what they're having a hissy about.' She pulled aside the curtains and checked the window locks. 'I'll just have a look through in the kitchen and check the back door and windows through there. I take it you have a cat flap for this pair of tearaways?'

'Yes, it's quite basic but it does the job.'

'Do you lock it at night?'

'No, they're free to come and go as they please, though they're more in than out in the colder months.' Beth opened the door into the kitchen and left her to it.

A few minutes later she was back.

'That's me done.' She smiled, putting her notebook away. 'There's definitely room for improvement on the security front. I'll get a written report round to you tomorrow.'

'Thank you, I appreciate you taking the time,' she replied, getting up to see her out.

'You have a good night now,' she said. 'Don't forget to lock the door behind me.'

'I won't. Good night.' Beth smiled, eager to get the house to herself again. Mindful of the officer's advice, she turned the key in the lock immediately after closing the door.

When was all this going to be over so she could get back to living a normal life again?

Turning off the lights, she headed straight up to bed, followed by the cats. Usually, she didn't draw her curtains as she preferred to wake up to natural light. Tonight, she pulled them closed.

She read until she was so tired that she couldn't hold her book up then turned off her bedside light and fell deeply asleep.

FORTY-TWO

Beth woke with a start, her heart hammering in her chest. Glancing at her watch she saw it was 3am. Was it the nightmare she'd been having that woke her or something else? Maybe the sound of her letterbox?

She could smell smoke.

Throwing on her dressing gown she crept downstairs, every creak of the old wooden stairs sounding like a thunderclap. As she advanced, the smell of smoke grew stronger. She'd closed the door of the living room to keep the heat in. Hesitantly, she put her hand up to it then withdrew it hastily with an involuntary yelp. It was boiling hot.

She had to get out. Her house was on fire.

The cats! Fortunately, they'd spent the night sleeping on her bed or they could have been trapped in the fire. Hastily, she ran back upstairs and bundled them protesting into her heavy cotton laundry bag, zipping it right up. There was lots of hissing and growling but at least she knew they were safe. If they'd decided to evade her clutches, she'd have been trying to catch them for ever. She stuffed her feet into trainers, grabbed her phone and ran back downstairs with the cats. Rushing to the front door, she tried to unlock it. It refused to budge, no matter how hard she tried.

'No, No, NO!' she yelled.

She was scared to open the sitting room door in case the flames, which she could now hear crackling, exploded into the hall. There was a fire extinguisher, but she suspected the fire was burning too fiercely for that to be effective. In any event it was in the kitchen on the other side of the flames. Hurriedly, she called the fire brigade, praying they would be able to reach her in time.

Racing back upstairs with howls of protest coming from the wriggling cats in the bag, she darted to the bedroom window and tried to open it. It didn't budge. Panicked now, she headed into the spare bedroom and the bathroom. None of the windows would open. It was as if they'd been glued shut.

Despite the increasing heat and thickening smoke, Beth forced herself to calm down and think logically. She needed to get the cats out right away. Casting around, she grabbed her solid glass bedside light and hurled it at her bedroom window. It cracked then she was able to bash all the glass out of the lower pane. She couldn't jump because there was a stone patio directly underneath.

The wail of sirens setting out from the town carried on the frozen night air. Help was on its way. Throwing off her duvet, she pulled the fitted sheet off the bed and knotted it to the duvet cover, making a makeshift rope. Tying it round the handle of the washing bag she carefully lowered the cats out of the small sash window, leaning out over the ledge against the jagged glass until she felt the bag nudge the ground. Now, how was *she* going to escape? Running into the bathroom, she soaked a towel in water and, holding it to her face, she went back onto the landing.

With an almighty crack the door to the sitting room gave way and the fire roared out into the hallway. Screaming in terror she ran back into the bedroom and slammed the door shut behind her. The sirens were louder now. She crouched down underneath the window and waited.

It was out of her hands.

As soon as she heard the fire engine screech to a halt she jumped up and hung out of the window shouting and waving to get their attention. In no time at all there was a metal ladder extending up towards her with a burly fireman there to assist her down to safety. She grabbed the bag of cats who sounded subdued and sorry for themselves and hugged it to her.

'There's no one inside,' she quickly informed the senior fire officer, who was already barking orders to the other firefighters. 'I don't know how the fire started but I think it may have been deliberate.' Her words were interrupted by a hacking cough.

'You need to get that looked at,' he said, before radioing for an ambulance.

Beth stumbled over to the low wall across from her cottage and sat down with a thump, clutching the bag of cats to her, afraid to let them out in case they ran back into the fire. The blue flashing lights gave the scene a cinematic feel. She felt detached as though she were dreaming. Nothing felt real.

By now, hoses were being trained on the roof. Two firefighters, with breathing apparatus on, headed for the front door carrying hoses.

More blue lights appeared in the distance. *This can't be happening*, she thought dully. Her whole life was going up in flames. Her photos of her beloved mum, her treasured books, she literally had only what she was wearing on her back. And the cats, of course. Thank God she'd managed to get them out safely. She made sure that they had sufficient air, allowing their heads to poke out but keeping them firmly anchored in the bag as she spoke gently to them. A few plaintive yowls added to the ruckus.

An ambulance drew up, and a kind but gruff paramedic ushered her into the back. She struggled to blow into his tube without coughing.

'I don't think you've suffered too much in the way of smoke inhalation but I'm going to take you in just to be sure.'

'I can't,' she said, panicked. 'I need to look after my cats. If they run away now, I might never see them again.'

A car drew up with a blue flashing light on the roof but no siren. The door opened and out jumped DS Hunter. She was so pleased to see him it triggered more tears. He ran straight over to her.

'Beth! What happened? Are you alright?'

'My house is on fire,' she sobbed. 'I got the cats out but nothing else. I think someone did it deliberately.'

'By rights she should go to hospital and get checked out,' said the paramedic. 'She's suffering from the effects of smoke inhalation, but she won't relinquish her cats to go to the hospital.' He shook his head at such folly.

'I'll take her myself,' DS Hunter decided. 'There's a squad car on the way. As luck would have it, I've a vet staying with me so he can sort the cats out and determine what they need.'

'She's all yours then.' The gruff paramedic nodded. 'Take care, Beth.'

Logan Hunter led her over to his car, putting the cats in the boot and opening the passenger door for her.

'Thanks,' she said, her voice rasping. Her defences completely down, she whispered, 'It's so good to see you.'

He clasped her hand and squeezed it. 'When I heard that your house was on fire, I feared the worst,' he said, his voice low. 'Anyway,' he added more brusquely, 'let's get you checked at the hospital. You'll be pleased to hear that Grant's up staying with me.' His eyes were firmly on the road. 'He'll make sure they're taken care of.'

'Grant and I, we're...'

'Whatever,' he said firmly. 'What you and Grant get up to is none of my concern. He's a great guy.'

But he's not you, a little voice whispered sadly in her head. She didn't have the energy to put him straight.

The hospital was quiet at that time, so she was seen right away and put on oxygen.

'No major damage,' Dr Jones said, after she'd carried out some tests. 'I think the cough is down to inhalation of some chemical irritants, but I'm seeing nothing to give me major cause for concern. The hoarseness is already improving after hydration. I can keep you in for the rest of the night or I can discharge you if you've got somewhere to go?'

Beth couldn't countenance waking anyone up in the middle of the night. She'd just have to stay and sort out the whole mess in the morning.

'She can stay at mine,' Logan Hunter muttered.

The doctor raised her eyebrows in surprise and looked over at Beth as if seeking guidance.

'My brother is up staying with me and he's a friend of hers. As he's a vet we're dropping her cats off with him anyway to determine if they need any treatment themselves. Also' – he lowered his voice – 'there's a strong possibility this fire was started deliberately. It might be safer if she stays with us so I can keep an eye on her, in case someone decides to try and finish what they started.'

'What about Poppy?' Beth asked, not wanting to bring any trouble to the little girl's door.

'It's the school holidays. She's off with my mother for a week.'

'In that case, I gratefully accept,' she said, smiling her thanks.

'I'll process the paperwork,' said Dr Jones, trying to hide her surprise.

FORTY-THREE

A few minutes later they were out in the cool, fresh air which triggered another bout of coughing. As they turned into Logan's driveway, Grant ran out to the car, opening the door for her and helping her out.

'Beth! I've been so worried since my brother phoned. Glad to see you're well enough to get out. I understand you've two patients for me?'

'Yes, they're in the boot,' she said, leading him round. 'I'll grab Toby, the black one, while you take Marmalade. They were well enough to be hissing and yowling at me, so I think they escaped the worst of it by being in the laundry bag.'

'I've improvised a litter tray in the kitchen with soil from the garden,' he said.

Logan opened up the boot while Grant and Beth each lunged for a cat before the animals could entertain ideas of staging an escape.

'Who's a beautiful boy then?' she heard him crooning to Marmalade, who relaxed against his broad chest and started purring.

Toby glared at Beth then looked at Grant as though trying to work out who had got the better deal.

'You're so fickle.' She grinned at him, stroking him until he gave it up and purred.

'Blimey, I'm glad I only have a six-year-old girl to look after,' scoffed Logan. 'This pair look like the definition of high maintenance.'

'Just ignore the nasty man,' Grant whispered into Marmalade's ear. 'He's just jealous.'

Logan walked ahead of them into the house, shaking his head. 'I'll run you a bath, Beth, and get you some clean clothes,' he said over his shoulder. 'My mother keeps a few bits and pieces in the top drawer in the spare room. Just help yourself to whatever you need.'

'Thanks,' she said, her customary awkwardness around him slowly seeping back.

She suddenly realised that she was reeking of smoke.

Grant examined both pets one at a time on the kitchen table. Beth admired the easy rapport he had with the animals. He'd be a great catch for someone, she thought wistfully.

'They're going to be fine,' he announced after a while. 'The thick cotton of the laundry bag kept them from the worst of it. It sounds as though you'll be out of your accommodation for a while though?'

'Yes, I'll sort something out in the morning, once I've grabbed some sleep. I think my brother's mother will be able to put us up meantime.'

Logan reappeared with a long baggy T-shirt and a striped dressing gown. 'You'd best take these in with you. Once you're done, just leave your clothes on the floor and I'll stick them in the wash.'

'My brother, the domestic goddess,' teased Grant.

'You're hilarious,' Logan shot back.

Beth could see the close relationship they had and was glad that she hadn't inadvertently come between them.

'That's your bath ready,' said Logan. 'I've put Poppy's hairdryer on your bed.'

'Thanks, guys, I really appreciate everything you've done for me,' she said quietly.

Heading into the bathroom, she sank into the tub which had been filled with fragrant bubbles with a refreshing masculine scent. She ducked her head under the water and applied liberal amounts of shampoo to her long curly hair before rinsing it off and pulling it up in a sparkly bobble that must be Poppy's. By the time she got out of the tub, she was feeling more like herself again but so tired she could hardly keep her eyes open. She carried her stinking clothes at arms' length into the kitchen and hurriedly stuck them in the washing machine along with copious amounts of soap powder before Logan could get them off her.

'Grant's gone to bed,' he said quietly, offering her a mug of hot chocolate. He picked up his own mug and led her through to the sitting room where the cats had crashed out curled up together on a comfy chair. They still reeked of smoke.

'Grant didn't dare bath them.' He grinned. 'He felt that he might lose some fingers in the process.'

They both sank down onto the couch, their hands curled round their mugs.

'You've both been so kind,' said Beth. 'Once things are back to normal, I'm going to take you both out for a slap-up meal to thank you.'

'That won't be necessary,' Logan said. 'Best to simply go with Grant.'

'You do know we're not together?' she said, sliding her eyes towards him. 'I think of him as a friend but nothing more than that.'

'It's none of my business,' he said shortly. 'I'm too busy to worry about such things.' He turned away from her.

'But you weren't too busy to be out on a date after you'd been to mine for dinner,' she said under her breath.

'That...' he said, shooting her a weary glance, 'was a mistake.' He glanced out of the window. The sky was getting lighter. 'Sleep in as long as you like in the morning,' he said. 'It's my day off but

I'll check in with the station to see what the fire investigators have discovered. Come on, I'll show you to your room.'

They quietly went upstairs, hearing loud snores emanating from the door to the right of the stairwell.

'You're in here,' said Logan, turning to her in the half light, his face in shadow.

'Night, Logan,' she said softly, opening her arms to give him a brief hug.

He wrapped his arms around her with a sigh and looked down at her, his eyes unreadable. She could feel the heat coming off him in waves and held her breath as he gently touched his lips to hers. Tentatively, she kissed him back, her heart racing. As he encircled her with his arms, she had never felt so utterly safe. Gently, he disengaged and she felt his fingers stroking her cheek.

'You're crying?' he said, sounding worried. 'I shouldn't have...'

A low sob hiccoughed out of her as she shook her head. 'No, I wanted to...' she said. 'It's just, I've never done this before.'

'What, never?' he asked, startled.

Dropping her eyes she shook her head, feeling mortified. 'I've always kept people at arms' length after what happened to me. It felt safer...'

With a sigh, he hugged her. 'I'm an idiot. After everything you've been through with the fire tonight, no wonder you're all over the place. I should never have...'

'Are you kidding me?' she said with a tremulous grin. 'Best kiss I've ever had! It was all just a bit overwhelming.'

'I hope it was worth waiting for,' he added softly.

Beth swayed on her feet. She was beyond exhausted.

He gently pulled away from her. 'You're dead beat. It's time you got some sleep.' With that he opened the door to her room and then once she'd entered, quietly closed it behind him.

A wave of exhaustion swept over Beth and her eyes closed. Suddenly they flicked open again. She groaned and buried her face in her hands. Logan had kissed her, and it had been... amazing. It had taken her completely by surprise and the rush of emotion had manifested as tears. She didn't know whether to laugh or cry. He must think she was a complete moron. No wonder he hadn't been able to get out the door fast enough. How was she ever going to live it down?

FORTY-FOUR

Beth woke early the next morning and was about to turn round and go back to sleep when the events of last night hit her like a sledge-hammer. Sitting up, she hurriedly threw on Logan's dressing gown and hurried downstairs to check on the cats. She discovered them eating breakfast but still looking edgy and unsettled. Cats were not big fans of change and Marmalade had already moved houses once in the recent past. Her clothes had been dried and were sitting folded in a neat pile on top of the tumble dryer. Beth could still smell smoke off them but at least they were now clean. Logan was nowhere to be seen and his car was missing from the driveway.

She hurriedly got dressed. Making a pot of coffee, she sat down at the kitchen table and turned her phone on to see that it had blown up with notifications from concerned friends and colleagues. Everyone at the bookshop had offered to take in her and the cats, even Lachlan, who was probably biting his nails in case she said yes. She chuckled at the very idea. He was a creature of routine and she had no intention of accepting his offer, bless him. Harris was insisting that she stayed with them, and her sister Fiona had indicated she could raid her wardrobe for clothes until she managed to get some replacements. Fiona Kincaid was a lot taller than her but apart from that they were roughly the same size.

She was on the verge of leaving when Logan Hunter's car turned into the drive. He strode into the house and seemed startled to see her.

'I didn't think you'd be up yet,' he said. 'You'd better sit back down. There's been a few developments in the case.'

He looked terrible. His eyes were red and his complexion grey.

'Have you even been to bed?' she asked tentatively.

'Not yet,' he said shortly. 'It's perfectly normal in this line of work to miss the odd night's sleep.'

Beth perched on a chair and waited until he sat down opposite her.

'The fire investigation team have found traces of accelerant which confirmed our suspicion that the fire was started deliberately. It appears to have been started via your cat flap.'

'Thank goodness the cats slept with me last night.' Beth shivered. 'By the way, I meant to thank you for sending PC Townsend to check my locks and stuff yesterday. Shame her work is a bit redundant now.'

Logan shrugged. 'It wasn't me. I didn't send anybody, and I've never heard of a PC Townsend. It must have been one of the Glasgow crew that sent her.'

'She did say she's only been up here a couple of weeks.'

'Beth, Maria worked with the sketch artist sent up from Glasgow and Saunders' image is being circulated to the nationals and news channels as we speak. It's only a matter of time until we have the bastard under lock and key.'

As Logan showed her the monochrome image on his work iPad, she felt a frisson of fear.

'I'll ping a copy of this on to your phone, Beth. You need to stay alert. Last night was a deliberate attempt on your life. Next time, you might not be so lucky.'

Beth nodded, trying to fight back tears. She felt terrified but she couldn't stay here forever. This was something that had to be faced. She stood up.

'But why are they targeting me?' she burst out. 'I admit I've been poking my nose into their business but that shouldn't be enough to make me a target. They're supposedly all about justice, righting old wrongs, etc.'

'We don't know,' Logan admitted. 'Our working theory at the moment is that Saunders may be related to the person who died in the hit and run. The family is scattered now and we're trying to track them down as a matter of urgency. The cold case file has been reopened, and the files will be arriving from Aberdeen later this morning.'

'Where am I going to live in the meantime?' Beth said bleakly. 'I can't put my family or friends at risk.'

'We've discussed it at the station and with the investigative team up from Glasgow, and it's been agreed that we need to offer you protection. DC Quinn and I are both firearms trained and have been reassigned to guard you round the clock. If we manage to bring this guy down, you'll be an important witness for the prosecution.'

'What about Poppy?' she asked, worried.

'She's staying with my mother for the duration. Hopefully, we'll run him down in the next few days. Once your photo is out on social media there's nowhere to hide. There's a whole team assigned simply to go through CCTV.'

'It's a lot to take in,' Beth said in a low voice.

She wanted her life back. Would her cottage even be habitable once this was all over or would it need to be completely rebuilt?

'So, where am I going to live?' she asked quietly.

'There's an empty flat in Albany Street just a few doors up from the police station,' he said. 'My boss knows the landlord. Here's the details.'

He handed her a piece of paper. 'If you contact your insurance company, they can call my boss, Chief Inspector Angus McSorley, who can confirm the current threat level etc.'

'What about the bookshop? Am I allowed to work?' asked Beth.

'Yes, although DC Rhona Quinn will accompany you. Think of her as an extra member of staff.'

'Oh, she'll love that,' said Beth, smiling, despite the seriousness of the situation.

'She's not as bad as you think,' he admonished her. 'She's a dedicated officer and she's got a vested interest in your safety.'

'Oh, and what's that?' asked Beth, sceptically.

'You don't know?' he asked, incredulously.

'Know what?' asked Beth in alarm.

'She's been dating your brother. It's quite serious, I understand.'

'Heavens!' said Beth faintly. She wasn't quite sure how she felt about that. Why on earth hadn't Harris told her? And who had DS Hunter been dating if it wasn't Rhona Quinn?

'I'll take the night shift,' DS Hunter continued. 'What do you want to do about the cats?'

'They'll have to live in the shop until this is done,' Beth decided. 'At least it's a familiar environment and its already set up for them.'

There was a knock at the door.

'I take it that's my babysitter,' Beth said with a smile.

They both stood up. She took a small step towards him. She was thoroughly rattled and desperately wanted him to take her in his arms once more for reassurance, but he turned away from her, back in professional mode. As DC Rhona Quinn entered the room with a brisk smile, Beth smiled back and picked up the cats' carriers.

When on earth was her life ever going to get back to normal?

FORTY-FIVE

It was well before nine when Beth rocked up to the bookshop with two disgruntled cats and DC Rhona Quinn in tow. She was pleased to see all her staff already gathered. They rushed towards her, everyone talking at once. The girls took the cats off her, letting them out and making a fuss of them. DC Quinn looked astonished to see the chicks, chirping away as they attacked their seed and jostled for a place under the heat lamp. Lachlan led Beth over to the table to a pot of freshly brewed tea. Morna and Chloe joined them. DC Quinn wandered over to take a seat as well. The staff gawped at her as they were aware that their boss and the feisty officer were not known for getting along.

'We have a new member of staff,' said Beth, waving a hand in Rhona's direction.

Jaws dropped collectively.

'For real?' said Chloe faintly.

'You know that my house burned down last night?'

'Yes, of course,' said Morna. 'It was all over Facebook.'

'Well, it looks as though it was deliberate and the police believe that Nora's murderer is potentially to blame. DC Rhona Quinn has been tasked with protecting me during the day.'

'And at night?' asked Lachlan, looking concerned.

Don't blush, don't blush... she told herself fiercely, and with only partial success.

'DS Hunter will be looking after me at night,' she said.

Chloe smirked and got a subtle dig in the ribs from Morna.

'That puts my mind at rest somewhat,' said Lachlan, oblivious.

'Just think of me as another member of staff,' said the officer. 'In here, call me Rhona and give me jobs to do as long as I can keep eyes on Beth. Where she goes, I go, until this dangerous man is behind bars.' She called up the colour image arrived at by the police sketch artist on her phone. It showed a handsome man with cold eyes, short, straight, dark hair and thin lips with a Roman nose. He looked as though he might be in his late forties or early fifties.

'Everyone crowded round to look, the consensus being that they hadn't laid eyes on him before.

'Before long, his face will be plastered all over town, not to mention in the local and national press. He can run but he won't be able to hide for long,' said DC Quinn, her expression grim.

'Why's it not in colour?' asked Chloe. 'Didn't Maria remember the colour of his eyes?'

'Yes, they're believed to be blue, but these sketches are monochrome to allow for a more accurate representation,' replied DC Quinn.

'What about Maria?' asked Beth. 'If she's the only one who can now identify him, isn't she even more at risk?'

'And what about her visa?' chimed in Morna.

'That's all been taken care of,' said Rhona Quinn. 'She's now been placed in a safe house far from here. The Home Office have agreed to renew and extend her visa in the circumstances.'

'That only leaves Kathleen unaccounted for,' said Beth. 'I can't help feeling a bit responsible for her plight. If it wasn't for my subscription boxes...'

'You can't think like that,' said Rhona Quinn briskly. 'We're still working to locate her whereabouts and have circulated her description to forces across the Unted Kingdom and Ireland. It's still entirely possible she's off somewhere, completely oblivious that we want to speak to her.'

'We'll need to be careful not to let the cats out,' said Beth, her face creasing with worry. 'I've put their litter tray beside the back door and their food is in the kitchen, but we'll need to watch them once we open or they'll be off out the front door and back to the house. They can stay there for the duration.'

She glanced at her watch prompted by the impatient knock on the door.

'Right, as far as our customers go, it's business as usual,' said Beth.

'What if they recognise, DC... er... Rhona?' asked Chloe.

'It's unlikely,' answered the detective. 'But, if they do, we tell them that I'm rotating round local businesses to deter shoplifters as part of a community policing initiative.'

'Wow, you've thought of everything,' Chloe replied, duly impressed.

As the customers trickled in, Beth and Rhona busied themselves in the kitchen, making scones, empire biscuits and chocolate chip cookies for the morning coffee crowd. Beth was impressed with how Rhona threw herself into helping whilst clearly still being alert to any possible danger. The slight bulge in her jacket told Beth that she was carrying a weapon, and she didn't doubt that she would whip it out to defend her in an instant. Small talk was kept to a minimum as the detective's restless eyes were constantly flicking around as she remained alert, slipping through every few minutes to wander round the café assessing all the customers without appearing to do so. Beth had to admit that she was impressive. Maybe she'd had her all wrong.

After putting the scones and cookies in the oven, Beth walked through into the main part of the shop. Chloe was behind the till whilst keeping an eagle eye on the chicks, Morna was serving in the café and Lachlan was speaking to customers on the shop floor. She felt a thrill of pride in her team for the way they always pulled together in a crisis.

Mike walked through the door, pausing in front of the table with an eye-catching display of his bestselling novel.

'How are you holding up, Beth?' he asked, his eyes concerned. 'I hear your house burned down. If you need a place to stay in the meantime...'

'That's so kind, but I'm sorted, thanks,' she said with as bright a smile as she could muster. Perceptive as ever, he clocked DC Quinn walking by carrying a pile of books. His eyes widened in surprise.

'Community policing initiative,' she hissed under her breath.

'Not buying it,' he hissed back. 'Are you in trouble, Beth? Is there anything I can do to help? If there is, just say the word.'

'Yes, I'm in trouble,' she admitted, 'but it's being handled. I'll shout if I need anything.'

'You'd better,' he said, giving her arm a squeeze and wandering over to the crime section. Lachlan followed him to discreetly fill him in on what had been happening.

The rest of the day flew by until Beth was dead on her feet, the disturbed sleep of the previous night catching up with her. Once the door was locked behind the last customer, they all slumped in relief. It had been an effort keeping up appearances when they were all so worried about what might happen next.

DC Quinn had parked her unmarked police car round the back of the shop and after a perimeter check, they set off. After a few minutes of driving, Beth turned to her.

'Where are we going? I thought we were going to Albany Street?'

'We are,' DC Quinn replied coolly.' I'm just making sure we're not being followed first.'

'Oh.' Beth sank back in her seat quietly.

This was a whole new world she'd entered, and she didn't like it one little bit.

FORTY-SIX

Beth stood quietly during the handover which occurred up inside the third-floor sandstone flat. DS Hunter looked more rested, but his face was still taut with tension as DC Quinn briefed him on the day.

'I did think for a few moments that we were being followed here,' she said to him. 'However, I took a circuitous route, and the suspect's car peeled off and took the road for Fort William, so it was most likely a false alarm.'

'If he's any sense, surely he'll be long gone?' Beth interjected. 'Why would he hang around up here? He's achieved his objective and is wanted for murder. Unless there's something you're not telling me?'

The two officers glanced at each other. Beth was immediately worried.

'You don't think that burning down the cottage was the end of it?' Beth asked.

'Impossible to say,' DS Hunter replied. 'We're going to do everything we can to keep you safe until those responsible are behind bars.'

'How close are you to catching Oliver Saunders?' Beth asked, flopping down into a chair, her legs weak and shaky.

'We've identified him now, thanks to Maria,' he replied. 'His real name is Aidan Rafferty and he's the son of Lorna Rafferty, the woman who was killed in 1979. You're not going to believe this but he's actually a serving police officer, works in a cold cases unit in Glasgow. I'm struggling to wrap my head around it myself.'

'That's crazy! Talk about hiding in plain sight,' murmured Beth.

'We believe that what happened to his mother festered inside him for years, but it was only once his father died that he seems to have been galvanised into taking direct action. His father was in the army but discharged on medical grounds five years after his mother was mown down. He was a corporal, so we think that posing as an army officer was Aiden Rafferty's twisted way of honouring his father. We also suspect he may have attempted to recruit others to seek revenge for wrongs that have gone unpunished.'

'Surely, he's not coming after me for what happened when I was thirteen?' said Beth, fighting down a sudden wave of nausea. 'It was an accident. I was just trying to get away from the people bullying me. Killing Jill was the furthest thing from my mind. In any event, I was convicted and served my time. I've paid for my crime.'

'Hopefully, we'll know more soon,' said DC Quinn. 'Anyway, I'd best get off and leave you in the capable hands of DS Hunter, Beth. Logan, I'll keep my phone on all night. Shout if you need me and I'll be down like a shot.' With that she left them to it.

An uncomfortable silence descended.

'Where will I be sleeping?' Beth managed.

'If you take the bigger of the two rooms, I'll probably doze on the couch mainly. Just... you know, in case. The police station is only a few doors down and we've got surveillance on the front door, so we should be fine. A camera has been fitted on the door to this flat and there's an entry code for the door downstairs.'

Beth started to feel safer. She took her bag of stuff through to the bedroom then came back.

'Are you hungry? I can cook us something,' she offered. She opened the kitchen doors and found them to be fairly well equipped with basics such as pasta. Opening the fridge, she found a bottle of chardonnay and some beers as well as milk, cheese, ham and tomatoes.

'That would be good,' he said with a tense smile that flickered on and off too quickly.

'Beer?' she asked, opening the wine and pouring herself a glass.

'No, thanks, I'm on the job,' he replied tersely.

Was that all she was to him? A job? Was this growing closeness between them all in her head?

A few minutes later she was serving up bowls of steaming lemon scented pasta with chunks of fresh bread.

'That smells great,' he said appreciatively, looking carefully out of the bay window before sitting down at the table. 'I think I forgot to eat today.'

'I'm sorry for causing you so much trouble,' she said, her eyes filling with tears. She truly felt awful for what she was putting him through. He was apart from his little girl, and it was all her fault for sticking her nose into the case in the first place.

'This isn't your fault,' he said, leaning over to take her hand then thinking better of it and giving it an awkward pat instead. 'If it wasn't for you, we might not even have caught up with Maria, which enabled us to identify Rafferty. Nora's murder might have been passed off as some failed romance scam.'

'It just feels like I set everything in motion with my subscription boxes,' she said miserably, putting down her fork, her appetite dwindling.

'Hardly,' he scoffed. 'The books didn't kill Nora Kelly, and even the mushroom tea supplied by Kathleen Boyle wasn't what killed her. It was merely a cover for Aiden Rafferty deliberately poisoning her with a lethal dose of deadly mushrooms. This problem is not of your making.'

'Talking of Kathleen,' Beth said. 'Has she turned up yet? I can't shake the feeling that something really awful has happened to her.'

'Not yet, there's been no sightings of her whatsoever, which is concerning. We've been unable to trace any family or next of kin for her either.'

After their meal, Beth washed up having refused Logan's offer of help. She carried across a pot of coffee for him and another glass of wine for herself. The couch was big and sprawling so she settled down on it, pulling a throw over from the back.

'I can light a fire, if you're cold,' he said, putting down his cup.

'No, it's fine.' Beth shuddered. 'Fire is all I can see when I close my eyes. If I hadn't closed the sitting room door when I went to bed last night, I might not be here today. The smoke inhalation would have done for me before the flames made it up the stairs. Thank God the cats were in with me. I couldn't have borne it if they hadn't made it out,' she said.

'I'm not going to let anything happen to you, Beth,' he said, stretching out his arm to wrap her hand inside his. 'I've got you.'

His hand was firm and reassuring. She could have held on to it all night but already she could feel him tensing up, wanting to remain on guard to fight whatever might be coming. She gave it a final squeeze and released him. He jumped up and did a sweep of the apartment, checking all the windows and testing the front door was secure. It was already dark. His radio buzzed and he updated the station.

'All's quiet down there,' he said. 'Try and get some sleep. You've had a long day. Things will look better in the morning.'

Beth highly doubted that but wished him good night. She wanted to seek the reassurance of his arms with a hug, but she sensed he didn't want that. Tonight, he was tasked with protecting her and the last thing he needed was for her to make his job any more difficult.

She closed the bedroom door and lay awake on her bed, alert to every creak and groan of this unfamiliar place. Eventually, her eyes could stay open no longer and she fell into a troubled sleep. Was this nightmare ever going to end?

FORTY-SEVEN

As she pushed open the door of the shop the following morning, DC Quinn following her in, the care and concern on the faces of her staff and friends made her briefly tear up. Both cats rushed towards her, each jealously staking their claim by winding in and out of her legs until she almost fell over. She picked them up one a time to give them a cuddle, taking care to safeguard Toby's position as top cat by giving him a cuddle first.

'Wish I got a greeting like that when I walked into the nick every morning,' DC Quinn said sardonically.

There was still half an hour to opening so they sat down at the table and Lachlan rushed through with a big pot of tea wrapped in her mother's tea cosy. As her eyes settled on it, Beth wondered what her poor mum would make of all this drama. Her eyebrows would be so far up her hairline they'd never be seen again. She'd caught her staff up on the developments in the case last night in their WhatsApp group.

'What was it like spending the night with DS Hunter?' Chloe said in a voice she probably thought was sotto voce. 'I'm getting real *Bodyguard* vibes.'

Beth coloured and shot an agonised look at DC Quinn who let out a short laugh.

'Hey, don't mind me. Logan and I don't talk about stuff like that. None of my beeswax.'

She got up and prowled around the shop, checking all was as it should be. The cats followed her, tails up, like they considered they were on the job, too.

'Oops, sorry,' said Chloe, a hand over her mouth.

'You moron,' hissed Morna, rolling her eyes at Chloe.

'Nothing to tell,' said Beth, giving a shrug. 'He was on the job. It wasn't a social event or "hook up",' she said, wiggling her fingers, making fun of Chloe to lighten the atmosphere. 'Both he and DC Quinn have been brilliant, actually. I feel a lot safer with either of them around. I'm hoping that burning my house down was the last throw of the dice before Aiden Rafferty ran for the hills. It would be insane for him to hang around and wait for the police to catch him. I had nothing to do with what Nora or Darragh did back in the day. I think he was just furious with me for getting in his way and placing him on the radar of the police.'

'Well, he should have thought about that before,' grumbled Lachlan. 'I still can't believe he's a serving policeman. What's the world coming to?'

'He did lose his mother in his formative years due to those two,' Beth reminded him. 'Some wounds never heal, and I think that a world of pain spawned this particular crime.'

'Tell me you're not actually feeling sorry for him,' said Lachlan, looking cross.

'Not exactly,' sighed Beth. 'But you've got to see people's actions in context, don't you think?'

'I don't have to see anything of the sort,' said Lachlan, shaking his head and gathering up the tea things to avoid arguing further.

'Someone got out of bed the wrong side this morning,' said Morna, raising her eyebrows at Chloe once Lachlan had disappeared off into the back.

'I think the strain is getting to him. We should be mindful of that. Thanks so much for picking up the slack, you two,' she said, taking in the tidy bookshop and the pleasant smells drifting through from the kitchen.

'Chloe's turned into a regular domestic goddess while you've been out of action.' Morna grinned. 'It's like *Invasion of the Body Snatchers* or something. Either that or she's trying to impress Joe with her credentials for becoming a farmer's wife.'

Chloe kicked her under the table and scowled.

Beth felt her body relax as the two continued to bicker. It felt like life was slowly returning to normal. She glanced at her watch and nodded to DC Quinn who had returned to the table, her eyes watchful.

'I'm opening up now. Is that okay?'

'Let me do it,' the detective said, walking over to the door. She opened it and slid outside, looking to left and right then came back inside flipping the sign to Open.

'Stay alert, everyone,' DC Quinn warned. 'I'm not expecting any problems in such a public place but keep your wits about you, nevertheless.'

'It's our big day tomorrow. Have we bought everything we need?' she asked Chloe and Morna. 'I can't believe we're doing this with everything else that's been going on.'

'What choice do we have?' Lachlan shrugged, walking over to join them. 'We advertised it so well that the whole town's going to be here, I reckon.'

'The kids will be completely hyper from all that sugar,' said Chloe, her eyes sparkling. Dealing with the youngsters who came into the bookshop was her favourite part of the job.

'I've got to get through this stupid TV interview first,' grumbled Morna.

'That's tonight?' said Beth, aghast. 'I'm so sorry, Morna, I'd completely forgotten.'

'I'm not surprised,' said Morna drily.

'Have you decided what to do yet?' asked Chloe. 'Stepford daughter or tell it like it really is?'

'No,' said Morna, her face etched in misery.

'It's a choice you shouldn't even have to make, lass,' said Lachlan, shaking his head.

'How has it been, seeing more of your family recently?' asked Beth.

'It's been good,' Morna admitted with a sad smile. 'For years, I'd bricked them up behind a wall in my mind. It was easier that way. But seeing them again, it made me realise how much I'd missed being part of a family, even if that family didn't attach any value to me. It was still there in the background.'

'Have you tried to talk to any of them about how you feel?' prompted Beth.

'I've tried but the words get stuck in my throat,' Morna said, looking away.

'Why don't you phone Cassandra and ask her to come in?' asked Chloe. 'You could lay it on the line for her, put across your whole point of view and see what she says? She's your sister and likely to be more open-minded. Your parents are probably a bit stuck in the past.'

'It's worth a try,' said Beth. 'It might help make your mind up one way or the other.'

'How has your new image made you feel?' asked Chloe, curious as ever.

'It's made me feel seen. Too seen,' said Morna. 'Before, people's eyes would slide right over me and that's the way I like it. I feel like I'm acting in a play dressed like this. It's excruciating.'

'Each to their own,' said Lachlan. 'It would be a boring world if we were all the same.'

'I'll phone her now,' said Morna, walking away.

'I'm really worried about her,' confided Chloe, as her friend and colleague walked away. 'Her family near destroyed her once. What if they do it again and she can't recover? I can't believe that Cassandra had me eating out of her hand when I first met her.'

'She had me fooled for a bit, too, if it makes you feel any better.' Lachlan sighed.

The bell tinkled and a gaggle of children from the nearby

nursery trooped in, squealing with delight at the sight of the chicks. After their attention started to wane, Chloe took them through to the café for some free orange squash and mini birds' nests. She then read them a story before sending them on their way with their grateful teacher and assistants, who promised to stick leaflets about the event tomorrow in their bags before home time.

DC Quinn sidled up to Beth. 'I don't know how you do it. This job is exhausting. Give me police work any day.'

Beth laughed at her. 'What? You'd rather go toe to toe with criminals than a nursery class of little kids?'

'Every time,' the officer said fervently.

The bell tinkled and they both looked towards the door, stiffening as Jane Guthrie hesitated on the threshold, then, with a worried look behind her, stepped fully in to the shop.

FORTY-EIGHT

'I need to talk to you,' said Jane Guthrie. Her eyes were wide and frightened, and a fine sheen of sweat misted her forehead. Beth got a waft of stale wine from her.

DC Quinn had turned away and was ostensibly straightening books on a shelf with her back to them. Beth assumed that Jane hadn't seen her yet.

'We can talk in the office,' she said, her heart thumping with nerves as she turned to lead the way. Out of the corner of her eye, she could see that her staff had stiffened and were aware of what was going on.

They had just sat down on opposite sides of her desk when DC Quinn entered and took up position inside the door, allowing her jacket to fall open so that Jane caught a glimpse of her upholstered firearm. She sprang to her feet.

'Whoa, is this some kind of set up? I should never have come.' She looked about wildly, trying to work out if she could get past the officer at the door.

'You wanted to talk to me,' Beth said, trying to keep her voice level. 'DC Quinn's here to protect me. She thinks I'm in danger. This isn't a trap,' she said, unmoving in her chair.

'Well, Miss Guthrie? What's it to be?' asked DC Quinn, adopting a more relaxed posture.

Jane thumped back into the chair, looking defeated.

'What was it you wanted to talk to me about? You're aware that my house was set on fire last night?'

'I heard about it,' replied Jane. 'It was nothing to do with me, if that's what you're thinking.'

'We know all about Aiden Rafferty,' said Beth with a confidence she didn't feel.

'You do?' said Jane, looking relieved. 'It's gone too far. I want no part of it. Aiden needs to be stopped. What was done to you. It wasn't right. You paid for your crime. I read all about it in the paper at the end of last year when it was raked up again.'

Beth was getting completely out of her depth. Surely, this was a job for the police. She glanced up at DC Quinn who gave her a slight nod to continue. She was no doubt thinking that if Jane was primed to talk to her here and now, she might clam up if they moved her to the more formal setting of the police station. No pressure then.

'What happened to you as a baby was terrible,' Beth said softly. 'I can see why you harboured a grudge against Nora Kelly.'

'Of course I did! Have you any idea how tormented I've been over the years thinking about what my poor mother went through? How I was denied the chance to have that secure maternal attachment that is everyone's right?'

'I can't even imagine...' said Beth, feeling a good deal of sympathy for the hard-faced, brittle woman in front of her.

'Then to cap it all, once she got me, she rejected me outright! Can you believe the cheek of her? It screwed me up so much I've never even contemplated motherhood myself.'

Beth could still hear the anger in her voice bubbling below the surface.

'Darragh Brennan suffered, too,' she said quietly. 'He wasn't party to the deception. He loved you as his own child, then you were snatched away from him. He had no other children. He asked me to give you this, should I manage to speak to you again.'

She reached into a drawer and pulled out the sealed letter which she handed across to Jane.

The woman opened the letter, tears rolling down her face as she read it. After she was done, she folded it away and placed it back in the envelope with shaking hands.

'He's left me everything,' she said. 'He said I'm the only child he ever had and the pain of losing me stayed with him. He explained about how ill Nora was at the time and asks me to find it in my heart to forgive her, so I don't carry that anger with me further into the future.'

She looked up, her face anguished. 'I didn't want this.' She sobbed. 'I never even got to see him one more time. I should have gone to see him sooner. I know that he had no part in what happened to me.'

'Darragh Brennan admitted to Beth that he'd been responsible back in 1979 for a hit and run involving the death of a young pregnant woman. Both he and Nora had been drinking. She wanted to report it, but he persuaded her to stay silent. The crime went unpunished,' said DC Quinn from her position by the door. 'You say that Aiden Rafferty has gone too far. Are you willing to help us to bring this to an end, Jane?'

Jane nodded tearfully. 'Yes. What can I do? I don't want anyone else to be harmed, least of all Beth.'

'What about Callum?' asked Beth. 'Is he part of it?'

'Callum? Not as far as I'm aware,' she replied. 'The only person I had any direct dealings with was Aiden Rafferty. If he involved anyone else, I wasn't privy to it.'

'How deep were you in with them?' asked DC Quinn.

'You're making it sound like it was some kind of terrorist organisation,' Jane said with a sigh. 'Believe it or not, it all started a couple of years ago with a grief counselling and support group in Glasgow for people who had been affected by crime. One day they were banging on about acceptance and forgiveness, and it just got too much for me. I thought "Sod this!" and stormed out. Aiden Rafferty walked out with me. He was furious as well. We went for coffee, and he told me about this small group he was putting together to make sure that people got their just desserts. At the time, it resonated with me. But I never thought at that stage that "just desserts" meant murder. It was meant to be a way of taking back some power. I was done with being seen as a passive victim. Aiden and I trusted each other. I felt safe with him. We shared a common goal, or I thought we did. For me, it was about bringing pressure to bear on the police and changing the law to recognise that for certain crimes, people should remain accountable. Nora was released from the state mental hospital after just two years, but she left me with a life of trauma. It galled me to realise that she was then, effectively, allowed to pick up her life as if nothing had happened.

'But then, in the last few months, Aiden found out who had run over his mother and we were shocked to discover it was the same person who had kidnapped me. He changed. I think he might even have become a little unhinged. He started talking about designing a logo, V for Vendetta, and became totally obsessed. The whole thing was growing arms and legs. He saw it in terms of starting a movement, something that would grow and expand. I didn't know what to do. I tried to distance myself, made excuses when he wanted to meet up. I then heard from my social worker who'd kept in touch with me over the years that Nora had died. She thought it would bring me peace. But instinctively I knew it was him. I came up to Oban the very next day. I was worried that I was, somehow, complicit.' Jane wrung her hands, her face anguished.

'I can see how that could happen,' said DC Quinn. 'I suppose the question now is, do you want to continue to be part of the problem, or do you want to be part of the solution?'

'I didn't murder Nora Kelly,' Jane said. 'But I did suspect that she was going to be murdered at some point and did nothing to stop it. When I heard she was dead, I admit I was relieved. It felt like closure. When I heard that you'd found the body, Beth, I introduced myself. I even thought that if everything went my way I might inherit her estate as next of kin. I still had my old extract of the birth certificate, although the principal register was amended years later. Then I discovered she'd made a will and left everything to you. At first, I was angry but then I realised I had no right to be. I was not, and never had been, her daughter. No amount of money could ever make right what she did to me.'

'But for three years at least you had a father who truly loved you,' said Beth, 'and those feelings never went away. You were treasured by Darragh Brennan. He had photos of you all over his house. He went to his grave loving you.'

'And I still remember that I loved him. I believe that Aiden Rafferty murdered him,' Jane said quietly, slumping back in her seat as if getting it all out had exhausted her.

'Jane, you've been very brave coming forward but I need you to tell the team of officers up from Glasgow what you've just told us under caution. Can you do that?' asked DC Quinn.

'Yes,' replied Jane after a moment. 'Can you be there, too?'

DC Quinn looked torn.

'Go with her,' said Beth. 'I'll be here for the rest of the afternoon. Nothing's going to happen to me in the shop, is it? This is too important.'

'Fine,' said DC Quinn reluctantly. 'But don't leave the shop without either myself or DS Hunter by your side. Is that absolutely clear?'

'Crystal,' replied Beth, with a mock salute.

'We'll leave through the back,' DC Quinn announced. 'Lock the door behind us.'

'I don't suppose I'll see you again,' said Jane, turning to look at Beth as she was about to exit the premises.

'No,' said Beth. 'I wish you all the best, truly, I do.'

'Likewise,' said Jane. 'Take care of those crazy cats.'

Beth locked the rear door behind them and leaned her head on it, utterly exhausted. Then, she pulled herself together and went back through into the shop. Things were coming to a head and she hoped she was going to make it through to the other side.

FORTY-NINE

Beth walked back into the shop. She didn't know how she was going to find the strength to keep going until closing time. A deep weariness had settled into her very bones.

'Coffee?' Lachlan asked, seeing her frozen expression.

'Please,' she said.

Moments later he returned with a large mug. Gratefully, she wrapped her fingers around it and took a glug.

'Where's DC Quinn?' he asked, sounding worried.

'Jane is now cooperating with the police,' Beth explained. 'DC Quinn had to go to the station to interview her. She didn't have a choice. Anyway, the odds of someone coming in here to start something are very low.'

'Jane killed Nora?' he asked, surprised.

'Not exactly.' She caught him up on what Jane had revealed about the way Aiden Rafferty had sucked her in.

'So, Aidan Rafferty is still at large?'

'Hopefully, not for much longer.' Beth shivered.

'I'd tell you to get off home,' said Lachlan, looking at her in concern, 'but that's not really an option, is it?'

'No, I have to stay put until I'm collected by DS Hunter. I feel a bit like a child with two overzealous parents right now.' She smiled ruefully.

The bell tinkled and in marched Cassandra. She was obviously trying to go incognito, and it was backfiring spectacularly. Her lustrous locks were hidden under a baseball cap, and her designer sunglasses were huge and covered most of her face. Clad in designer labels from head to toe, she still looked way more exotic than people in Oban were accustomed to seeing. Everything about her screamed *I'm a celebrity, get me out of here!*

'Oh boy,' sighed Lachlan. 'Here we go again. I'll mind the floor. I haven't got the stomach for this carry on.'

Beth followed the girls into the café, taking up position behind the counter in case Morna needed her.

Seeing there was no one else in, Cassandra took off her cap and shook out her long mane of hair.

'You look like one of those shampoo ads,' said Chloe, but there was no admiration in her voice this time.

'Look, Morna, can't we do this in private?' Cassandra asked, looking at the rest of them with disdain.

'Anything you want to say to me you can say in front of them,' Morna answered, folding her arms.

'Very well,' Cassandra huffed. 'What's this about anyway? We've got to leave for the studio soon.'

'I think it's time this family accepted me for who I really am,' Morna said, her voice strong.

'And who she is, is completely frickin' awesome,' said Chloe, folding her arms also.

'Look,' hissed Cassandra, 'it was you who turned your back on us, not the other way round. We're just asking you to show up for us until our father gets elected then you can disappear off again into the weird world you choose to inhabit. Where's your loyalty?'

'No,' ground out Morna, her eyes burning with rage. 'Where's yours? This family has treated me like faulty goods from the very beginning. Can you even imagine what it felt like to be left alone at that hideous boarding school in the holidays on some pretext whilst they took you home or off on some foreign jaunt without me. I was your little sister. Why didn't you stand up for me? Why didn't you ask them to let me come home?'

'Yeah, why didn't you, Cassandra?' chimed in Chloe, her eyes narrowed in anger.

'Look, it wasn't as easy as you think,' shot back Cassandra, sitting back in her chair. 'You think that they loved *me* unconditionally? Think again. I could never be a typical kid. I wasn't allowed an off day. I had to be *perfect* every single day or they threatened to send me away. It was exhausting. It still *is* exhausting. Maybe I thought you were better off out of it, away from all the pressure.'

'That's a cop out,' said Chloe coldly. 'You're a grown woman. You have choices. You're just not brave enough to make them because you're addicted to all your celebrity bullshit. Admit it!'

'I could do with a friend like you in my corner,' said Cassandra with a half-smile.

'Takes no prisoners once she gets going,' agreed Morna, shooting Chloe a grateful grin.

'Still here, guys!' huffed Chloe.

'So, what *are* you going to do?' asked Cassandra. 'They'll blame me if you don't show up ready to tow the party line.'

'Did you know that they threatened to hound Beth out of business by any means possible, if I didn't agree to a stupid makeover in their likeness?' asked Morna conversationally.

'What?' asked Beth, startled.

'That's outrageous!' exclaimed Chloe. 'I couldn't understand why you gave in without a fight, Morna. Now it makes perfect sense.'

'I didn't know,' said Cassandra. 'But I can't honestly say that I'm surprised.'

'It's become increasingly clear to me that your earlier instincts were correct, Morna,' said Beth. 'They don't deserve you. I expect you to turn up tomorrow dressed in whatever way makes *you* happy. Don't worry about the shop, I'd like to see them try. They're bullies making empty threats, and I refuse to be intimidated by them.'

'What are you going to do about the interview, Morna?' asked Chloe.

Morna thought long and hard before looking up at them, her eyes glinting with determination.

'Tell them they've never showed up for me, so I don't intend to show up for them. If they can't accept me for who I am then as far as I'm concerned that's their loss. I'm done.'

'What about me?' asked Cassandra.

'What about you?' replied Morna, looking at her through narrowed eyes.

'Can we still see each other from time to time? Chloe's right. I'm too old for my parents to dictate my relationships. In fact, I'm thinking of taking a leaf out of your book.'

'Maybe,' said Morna. 'But no more ambushes?'

'Agreed,' said Cassandra with a smile that finally reached her eyes. She gathered up her things and turned to leave. 'Time to face Armageddon.' She grinned.

Morna submitted to a brief hug before Cassandra left in a cloud of designer perfume.

'Wow, that was intense,' breathed Chloe.

'Thanks for having my back,' muttered Morna. She rushed off to the fantasy section to regain her equilibrium.

Lachlan hovered in the doorway, clutching a mug of tea as though his life depended on it.

'Is the lass okay?' he asked softly.

'She will be, Lachlan.' Beth smiled.

As she moved around the shop advising customers, Beth reflected on how precious life had become since she'd moved up to Oban. Her life was fuller than she had ever imagined it could be. If only she could rid herself of the unsettling feeling that she was living on borrowed time.

FIFTY

Despite being exhausted, Beth had slept only fitfully, tormented by dreams involving the fire. At one point she had shouted out in her sleep and DS Hunter had appeared in her doorway to check on her. She'd slept better after that, feeling safer that he was there.

She cooked them both breakfast, her stomach tied in knots about the day ahead. It was Easter Saturday and instead of feeling the usual sense of joy and anticipation that tomorrow usually brought her, she was being guarded round the clock. As she sat down to eat, she poured them both some coffee.

'Are you sure you don't want to grab a quick shower and change your clothes?' she asked. 'I'll be fine on my own for a few minutes.'

He looked drawn and exhausted. Clearly the strain was getting to him, too.

'Famous last words. That's not how it works.' He grimaced, chugging down some coffee. 'There'll be time for all that when DC Quinn arrives.'

Beth nodded and smiled but although she appreciated the efforts being made to keep her safe, she was craving some time on her own.

'Are they any nearer to catching Aiden Rafferty after interviewing Jane?' she asked.

'They've promised her immunity from prosecution provided she helps them to bait a trap. She jumped at the chance. She was in way over her head and happy to grasp any lifeline that will enable her to move on from the events of her past. It's meant to be going down sometime today.'

'Will you be involved?' she asked, worried.

'Yes, but the Major Crime Unit will be in charge. I'll just be backing them up.'

'I can't wait for this nightmare to be over,' said Beth.

'You and me both,' he said. 'You'll be sick of the sight of me.'

'Never!' Beth laughed. 'But I can't wait to do normal things again, without looking over my shoulder all the time.'

'I know what you mean,' he said. 'I've missed Poppy something fierce. She'll be cross about missing the shindig at the shop today. She was looking forward to it.'

'We'll have to find a way to make it up to her.' Her smile faded. That was rather presumptuous of her. He'd probably had enough of her company by now to last a lifetime.

The doorbell rang. DS Logan jumped to his feet and ascertained it was DC Quinn before opening the door. Beth swallowed the last of the coffee and grabbed her bag.

'Ready for another exciting day in the book trade?' she said cheerily to DC Quinn.

'Can't wait,' the officer replied drily, rolling her eyes at DS Hunter.

They arrived at the shop to find everyone there putting the finishing touches to the planned activities. Lachlan bounded through from the kitchen in his rabbit outfit, startling her.

'It's roasting inside this costume,' he complained.

'But it'll make a lot of kids very happy,' soothed Beth.

Still grumbling, he unzipped the head so he could drink his tea.

Chloe flitted over to join them. She was wearing a sparkling white tutu with rabbit ears and face paint. Beth had dressed as an Easter egg since she liked eating them so much.

'I hope there won't be too many copycat Easter bunnies,' said Chloe. 'It'll get too confusing.'

'What do you mean?' asked DC Quinn. 'Tell me this event isn't fancy dress? I thought it was just you lot who were dressing up?'

'It's not mandatory,' said Beth, 'but we do have prizes for best adult and best kid.'

'But that's going to be a nightmare to police,' groaned DC Quinn. 'Potentially, Aiden Rafferty could slip in amongst us and we wouldn't see him coming. You have to cancel it!'

'I'm afraid that's not possible,' said Beth firmly. 'Our customers have been looking forward to it, particularly the little ones. I can't possibly disappoint them. It wouldn't be right.'

'It's too late anyway,' said Morna. 'They're due to start arriving any minute now.'

Lachlan drained the dregs of his tea then shoved his head back on.

'You lot don't make my life any easier,' snapped DC Quinn. 'Be on your guard, everyone.'

A stream of little kids entered the shop, dressed variously as Easter rabbits, Easter eggs and Easter chicks. There were a number of adults dressed up as well, who DC Quinn made a point of engaging in conversation and watching closely. Chloe had given her some rabbit ears and a bunny tabard which she'd donned with bad grace.

After a while Chloe glanced at the clock. 'Right, children, everyone ready for an Easter egg hunt?' she asked.

'Yesssss,' came a straggle of voices.

'I can't hear you,' said Chloe sweetly, putting her hand to her ear.

This time the kids raised the roof. Toby and Marmalade shot up to the top of the bookcases in panic, looking horrified at this sudden turn of events. The children were each given a little wicker basket and the race was on to see how many eggs they could find in the next twenty minutes. Chloe blew a whistle to start them off. Some late arrivals, the adults in fancy dress and excited kids, crowded into the shop.

'Sorry we're late,' one harried mum said breathlessly, clutching the hands of two little girls, grinning from ear to ear.

'Wouldn't have missed it for the world,' muttered one dad, clearly meaning exactly the opposite.

Beth didn't have the heart to turn them away and soon they, too, were caught up, charging around with their little baskets.

'There's so many more here than I thought would come,' Beth whispered to Chloe. 'Have we even enough Easter eggs for them to find?'

'Bought way more than I thought we'd need,' said Chloe, 'so I think we'll be fine.'

Beth was touched by how many of the locals had turned up to support the event after the previous bad publicity in relation to the subscription boxes. Her mother had been right about the community spirit in this town.

'I'll stay by the chicks,' said Morna, 'just in case any of the little tykes decides a chocolate treat isn't enough.'

'Joe would kill me if I lost any of them,' said a worried Chloe.

DC Rhona Quinn appeared. She radiated tenson. 'There's at least six bloody Easter bunnies in the café and wandering around,' she said in a low voice. 'Anyone could be hiding inside a costume like that. I don't like it. I don't like it at all.'

Beth's heart sank. She was right but there was nothing they could do about it now the event was in full swing. Surely, Aiden Rafferty wouldn't dare come in here, would he? Her heart rate accelerated as she, too, looked around, trying to pick up on any potential threats.

A tall Easter bunny approached her and Beth stiffened, backing up against the nearest bookcase. She saw DC Quinn's hand reach for her holster and shook her head frantically whilst smiling a rictus grin. There was no way she was having a blood bath in the shop at an Easter event. The kids would be traumatised for life, not to mention the adults.

'I should get danger money for this,' the Easter bunny grumbled. 'I was rugby tackled from behind by two kids wanting me to help them reach more eggs.'

'Oh dear,' DC Quinn sympathised, turning on the charm. 'Come with me and we'll find you a quiet corner in the café where you can take a breather with a cool drink.'

'Great idea,' said Beth, instantly getting where the detective was going with this. She spoke through a loudspeaker. 'Attention, everyone! Would all the adults in fancy dress please go into the café for judging? Once that's done there will be free cold drinks served and a group photo.'

She then whispered in Chloe's ear, 'Can you keep the little ones entertained for ten minutes and away from the café area?'

Chloe nodded and sped away, weaving her usual magic round the little ones, as Beth chivvied the adults into the café where she awarded prizes to the top three best costumes.

'Right, everyone,' she said in a singsong voice, 'masks and heads off for the group photo.' Everyone complied and Beth took her time getting them all lined up so that DC Quinn could check that Aidan Rafferty wasn't hiding in plain sight. As they all revealed themselves to be hot and sweaty but otherwise innocent mothers and fathers, she heaved a sigh of relief. Afterwards she walked amongst them congratulating the winners and commiserating with the losers, casually affixing small red stickers to everyone's back. It was the best she could do to ensure that everyone had been accounted for.

A few minutes later, the Easter egg hunters came running in, followed by an exhausted Chloe. The winner received a huge Easter egg but there were consolation prizes as well. After snack time, Chloe gathered them all up in the children's section and read them a story.

'How does she do it?' marvelled Morna. 'They're all hanging on her every word. I tell them something and they completely ignore me, like I'm invisible or something.'

'She has the knack,' agreed Beth, starting to relax now that it was nearly all over. Soon, they were waving the children and their parents out of the door. Beth gave a sigh of relief and locked the door behind them.

'Tea?' she asked faintly. They all nodded vigorously and she headed towards the kitchen.

DC Quinn poked her head around the door. 'Beth, I need to head to the station for a lunchtime debrief. I'll be back before 2pm when the shop opens again.'

'Fine, see you then.' Beth smiled. Although they'd got off to a bad start last year, the young detective was growing on her. Perhaps she had mellowed as a result of going out with Harris.

As well as the tea, Beth brought through a tray of sandwiches and cakes left over from the event along with a few chocolate bunnies she'd squirrelled away. 'That went well, I thought.' She smiled at her staff who looked like partially deflated balloons.

'That costume was sweltering,' said Lachlan, fanning his hot head with an improvised fan.

'The chicks are all present and correct,' said Morna, walking in from the main part of the shop.

'What about the cats?' asked Beth, frowning as her eyes searched the bookcases for them. She called for them but to no avail. Sighing, she searched out a packet of Dreamies and shook it. No answering miaows. That could only mean one thing. They were no longer on the premises. They must have sneaked out the door under cover of everyone leaving. No doubt they were heading for the cottage at this very moment.

Sighing, she opened the door into her office to check they hadn't been shut inside. No sign of them. She could, however, smell perfume. The scent smelled familiar. When had she been around that scent before? Had someone been in here nosing around? Some people had no notion of boundaries, she huffed, checking the drawers in her desk. Fortunately, anything important was kept in the safe in the corner. It left her feeling vaguely uneasy.

FIFTY-ONE

Beth locked the office door behind her, having pulled the blinds so the small room was in darkness. She'd decided against telling her staff as she didn't want to worry them. It could be something or nothing. She had to get out of here. She needed to clear her head.

'I'm just heading out to Boots to pick up a few bits and bobs,' she fibbed.

Her staff looked at her then at each other.

'That's not a good idea,' said Lachlan. 'Wait until DC Quinn gets back. She can accompany you.'

'Don't fuss, Lachlan,' she said, more sharply than she had intended.

Morna stood up. 'I'll come with you. It's not safe for you to be wandering about on your own.'

'Think what DS Hunter would say,' chimed in Chloe.

Beth cringed inwardly. He'd blister her ears for even daring to mention it.

'Honestly, Morna, it's fine. I've had the police monitoring me round the clock for a couple of days now. Not to mention the craziness of this morning. I just need a bit of alone time and some fresh air. I won't be long. Where's the harm? I might even catch the cats looking for scraps down by the harbour. I'll be back before you know it.'

'I suppose we can't stop you,' said Lachlan with a frown that made his views on the matter clear.

Beth walked away from the shop and felt like she was able to breathe properly for the first time in days. Her shoulders came down from around her ears, and she filled her lungs with fresh sea air. She popped into Boots so as not to make a lie of her words then carried on towards the harbour intending to search for the cats there.

Suddenly a number of loud bangs rent the air. One might be a car backfiring. Several indicated gunfire. She froze to the spot, all the hustle and bustle quietening around her as though time itself was standing still. Logan! Whatever had gone down, he was sure to be in the thick of it. Dread twisted her gut. If anything had happened to him...

A few minutes later, a cacophony of sirens began behind her coming from the houses above the bay. The noise swelled and she covered her ears as two ambulances and three police cars sped past her, their primal wail causing her to throb with anxiety. What on earth was happening? Her phone rang and she snatched it up. It was DC Quinn.

'Yes?'

'We've got him, Beth. Aidan Rafferty is in police custody.'

Something was wrong. Beth could hear it in her voice, a whisper of tears.

'What happened?' she asked quietly, her knuckles white, as she gripped the phone hard, bracing herself. *Please don't let it be Logan...*

'I shouldn't really...'

'Please,' said Beth. 'Tell me...'

'Rafferty was holed up in Nora Kelly's house. Been living there for days apparently. He'd got in through a window at the back of the house. We tried to talk him down. He was having none of it. Shots were exchanged. Two of them hit Logan, one in the chest and one in the shoulder. When I saw him lying there, Beth, I honestly thought he was dead.'

Beth felt her heart thud in alarm. The thought of how close he had come to death terrified her. She felt for DC Quinn. It must have been a harrowing ordeal.

'Is he going to be alright?' she asked in alarm. 'Is there anything I can do?' She was struggling to focus on what practical help she could offer. 'He has a case of stuff at the flat. How about if I grab some of his things and take them to the hospital?'

'I don't really know how he is yet. All that I know is he's stable for now. It would be helpful if you could do that,' DC Quinn said. 'Now that we have Aiden Rafferty in custody, you should be safe. I'll need to go back to the station to help out where I'm needed.'

'Do what you have to do, Rhona,' said Beth, using her first name. 'And, please, take care.'

Beth walked back to the flat, feeling like she was walking through treacle. The last few days were catching up with her. As she walked up Albany Street, she could see the increased police presence. Two armed officers stood in full body armour either side of the door into the police station. Inside there was a mass of bodies crammed into the small reception area. Keeping her head down she carried on past before reaching the imposing block of sandstone flats. Trudging up the stairs she made it to the third floor without encountering anyone and let herself in through the door.

The breakfast dishes still lay unwashed in the sink from this morning. As she noticed Logan's mug and plate, she felt a wave of emotion swell up that she fought to contain. Up until now she hadn't really thought that his job was particularly dangerous. Oban was a small Highland town with barely a hint of the extreme violence that could flare up in a city. Now, however, he would be waking up to a different reality in hospital. His little girl could have lost her father. At least it was all over now and there'd be no more looking over her shoulder. Aidan Rafferty couldn't hurt anyone else.

Hesitantly, she pushed open the door into his room. The bed

was rumpled and she could detect a faint hint of the lemon and ginger soap he used. She found a small holdall in the wardrobe and put a couple of changes of clothes into it. She also scooped up a framed photo of Poppy and added it to the pile. She couldn't find any pyjamas but added in his dressing gown and a couple of extra T-shirts. Walking through to the bathroom, she extracted his wash bag, checking it contained everything he was likely to need. That should do it. She wasn't sure if she'd be allowed to spend another night here or not but left her own things meantime for want of anywhere else to put them. Letting herself out, she ran back down the stairs and set off for the hospital. It was a fair walk and would give her time to get her scattered wits together. Although she was relieved that Aidan Rafferty had been caught, she knew that she wouldn't be happy until she could see with her own eyes that Logan Hunter was going to be okay. She'd even gladly submit to one of his usual tongue lashings if that was what it took. Though, she conceded, they seemed to have recently moved past that stage.

It suddenly occurred to her that her staff would be worried and wondering what on earth was going on, with both her and DC Quinn failing to show and the wailing of the sirens earlier. Taking out her phone, she quickly brought Lachlan up to speed on her whereabouts and the fact that Aiden Rafferty was now in custody.

'The shooting is the talk of the town,' said Lachlan. 'We've started doing a brisk trade in get-well cards for the detective sergeant. The jungle drums have been beating. Do give DS Hunter our best wishes for a speedy recovery.'

'I take it the cats haven't turned up yet?' she asked.

'No sign of them,' admitted Lachlan. 'I dare say they'll be back when they're hungry.'

'I'll walk out to the cottage after I've been up to the hospital, see if I can find them skulking around. Poor Marmalade is going to need therapy after all this upheaval.'

'Him and me both,' said Lachlan. 'At this rate I'm going to need to move to the city for a quieter life.'

'Don't you dare,' laughed Beth, hanging up.

Beth arrived at the hospital to find a number of police officers conversing in the reception area. There were only a couple of familiar faces. Suddenly, she spied Chloe's friend, PC Jenny Clark, who was talking to an older woman. Beth walked across and hovered until she noticed her.

The young officer excused herself and turned to her. 'Beth! You must be so relieved to know that he's been caught.'

'Yes.' Beth smiled. 'You can say that again. Although I was very worried to hear that DS Hunter had been shot. I was wondering if it would be possible to see him? I've brought him a bag of stuff from the flat that I thought he might need.'

'We're not really meant to let anyone in to see him,' said Jenny apologetically. 'If you give the bag to me, I'll make sure that he gets it.'

Just then a little girl ran across to Beth. 'Hi, Beth, have you come to see my daddy? He's been shot! But Grandma says he's going to be alright,' she said, walking over to tuck her small hand into the one offered by the woman Jenny had been chatting to.

'Ah, so you're the famous Beth.' The woman smiled, her brown eyes crinkling at the corners. 'I've heard all about you from this one. She was very put out to miss the fun in your shop this morning but in light of what happened next, I'm rather glad that she did.'

'Oh!' Beth blushed. 'Nice to meet you. I'm, er, a sort of friend of your son.'

'Indeed.' She smiled, her eyes twinkling. 'I couldn't help overhearing your conversation with PC Clark. I'm sure he would be happy to see you for a few minutes and take receipt of that bag you so thoughtfully provided. This young lady and I are off for ice cream.'

'If you're sure,' said Beth, immediately liking this warm woman. She waved goodbye to Poppy, and PC Clark escorted her to the door of the ward.

Tears sprang unbidden into Beth's eyes as she saw the invincible Logan Hunter lying limply against the pillows, his complexion grey, his face screwed up in pain and his shoulder strapped, with blood still leaking through the dressing. His chest was bare and covered in a huge bruise that was starting to darken. His eyes sparked into life when he saw her.

'Beth! What are you doing here? What's happened? Why are you crying?' He tried to struggle to a sitting position, but Beth hurriedly held up her hand to stop him.

'You're what happened, you idiot.' She laughed through her tears. 'I've been so worried about you since I heard you'd been shot.'

Logan shrugged then winced. 'Honestly, it's just a graze. It looks way worse than it is. Don't worry,' he said softly, giving her hand a quick squeeze with his good arm. 'I was wearing a vest so the shot to the chest just winded me and broke a couple of ribs. I might be black and blue for a bit but no lasting damage. The one to the shoulder didn't nick anything major. After surgery, I'll be right as rain. It's a lot of fuss about nothing. This place is already doing my head in.' The fact that he was grumbling reassured her more than anything else.

'I met your mother,' she said, raising her eyebrows.

'Oh, you did, did you?' He looked mortified.

'Anyway, I told DC Quinn I'd bring you some stuff in.'

She unpacked the bag, letting him see what she'd brought. His face lightened to see the photo of his daughter, and she placed it on his cabinet where he could see it by turning his head.

'I couldn't find any pyjamas,' she announced after putting away the rest of his stuff. 'Would you like me to buy you some?'

'That won't be necessary.' He winced. 'My mother is on it. I'm going to be organised to within an inch of my life the minute I get out of here.'

Beth laughed. She got up to go seeing that he was struggling to keep his eyes open, as the adrenalin left his system and the pain meds kicked in.

'I'll come round and check on you when you're out,' she said, turning to go.

'I'd like that,' his sleepy voice followed her as she walked out of the door.

Seeing him so vulnerable had really tugged at her heart strings. If anything had happened to him... She forced the thought away. Walking out of the hospital and back into town, she realised there was no time to go back to the shop before it closed. She assumed the police wouldn't mind her spending another night in the flat. She'd figure something else out for tomorrow. But, in the meantime she had two cats to track down. Quickly she phoned Chloe just to check whether they'd pitched up at the shop. No such luck.

The sun was already setting over the bay. It would be nearly dark by the time she walked out to the cottage. Popping into the flat on the way for her cat carriers, she then continued on to Gallanach Road. She realised that part of the reason she was so tired was because after weeks of worry she could now relax and not be looking over her shoulder every five minutes. The darkness slowly swept over the bay as she walked out into the countryside, leaving the lights of the town behind her. She welcomed the peace and solitude after the stress of the last few weeks, the spring air cool on her cheeks. As she walked along the road, she periodically called out to the cats but there was no answering miaow. Although she knew that if push came to shove, Toby could fend indefinitely for himself, she suspected the same did not apply to his big soft friend. Marmalade had been doted upon and babied by Nora Kelly, which perhaps wasn't surprising given her sad history.

As the cottage came into view round the next bend, the white plastic shroud it was wrapped in billowed in the breeze making it look like some vengeful ghost. As the moon slid out from behind the clouds, she called out again for the cats, struggling to hear anything aside from the crackling plastic. Her poor cottage. She'd been told by the insurance assessor that it wasn't as bad as it looked but right now, she doubted if it would ever be a home again.

Suddenly, she froze. Calling out again, as the breeze died back briefly, she heard an answering wail. It was Toby. Seconds later she heard Marmalade, sounding deeply sorry for himself. Somehow, they must have got trapped inside.

'I'm coming, boys,' she cooed, walking up to where the front door should be, behind the plastic. Fumbling in her bag, she pulled out a nail file with which she managed to cut a slit she could widen to expose the door. Frustrated, she remembered it would be locked and she'd handed over the keys to the insurer meantime. The cats were louder now, knowing she was nearby. Frustrated now, she banged angrily on the door only for it to give way and swing inwards with a creak.

At that moment, the moon slid behind a cloud and the darkness intensified. It felt like creeping into the belly of a whale with nothing to light her way. The smoke and smell of charred wood was acrid and nipped at her eyes and throat. She swallowed hard as she thought of all that she had lost in the flames, the framed photos and mementos of her mother being the greatest loss of all. The cats sounded frantic now. Where on earth were they? Why weren't they seeking her out? Had they got trapped somewhere? At least with all the miaowing they couldn't be in too bad a way. She squeezed through the living room door, which was sitting at an angle, attached by only one hinge. She knew that the worst of the damage was concentrated there and in the kitchen. The smell of charred wood was stronger now. And something else. A faint trace of perfume... Bracing herself for the damage she would see, Beth turned the handle and pushed open the door, crooning to the cats to reassure them.

Puzzled, her eyes widened as she saw them. They were each in a separate cat carrier, sitting on the intact stone hearth amidst the charred remains of her furniture and belongings. Who could have placed them in there? Hurriedly, she stumbled over to them, almost tripping in her haste, the frantic cats wailing even louder on seeing her. But just as her hands were reaching for them, she experienced a crushing blow to the back of her head.

She could feel herself tipping forward as the blackness became absolute.

FIFTY-THREE

Beth came to slowly. She kept her eyes shut as she tried to process what had just happened. Could something have fallen on her head, weakened by the fire? She clung to that idea for a few seconds before dismissing it. That didn't explain the cats sitting there. A primal fear inched up her spine, drying her mouth. No, this was deliberate. The cats were bait, and like an idiot she'd walked straight into the trap. But who? Aiden Rafferty was in custody. Clearly, he hadn't been working alone.

Suddenly a bucket of icy cold water was thrown over her. Beth pushed herself up to a sitting position, gasping and spluttering. She spun round to face her attacker, her jaw sagging open in surprise. A number of candles had been lit so she could now see better. A young woman with black hair and red lipstick stood staring down at her, her eyes dripping with contempt. Beth felt confused and groggy. She couldn't work out what on earth was going on.

'Kathleen? What are you doing? I've been trying to find you. I thought you were dead.'

'Better for you if I was,' the young woman standing over her spat, the hatred in her eyes like a palpable living thing.

Beth vaguely realised that she didn't sound Irish anymore. She sounded... Now she had it. The accent coupled with the dimples.

And that necklace. The J had stood for Jill. Her mind spiralled back into the past. Her heart thumped with dread. It was Kathleen's perfume she'd been smelling.

'PC Townsend…' Beth said. 'The fire, it was you! You glued my windows shut. Then you put glue in the lock of my door after getting me to lock it behind you.'

'Well, you know what they say. The best laid plans and all that.' Kathleen produced a wicked looking knife from behind her back and held it out in front of her.

Beth flinched in terror. Kathleen smiled. A plaintive miaow sounded. The cats! What would happen to them if she gave up now?

'How did you know I'd be here?' she asked, playing for time.

'I know everything about you,' sneered Kathleen.

'Then you also know that I'm not the monster you've created in your head,' said Beth quietly.

'Says you,' Kathleen scoffed. 'Ever heard of air tags? I put them in your bag during your Easter nonsense then bundled up the cats and let myself out of the back door. You made it too easy for me.'

'One of our Easter bunnies?' asked Beth.

'Even smiled nicely for the camera, putting a light hand on the little girl in front of me,' mocked the young woman with blazing blue eyes. The knife came closer as Kathleen took a step forward. 'Amazing what a strawberry blonde wig can do.'

Beth suddenly felt a desperate calm come over her. She realised that she'd been waiting for this day to come for years. The day of reckoning. She'd thought those dimples and blue eyes had seemed familiar, but the black hair and Irish accent had thrown her.

'You're Jill's younger sister. That's why you have the "J" around your neck.'

'You don't get to speak her name!' the woman yelled, the hand pointing the knife towards her shaking. 'You took her life and got a few years' detention in a secure home. Boo-hoo! I'm here to balance up the scales.'

Beth nodded, still strangely calm now that her worst fears had come to be realised.

'Kathleen, we were only thirteen! We were children, for God's sake. Both of us! I was only trying to get past them and run to the safety of the classroom. She blocked my way and I swung the racket I was carrying. The wood connected with the side of her head. But that wasn't what killed her. She staggered and tripped over a step behind her which caused her to fall back, banging her head.'

Kathleen's grip tightened on the knife. 'Even now, you're still trying to blame her!' she shouted, taking a step forward.

'For what it's worth, not a day goes by that I don't think about her,' said Beth. 'If it was in my power to undo what happened, I'd do it.'

'Words are cheap,' Kathleen said scornfully. 'She never got the chance to grow up, get married, have a career, kids of her own. You, on the other hand, have everything you could possibly want. How do you think that makes me feel?'

'Angry? Bitter? I could hardly blame you for that,' sighed Beth. *So, this is where it ends*, she thought. All that struggle to end up dying in the ashes of her dream home.

Kathleen raised the knife. Her hand was still shaking. It was one thing fantasising about killing someone. It was quite another to look them in the eye while doing it.

Beth felt hope slice through her. She had to keep her talking, make her see that she was a person who had made a terrible mistake and not the monster who had no doubt inhabited her dreams.

'I take it you know that Aiden Rafferty has been arrested,' Beth said. 'He's behind bars where he belongs and looking at a life in prison. Aren't you worried he'll give you up for a reduced sentence?'

'What's that got to do with me?' Kathleeen scoffed. 'This has always only ever been about you and me.'

'But Nora was poisoned from mushroom tea,' said Beth. 'He purchased tea from you in cash in large quantities.'

'Bloody cheek of the man trying to get me involved in his shit,' snorted Kathleen. 'There was absolutely nothing wrong with my tea. I actually do this for a living. He knew I was coming up to deal with you and, when he saw the pop-up shop, he obviously decided to use it as a front. Here was me thinking he'd proper seen the light about my teas. Obviously, he must have got the actual poisonous mushrooms from another source. I was raging when I found out the way he'd done it. I had to up and leave before I'd managed to deal with you.'

'So, you're a member of Vendetta?' asked Beth faintly, her head spinning.

Kathleen rolled her eyes. 'No! That was all him. I met him at a grief therapy support group in Glasgow. We went for coffee afterwards a few times to have a rant. He wanted to turn our anger into some stupid kind of movement with a logo and a cool name. What a loser. All I wanted was justice for my sister. I didn't want to join this stupid group he was trying to start. Neither of us wanted to play nice and forgive those who wronged us. But after I've dealt with you, I want nothing more to do with him. He knows that.'

'So, how come you both ended up here at the same time?' asked Beth.

'I've been planning this since the end of last year, when I found out where you were living from the paper.' Kathleen shrugged. 'But Aiden only discovered recently it was Nora who had killed his mother.'

'Proper noble, killing an older woman who was in no position to defend herself,' said Beth.

'His pregnant mother was in no position to defend herself either but that didn't stop the pair of them driving off and leaving her to die alone.'

'If he was so righteous, how come he manipulated Nora Kelly into leaving me her entire estate so that it supplied a motive for murder?' asked Beth. 'Not exactly got the courage of his convictions, has he?'

'You're not *exactly* innocent,' mocked Kathleen. 'He knew you wouldn't be convicted at the end of the day, but it would blow up enough smoke for him to slip away undetected.'

'He had it all figured out,' said Beth, bitterly.

'You might not have murdered Nora, but you did murder my sister,' snapped Kathleen. 'I saw that article in *The Herald* last year. Everyone knows you're a murderer. What goes around comes around. That's how I found you.'

'Your sister was a bully, Kathleen. She was relentless and without a scrap of empathy for any of her victims. Jill made my life a living hell. She dissected me sliver by sliver until I lay eviscerated before her. My life was no longer my own, merely a prop for her sadistic enjoyment. On that last day, when she and her cronies had me cornered, I was so terrified that I lost control of my bladder. Thought they were going to see what I'd done and tell everybody. I had to get away.'

'You're lying,' Kathleen snapped. 'That's not how I remember her at all. The school, the other kids, they'd have said something. I only remember her sunny nature, how many friends she had, the glowing reports she brought home from school.'

'She could be charming, for sure,' agreed Beth. 'She had everyone at school, including the teachers, wrapped round her little finger. But, Kathleen, looking back at her from an adult perspective there was something inexplicable, something rotten beneath the surface. Something I can't account for. I like to think she'd have grown out of it but now, looking back, I'm not so sure.'

'Why are you saying these things?' ground out Kathleen. 'You should be on your knees begging for your life, not slagging off my dead sister.'

'If you're going to kill me, I'd rather go to my grave having told you the truth,' said Beth, lifting her chin defiantly. 'Have you even thought about your parents in all this? They've already lost one daughter. How do you think they'll feel when the other one is imprisoned for committing murder?'

'All I'm doing is righting the wrongs of the criminal justice system. It should be that if you take a life, you forfeit your own. Aiden was right about that.'

'Is that what you tell yourself?' Beth snapped right back at her. 'There's a good man, a policeman, lying in hospital because of your vigilante claptrap. He's the only parent of a little girl. How does that square with your so-called beliefs?'

'Yes, well, actions can sometimes have unintended consequences,' Kathleeen said, biting her lip and looking away.

'Which brings us to why we're here,' said Beth quietly. 'Look, I can see how you got carried away thinking this was a noble cause, but I can assure you that once you take the life of another person, you'll never be the same again. Take it from one who knows. Don't do that to yourself.' Beth could see that Kathleen was wavering.

She could hear the distant wail of a siren. It seemed to be coming closer. Kathleen leapt towards her. 'What have you done?' she shouted, her eyes wild with fear, the knife now perilously close to Beth's face.

Beth shrugged. 'I haven't done anything. You'd have seen me.'

The penny dropped.

'It must have been my watch. When you clobbered me, I fell hard. My watch would have registered it as a fall and so my phone called emergency services.'

Kathleen stood frozen, paralysed with indecision.

'Look, if you can swear to me that this thing between us is over, you can just go. Give me the knife. I'll get rid of it. I don't want anyone else getting hurt. You were never here. The police are chasing a ghost as, without me, they don't know your true identity.'

'Why would you do that for me?' asked Kathleen.

'I'm not doing it for you. I'm doing it for your sister. I'm gambling on the fact that we understand each other a little better now. This all ends now. You burned my house down. Take the win.

You get to go home. It's what your sister would have wanted for you.'

After a moment's hesitation, Kathleen nodded and handed Beth the knife. Then she spun round and slipped away into the darkness of the night. Beth had taken a calculated risk, but she believed that Kathleen would abide by their agreement. The siren was deafening now. Beth lay down, positioning her head near a piece of timber. For good measure she smeared some blood over it.

A few minutes later she heard the crackle of plastic as the paramedics arrived.

'In here,' she called faintly. 'I took a bit of a tumble when I came to collect my cats.'

FIFTY-FOUR

TWO WEEKS LATER

Beth sat outside in the spring sunshine, the flowers around her a riot of colour and the birds busy singing or nest building. The cats sat on a low wall staring at the birds, but they were too lazy to chase them. Harris appeared with a pitcher of lemonade, sent out by his mother who had taken in Beth and the cats until the repairs on the cottage were completed, which would take several months. He settled down beside her, pouring them a glass each.

'Are you a little disappointed that Nora's will turned out to be invalid?'

'Hardly.' Beth shuddered. 'I wanted nothing to do with it.'

'People often make the mistake of thinking the law in Scotland and England is more or less the same but in Scotland the will needs to be signed by the testator on every single page, or it's deemed to be invalid. When I first saw that photocopy, I suspected it would prove to be invalid, but I needed to examine the original to be sure. Mind you, invalid or not, it still served to provide you with a motive which is all that Aiden Rafferty was trying to achieve.'

'What will happen to her estate now?' asked Beth.

'The will is invalid so under the laws of intestate succession, it'll go to her biological child, Callum, who was innocent in all this. Normally, if the embryo had been donated through a clinic the right to inherit would be expressly removed. In this case, Nora chose to remove that clause.'

'I think Nora would have been happy with that outcome,' said Beth softly. 'However, he needn't think he's getting his hands on Marmalade!'

'Speaking of finances, I'm also pleased to report that the insurance company is going to cover all the repairs and redecoration costs in relation to the cottage,' Harris said.

'Phew!' said Beth, relieved. She reached for her brother's hand and squeezed it. 'I really don't know what I'd do without you, Harris.'

'All part of the service,' he said with a mock bow.

Susan Kincaid popped her head out the back door. 'Beth, I have a visitor for you, if you're up to it?'

Beth nodded and felt her lips split into a huge smile as she saw Logan Hunter appear alongside DC Quinn. His arm was strapped up in a sling, and he was still paler than normal, the pain of his injury etched on his face.

Harris immediately leapt up and disappeared inside with DC Quinn. She'd started joining them for meals now and then, and Beth was glad to see her brother happy again after the strains of last year.

'DC Quinn was updating me on the case and I decided to come along for the ride,' he said. 'I hope you don't mind. Poppy's at school and I've been going out of my mind with boredom stuck in the house every day.'

'Of course not, I'm happy to see you.' She smiled. 'How's the shoulder?'

'Not too bad. Fortunately, there doesn't seem to be any nerve damage. I'm back at work in another four weeks. I imagine that they'll stick me behind a desk for a bit. I thought you'd like to know that Aiden Rafferty's lawyer has confirmed he'll be pleading guilty. Apparently, he was able to track Nora down through a familial DNA match when Callum went on one of those ancestry sites. The police had worked out exactly which phone box the 999 call had come in from back in 1979. They found blood all over it and took samples, preserving them with the case files. Rafferty obtained access to it all through his job in the cold case unit. He was able to obtain a DNA profile years later. He then visited Callum and he gave him Nora's address so she could be ruled out, too.'

'That's terrible,' said Beth. 'Poor Callum! To think that he was the unwitting catalyst for her death. Does he know?'

'I don't think it's really sunk in yet. Hopefully, he doesn't fully join the dots. Certainly, no one will be keen to enlighten him on that point, poor lad.'

He shifted in his seat.

'What is it?' she asked, dreading what he might say next.

'DC Quinn filled me in on your statement at the hospital,' he said. 'The thing is, I'm not quite buying it.'

'Aren't you meant to be off-duty?' she asked crossly. 'I thought this was a social visit?'

'It is,' he said. 'It's just that I can't shake the feeling that something happened in the cottage that night that you're not telling us about. It worries me. I need to know that there's no loose ends that can come back and bite you, Beth.'

'There's nothing to worry about, I promise,' she said softly.

Like a dog with a bone, he continued, as if she hadn't spoken.

'The cats were on the hearth beyond where you apparently fell. If you fell on your way towards them, they wouldn't have been neatly parcelled up in their cat carriers. If you fell on the way out then they would have been lying near you, one on either side of where you fell and knocked yourself out. It doesn't add up.'

Beth let out a long sigh and dropped her eyes. She really didn't know what to tell him. All she knew was that the circle of hate had been interrupted and that could only be a good thing. She'd had a letter from Kathleen, sent to the shop two days ago. In it she said that she had been doing a lot of thinking and decided to undertake some one-to-one therapy to properly come to terms with what had happened to her sister. She wrote that while she wasn't there yet, she hoped to one day be able to forgive Beth for what she had done and find her way back to a normal life again, one that wasn't driven by the thirst for revenge.

'Okay,' she admitted, when the silence between them had stretched to breaking point. 'Maybe something did happen, but it's been dealt with and it's not in the public interest to do anything about it. I promise you, it's over.'

'Are you sure? I take it that means that whoever targeted you is still out there? Can you live with that? What if they change their mind and come after you again? I'd rest easier in my mind if they were locked up behind bars,' he said, his worried dark eyes boring in to hers.

'Let's just say we reached an understanding. I know that you think I can be naïve at times, but I've also got good instincts about people. I feel I can trust this person. Let's leave it at that. Any more bother and the gloves are off, I promise.'

'I suppose I'll have to accept that,' he said gruffly. 'For now.'

He shifted in his chair, furtively glancing back towards the house. 'Er... there was another reason I wanted to see you,' he admitted, his eyes rising to meet hers.

'Go on,' Beth said cautiously, her palms moistening with nerves. She'd been waiting for the axe to fall for some time now, sure that he was going to tell her that their kiss had been a mistake that he now regretted. Her heart flinched in anticipatory grief.

'I was wondering how you would feel about having dinner with me tomorrow night? My mother is taking Poppy to Glasgow to go shopping for some new clothes and they're staying overnight.'

'I'd love to,' Beth said, her face splitting into a smile.

'You would?' He swallowed hard, then his own smile answered his own.

'But only if you let me cook,' said Beth. 'You still need to take it easy. I'll come at six.'

'That's a... date... then,' he said, struggling to his feet as DC Quinn came back out of the house.

She looked from one to the other. 'Blimey, I don't want to know,' she said, shaking her head at them in mock severity.

'See you tomorrow,' he said, giving her a last lingering look as DC Quinn led the way back out to her car.

Later that same day, she made her way down the hill and walked along the bay to the bookshop. Although it had only been two weeks, it felt like a lifetime had passed since she was last here. Taking a deep breath, she opened the door and walked inside.

'Beth!' Chloe shrieked, running up and giving her a hug. 'We've missed you!'

'Tea?' asked Lachlan, raising an eyebrow.

Gratefully she nodded. 'It's so quiet in here without the chicks,' she laughed. 'It's good to be back to normal.' She smiled at Morna who was clad in her usual black, her fine features concealed behind a wall of makeup and a new tattoo snaking down her arm.

'Good to have you back.' Morna grinned. 'Business has started picking up again since *The Oban Times* ran that article completely exonerating our subscription boxes.'

As they sat at the table, drinking their tea, Beth felt peace steal over her. This was where she belonged. She could feel her energy flowing back. The thought of her date tomorrow night made her heart sing. The door tinkled and the two cats scooted in on the heels of a couple of women. All was as it should be.

With a contented sigh she scooped Toby onto her lap. 'So, Morna, about this fantasy festival you mentioned a few weeks ago...'

A LETTER FROM THE AUTHOR

Dear reader,

Huge thanks for reading *Poison at the Wild Haggis Bookshop*. I hope you were hooked on Beth Cunningham's journey. If you want to join other readers in hearing all about my new releases and bonus content, you can sign up here:

www.stormpublishing.co/jackie-baldwin

If you enjoyed this book and could spare a few moments to leave a review that would be hugely appreciated. Even a short review can make all the difference in encouraging a reader to discover my books for the first time. Thank you so much!

A lot of different elements came together to spark the ideas for this plot. With an amateur sleuth it is always a challenge as to how to insert your character into the heart of the investigation. Book subscription boxes are starting to take off now so I thought it would keep the connection to the shop but could deliver much more. I'm quite intrigued by mushrooms and their hidden mycelial world. There was also a case being played out in real life through the courts and press involving poisoning by death cap mushrooms. Having the Easter chicks in the shop was inspired by a memory from my childhood. There used to be a wonderful department store in Dumfries called Binn's. Every year, my mother would take me to see all the Easter chicks. All of this was thrown into the soup of the plot.

Thanks again for being part of this amazing journey with me and I hope you'll stay in touch – I have so many more stories and ideas to entertain you with!

Jackie

www.jackiebaldwin.co.uk

instagram.com/Jackie.baldwin.1088
facebook.com/JackieMBaldwin1
x.com/JackieMBaldwin1

ACKNOWLEDGMENTS

Writing the first draft of a book is a very solitary occupation but once it has been submitted it becomes much more of a team effort. I'm very grateful to have the wonderful team at Storm working hard to ensure that each book is the best it can possibly be before it arrives in your hands. Special thanks go to my brilliant editor, Kathryn Taussig, and her assistant editor, Naomi Knox, for the structural edit, the copyeditor, Liz Hurst, for her meticulous attention to detail, and proofreader, Amanda Raybould. Credit for my beautiful cover must go to the very talented Dawn Adams. I'd also like to thank Elke Desanghere for her beautiful marketing materials. I'm also grateful to Alexandra Begley for her role in production of the book. In relation to the audiobooks, I am so happy that Samara MacLaren agreed to be the narrator as her wonderful voice fits beautifully with the characters.

Thanks to Kelly Lacey at Love Books for organising my amazing blog tour. Special thanks are also due to Helen Boyce at The Book Club Reader Review Request group for her help in finding early readers.

Thanks to my friends and family for their generous support, including my writing partners in crime from Twisted Sisters. A special thank you to my daughter-in-law, Rhanna, for her unwavering support in reading and championing my books.

Finally, my thanks, as always, to my husband, Guy, for putting up with me when I have lost the plot!!

9781805088479